Back and Forth

Stay Back! Trilogy Book 2

Lynn Stewart

Up Wind Systems, LLC

CAMBRIDGE, MARYLAND

Lynn Stewart/Up Wind Systems, LLC
Cambridge, Maryland
lynnstewart.ink

Publisher's Note: This is a work of fiction. Names, characters, places, and incidents are a product of the author's imagination. Locales and public names are sometimes used for atmospheric purposes. Any resemblance to actual people, living or dead, or to businesses, companies, events, institutions, or locales is completely coincidental.

Book Layout © 2017 BookDesignTemplates.com
Cover Design by Books Covered

Back and Forth/ Lynn Stewart. - 1st ed.
ISBN 978-0-9998905-2-3

For Sweet Petunia

"...Names lifted from a hat or balanced on the tip of the tongue. Names wheeled into the dim warehouse of memory. So many names, there is barely room on the walls of the heart."

—BILLY COLLINS, THE NAMES

Contents

Prologue

I'VE NEVER BEEN ONE TO COMMEMORATE milestone events with a reenactment. Yeah, I'll mark the critical days in my mental calendar - you know, birthdays and such. My wedding anniversary. The day my wife was raped. The day I left her. And the day our divorce became a real living, breathing thing, like that bastard's baby she was carrying. Something that could never be undone. Oh, and the day about a year and a half later when I professed my undying love for her sister. We'd been on-again, off-again for a few months, but, in the end, well, let's just say getting mixed up with your ex-wife's sister is never a good idea. So there, I've rambled enough about that. I'm not really a sentimental fool when it comes to the time-marking rituals. But today, well, today seems somehow different. No, not somehow different. It just is. Different. In every way imaginable. It was terrible, this day last year. I wish I had the talent to turn a word or a phrase that would, in just a few utterances, convey the complete and utter horror of this day last year. Even Shorty, who never shuts up, was quiet this morning. He was with me that day and saw the same things I saw. He looked at me this morning, the first anniversary of all that, and whispered: *no words, man, no words.*

I didn't feel much like sailing this morning even though the conditions were perfect with a gentle southerly breeze. But to honor this day properly, I needed to sail, because sailing was what I was doing that morning last year. I was sailing when it happened. So, I dragged poor Shorty out this morning at the crack of dawn specifically to sail. Yeah, he was with me on the boat that morning last year. I don't even remember why we were sailing around the Hudson early on a Tuesday morning. But we were. And we saw everything. We watched in disbelief, just like everyone else. We dumped the sails and just sat there, not moving, not talking. When the World Trade Center's north tower disintegrated, and the vast cloud filled our existence I snapped into action, turning on the engine - full throttle - and then turning the boat around in a desperate attempt to get the hell out of there. As a retired cop, I wanted to be in those buildings with the first responders. I hate it that I had to retire early, especially since my leg has long since healed; the only evidence of the scuffle that broke it is a limp that I'll likely call my own forever.

As I watched what was going on across the river, I kept thinking about Nester, my partner, best friend, and now my ex-wife's live-in. Yeah, Nester's cousin, who might as well have been his brother was there. A firefighter. God, when I saw what was happening, I dropped to my knees in the cockpit and prayed that my buddy's cousin was okay. It turned out that he wasn't. He went in and never came out.

When the other tower came down, Shorty pushed me out of the way and grabbed the wheel. I fought him, gripping the wheel and throwing my body up against it. He eventually either over-powered me or I went limp and gave up. I don't remember which. Before I could even be pissed or upset, we were moving toward Lower Manhattan. It was pandemonium. We saw hundreds of people trying to get off the island - so desperate to escape the dust and fire that some were jumping in the water. Did I mention it was pandemonium? They were standing on what seemed like the edge of the earth, begging to be picked up. Shorty banged *Three-Ring Circus* against the pier and although it's a tiny boat - a thirty-five-foot fiberglass banana - we managed to pick up a dozen or so people. We didn't have a plan. And my reputation for knowing things before I knew them was strangely not working. I felt helpless and hapless and a million different things in between. We transported the people to Jersey City, right across the harbor. Back and forth we went. The people we ferried didn't seem to know what to do next or where to go or even care about what to do next or where to go. They only seemed to care that they were off that island. An island I never really thought of as an island. Until that day.

It's strange looking up at the sky today, seeing the same blue as that day. Maybe not as vivid, but close. Pretty damned close. The most significant difference is that there are planes flying to-day. As if it's the most normal thing in the world to fly into the city. On that day last year, by the time Shorty and I sat still long enough to even think about it, we realized the sky was silent. We were quiet too. After the initial shock and horror, there was a period of absolute silence. The atmosphere was mute. People were mute. Zombies. It was like we'd all turned into zombies. We were moving in slow motion. I remember thinking everyone was like a figure in a wax museum - we resembled ourselves but were anything but ourselves. We would never again be ourselves. Our former selves were gone. My stupid little yellow sailboat with its juggling, unicycle riding, grinning clown painted on both sides looked evil, as if it were laughing in the midst of tragedy.

Part 1 - Before

Intuition - Brenda

IT'S BEEN SAID THAT A PERSON'S gut reaction to something is the right one. Generally, Brenda Arnstein found this to be true. Over the years she's walked in and walked right out of restaurants because something undefinable and elusive made her recoil. Gut reaction. She had been sure her husband would divorce her on their first anniversary when she refused to walk into, let alone eat at what was supposed to be the best seafood restaurant on the East Coast. The fluorescent lights, linoleum floors, and cheap looking Formica tables were not part of the romantic tableau she'd been expecting. But it wasn't until she noticed a table of five men in hunting attire drinking pitchers of beer that she had her meltdown. Pitchers! She didn't want to go to this kind of place for her anniversary. What did Alec think when he made this reservation? She was incredulous that a dump like this even took reservations. She stood outside the front door and cried. Alec went in and had a brief conversation with the host. He came back out and, God bless him, didn't say a word. He put his arm around her and walked her back to the little Italian place that they'd seen near their hotel.

Years later she came to understand that the dive with the fluorescent lights and pitchers of beer was indeed the best seafood place on the East Coast and that its unique ambiance was part of its charm. She also came to understand that some gut reactions require a thoughtful assessment. Not all are to be trusted. If she'd only given that hole-in-the-wall dive a chance, she and Alec would have had a good time and lots of laughs. She is now confident of that. Because that's precisely what they did a year later, on their second anniversary, and every year after that until the place was flooded during a storm and never recovered, never re-opened.

Last week, she had an instantaneous gut reaction when she noticed a scaly bump on her left breast. She discovered it only after she realized she'd been mindlessly scratching there. She rationalized her fear away: it wasn't a lump, but more like dry, irritated skin. Brenda quickly ran her hands over both breasts, poked and prodded and decided that what she had was a rash, and that was that. She promised herself that she would be better about self-exams in the future.

She fastened her bra and decided to push aside any fear of disease. She would allow herself to enjoy the impending change from summer to fall. She would let it fill her with joy if she could even call it that. She hadn't felt joyful - genuinely joyful - in a long time. It was late August and still technically summer. Yet every twist and turn yielded a billboard or store window displaying wool sweaters and down-filled coats, clearly things you wouldn't need - even in New York - until much, much later. Henry's fifth-grade school supply list showed up in the mail one hot and sticky Wednesday shortly after the Fourth of July, and he begged Brenda to take him school-shopping. *Let's at least wait until next month, when all the cool notebooks and binders and pens will be lined up on shelves, waiting for little hands to grab them and take them home,* she'd tried to tell him. She even tried to appeal to his frugal side, a trait that she lacked, and explained to him that everything would be on sale for pretty much the entire month of August. But no. She was not one to let a ten-year-old run her life, but she delighted in his enthusiasm and how he seemed to blossom into a pretty good student last year. She allowed him to peruse the aisles with a list in his hand and his very own cart. Today, Henry was school clothes shopping with her sister Kathy in New Jersey. It was a tradition they'd started two years ago when Brenda was recovering from her knee surgery, and Alec was traveling for work.

She was leaning against the kitchen island looking up at the ceiling when Alec came home. He was one of the few therapists in Brooklyn with office hours on Saturday and always had a full schedule. She didn't acknowledge him when he slid up next to her at the counter and pressed his shoulder against her shoulder. She was fixated on the ceiling with one thing on her mind, and it wasn't the one thing she suspected Alec had on his mind.

"What's the plan?" he said with a playful wink in his voice. Brenda knew this voice, and it meant that he wanted sex. After twelve years of marriage, his voice-wink was one of the few things that hadn't changed. He was leaving in the morning for a psychology conference in Tokyo. He'd be giving a talk on how to write high impact papers and what to do if your manuscript is rejected. It was understandable that he would want her to provide him with a special sendoff - it was what they did before he traveled, but today she had more pressing things on her mind. Besides, she wasn't a huge fan of their routine lately. Something with their lovemaking had changed in the last few months. It was a subtle change that she couldn't articulate well enough to even start a conversation. This was one gut-reaction that she didn't want to ignore, so she decided that when Alec returned from his trip she would bring it up, even if she had to fumble her way through the words.

"This. All this is my plan." She pointed at the nine-foot ceiling in the kitchen, waving her arm around as if showing the apartment to prospective buyers, touting the many benefits of such elegant beauty. *Oh, such space! Oh, such a light and airy feeling! Where could you possibly find such space at such a price in an old Brooklyn apartment?* If only that was the reason for her arm gestures and not because sticky moth pods were dotting and lining the corners where the ceiling and wall intersected. Hundreds of them. Or so it seemed. Henry discovered them last weekend and pointed them out between bites of pizza. Matter-of-factly. Without a speck of judgment. Either that or ten-year-old boy indifference. Feed him, give him his favorite books and Legos, buy him his school supplies early, let him go to back-to-school shopping with Aunt Kathy. Dust? What's that? Residue and crumbs on the kitchen counter? No worries. Damp leaves tracked in and left behind on the floor like decals? Just part of life. Sticky moth pods lining the ceiling like carefully strung white Christmas lights? Something to ignore. The pods aren't hurting anyone, and the baby moths deserve a chance at life! Don't they?

"We'll deal with them later." Alec opened the fridge to reveal the bottle of chardonnay that he had apparently snuck in to chill. He grabbed the bottle with one hand, closed the refrigerator with his foot, and practically leaped over her to get to their favorite wine glasses. So yes, she had every expectation that her husband would want sex tonight. But then she remembered the moths. He handed her a glass and said "Cheers!" as he was pouring. She looked at him, incredulous. He clinked their glasses, a little too aggressively, she noted, and she took an obligatory sip.

Brenda set her glass down on the island and went to the laundry room to retrieve the broom. The duct tape wasn't where it was supposed to be - in the cabinet above the washing machine - and she felt her eyes suddenly grow heavy like they were holding in some secret that just needed to get out. She willed the tears back in, not even sure where they were coming from, but come they did, in gushes. She could hear Alec foraging for the pita chips and hummus that was their go-to pre-dinner (and sometimes pre-sex) nosh. The rustling of the chip bag. The individual clink-clanks of chips hitting the bottom of the ceramic bowl, sliding out of the bag as if in an amusement park, screaming all the way down the big, bad roller coaster. She grabbed a tee-shirt from the stack of dirty clothes and blew her nose into it. She looked around the tiny laundry room and suddenly felt ridiculous for trying to live up to the standards of what she saw in magazines. In a fit of pique, she scattered dirty clothes all over the floor.

* * *

The brilliant idea to declutter the entire house had come to her one day in late March - the same day she decided to try again for another baby. Of course, it would be weeks before she mustered enough courage to even broach the topic of another baby with Alec because she knew what his reaction would be.

She had become complacent about housekeeping over the years. Why? She wasn't quite sure. She grew up in a messy, cluttered home. Her mother's mantra - a Phyllis Diller quote - was canonized on a framed needlepoint hanging above the kitchen window: *Cleaning your house while your kids are still growing is like shoveling the walk before it stops snowing.* Brenda didn't entirely agree with Phyllis or her mother. To the casual observer, she and Alec kept a pretty tidy house. But she felt terribly disorganized and had a habit of collecting and holding onto things she didn't need. And she had a pattern of sowing piles. At some point in time the harvest would inevitably come in, and by then, reaping was out of the question. There were logic and purpose in every pile, so maybe she wasn't quite as disorganized as she thought. Plus, she kept the piles in good order; wayward papers rarely snuck out of any pile. Yet more piles always sprouted - weeds in the field, overtaking the original piles - and the thought of any sort of garden maintenance would soon become overwhelming. But the piles were logical in their placement and content. Brenda often reminded herself (and Alec) of this fact.

Then there were the closets. Every closet was overflowing with random this and random that. Bulging, in fact. The hall closet contained the winter coats that wouldn't fit on the coat rack, empty photo albums, rarely used office supplies such as large, padded mailing envelopes, a mishmash of varying sized letter holders, and boxes of hanging file folders still neatly wrapped in cellophane. Oh, and the toys. The "emergency" toys that were too young for Henry, but she kept on hand for when any of their various friends with little kids stopped by, or when (if) they had another baby.

Brenda had decided to start small that first decluttering day and selected the linen closet right outside of Henry's room. She set the kitchen timer for thirty minutes. Then she stood and stared. At everything. At nothing She felt overwhelmed, para-lyzed, and unable to take the first step. What was she thinking? She would never be Martha Stewart. Wouldn't want to be. She liked her disorganized self. To hell with the decluttering! After what seemed like an eternity, she touched the closet's cold, brass door handle. After a few more minutes she clutched it, wrapping her fingers around as if it was about to take off running. She felt like taking off running. But she stayed, determined to follow through. Eventually, she turned the handle and opened the door, peeking inside as if to find a monster hiding on the top shelf un-der the piles of mismatched sheets, pillowcases, and blankets. And eventually the kitchen timer beeped, but she ignored it. She had passed from complete and utter fear into a giddy, mania. She bagged things for The Salvation Army, bagged other items for the dumpster, and finally folded up what remained into neatly categorized packages - a top sheet inside the fitted sheet, inside the pillowcases. A bedding Turducken! The linen closet looked beautiful.

For the next three weeks, she set the kitchen timer for thirty minutes each evening and tackled one project. Just one. She forced herself to that limit. She liked structure and boundaries and rules. Big, open spaces overwhelmed her, even if that big, open space was a vast sea of unstructured time. When she was single, she sometimes dreaded the big, open space of the weekend and found herself wandering from room to room in her apartment, unsure what to do with herself. So, she learned to chunk her weekends up with planned activities, even if the activity was as mundane as walking three blocks to the corner market for an item she didn't need.

Brenda liked time boundaries around things too. If she didn't bound herself by time, that corner market excursion on a Saturday would turn into hours of time wasted wandering around the neighborhood, neglecting things that needed to be done. Thirty minutes to declutter a closet or a room was good, otherwise she might get distracted by a story in an old newspaper that was wrapped around a porcelain teacup. An hour later, she'd still be engrossed in the paper. Sure, she often broke the thirty-minute rule by staying after the bell rang, but she never broke her rule of only decluttering one space per day.

She worked herself from the linen closet to the master bedroom. She did her side of the walk-in closet, her designated dresser drawers, her side of the bathroom vanity. She made her way to the kitchen and tackled the junk drawer. And in the cupboard where she kept her baking supplies, she found just enough flour and cocoa to make brownies. Later that night, after handing Alec a warm brownie, she announced that she wanted to try for a second child. As soon as the words were out of her mouth, she regretted them. She didn't mean for the conversation to come up right then, and so casually. She hated that she had such poor control of her impulses.

"Another baby? But why? Why now? Henry is ten. He's in school all day and has activities almost every day in the summer." Alec paused long enough to shove half of a brownie into his mouth and swallow it whole. "Actually, it's time you started doing something. I mean really doing something. And doing something real."

"Art therapy isn't real?"

"Ah, come on Brenda. Dipping a paintbrush in a bucket of Tempera and handing it to a depressed geezer to splatter it on a piece of butcher paper? What is that?"

"It's not Tempera. We use artist-quality acrylic and proper canvas, you know that. Their masterpieces line the adult day care center walls. Some of the paintings are quite lovely." She couldn't believe she was having this conversation. She couldn't believe her calm, either. She was quite in awe of this out-of-character calm. Her normal reaction would have been to walk away, but she stayed and was ready to defend herself. "You've always seemed supportive of this. Why are you suddenly looking down your nose at what I'm doing? I love what I do." Her calm was beginning to evaporate. "You're a shrink! You should know this is good for people."

"People who matter. Kids. Productive adults recovering from trauma. Not a bunch of geezers who are never going home. It's not like you're preparing them to once again be contributing members of society."

"You know, Alec, a lot of these so-called geezers are actually vibrant, funny people who are completely aware of themselves and their surroundings. They just can't take care of themselves. Some of them have no family, or at least no family who wants anything to do with them. Painting makes them happy. Painting helps them deal with their feelings when their emotions are so bottled up they don't even know how to begin expressing them." Brenda looked at him, incredulous, all calm now gone. "I can't believe I'm having this conversation with you." She kept at it. "You of all people."

"You were supposed to start painting seriously again when Henry started preschool. Remember? That was our deal." She kept walking, and Alec kept talking. "Bringing another child into this house is just one more ploy to avoid getting serious, isn't it? You fill your life with excuses. When is your real life going to start, Brenda? We agreed a long time ago that I'd foot the bills until Henry was in school. Then you'd either start selling some paintings or get a full-time job and start contributing. Remember that?"

She stopped walking and turned around to face him. "Yeah. I remember." She walked away feeling defeated and weary.

***

Brenda emerged from the laundry room - eyes wet from crying - with the broom. She walked past Alec without looking at

• 16 •

him. He was leaning into the island, forearms resting on the newspaper, scanning the sports page. She could feel his eyes on her as she walked by and braced herself for a series of complaints. But none came. She found the duct tape on top of a pile of recipes yet to be filed. Alec finally looked at her.

"We'll deal with the moths later." He pulled the broom out of her hand and stood it against the counter. She didn't fight it. She let him take the duct tape. "Why are your eyes red? Have you been crying?" She shook her head but the tears came again. "Now what's wrong?"

"I'm going to miss you, is all. Tokyo seems far away. Well, it is far away, but you know what I mean. Plus, two weeks is a long time. A really long time." She took a deep breath and felt even more tears coming. She clenched her teeth in a feeble attempt to delay the inevitable.

"This won't work." Alec examined the broom-duct tape contraption and shook his head.

"Yes, it will, I'll show you." She tucked the broom under her arm and picked up a bar stool and carried it over to the far wall near the window. She climbed on the stool and stretched her arm as far skyward as it would go, dabbing at several moth pods with the sticky end of the duct tape. Nothing. She poked harder. Nothing. It was as if the moth pods were a permanent part of the wall. Cemented there to live in infamy. She turned to look at Alec, expecting some form or another of: *see didn't I tell you it wouldn't work?* But in instead found him on the other side of the kitchen with an extra-long paint roller in one hand and a screwdriver in the other. He quietly affixed the screwdriver to the roller with duct tape (whoever invented this stuff was a genius), then he stood on the bar stool. Instead of trying to yank the moth pods off the wall like you would pull unwanted hair with a strip of wax, he used the screwdriver to scrape them. It worked! Brenda grabbed the vacuum and sucked up the debris that floated down. They worked together in silence - teamwork at its best - for more than an hour before they decided to take a long enough break to order Chinese. By the time the food was delivered they had done the entire perimeter of the kitchen and believed they had destroyed every moth pod. Brenda even sucked up some live moths that were flying around amid the chaos. Her tears were long forgotten and world domination belonged to the team of Brenda and Alec Arnstein.

Japan - Brenda

BRENDA STOOD NAKED IN FRONT of the bathroom mirror listening to Alec belt out show tunes in the shower - a little too off key, a little too falsetto, and a bit too annoying. She studied her reflection, imagining herself a few months from now with a baby bump. Her period was two weeks late, but she didn't hang any hope on that, fearing the fluky cycles might mean she was entering menopause early, at thirty-eight, just like her mother and sister had.

The steam from the shower distorted her reflection. Like a mirage, her body came in and out of view. She yanked a tissue out of the decorative holder (a present she bought herself after decluttering her side of the vanity) and wiped away enough steam to reveal a version of her reflection. She brought her left breast up close and examined her rash. She felt a momentary surge of impending doom. Henry, motherless. Alec meeting someone new within the first year. She closed her eyes and willed herself back to the present moment and reminded herself to pick up some fragrance-free laundry detergent today.

She looked over her shoulder at Alec, who was shampooing his hair to the beat of his song, oblivious to anything else taking place around him. Brenda opened the medicine cabinet and pulled out the early pregnancy test kit, the scaly patch on her breast long forgotten. She opened the package and was about to remove the test stick from its protective foil wrapper when she noticed that Alec was no longer singing but was drying himself. She quickly shoved the test kit back into the cabinet. He stepped out of the shower and came up behind her, wrapping his arms around her and pressing himself against her back.

"A quickie?" He nuzzled her neck, and they laughed, knowing full well the cab would be here soon to take him to the airport.

**

"When's Henry coming home?" Alec fiddled with his cell phone, and Brenda held his hand in the backseat of the cab, a spur of the moment decision on her part to ride with him to the airport. She imagined the young lasses of yore trekking down to the beach to wave their white handkerchiefs as the jolly sailors they'd known only for a few short hours set sail for faraway lands. Brenda expressed interest in going with Alec to this conference, but he'd said no, that the timing wasn't ideal with school starting for Henry. She argued that Kathy could have come over and stayed with Henry. Both Kathy and Henry would have loved that. Alec still said no.

"I'm picking him up tomorrow, so Kathy doesn't have to schlep all the way over here."

"But it's okay for you to schlep all the way over there?" Alec shook his head, and she braced herself for a lecture, argument, disagreement, or divergence of opinion. She didn't want to have to beat herself up for the next several hours or days or at least until he was safely on Japanese ground and settled into his hotel room so she could grovel and apologize for letting her sister control everything, as Alec would imply. Brenda wanted her last moments with him to be sweet like the air had turned last night after they'd obliterated the moths. That's what she wanted him to remember. Yes, she was overly dramatic. Of this, she was painfully aware. She was acting like he was in the military, going off to war, never to be seen or heard from again. She was behaving as if cell phones, or even regular, ordinary telephones didn't exist. Or that by the time the Pony Express delivered her letter he would already be on his way home.

"You're right." She nestled her head in the crook of his arm. "What was I thinking? I'll call Kathy tonight and tell her that if she doesn't get her skinny butt on a train to Brooklyn tomorrow, she might as well just keep Henry. I'll send his things UPS." They both laughed, and she was pleased with herself for diverting the discussion to avoid a negative exchange. But then, before she could command her tongue to lay still: "Actually, she would have come over to stay with Henry. She would have happily come over for that. Henry would have been ecstatic. I don't understand why you wouldn't want me to join you in Japan."

"What would you do all day while I'm attending conference sessions? You'd be bored out of your mind."

"And you've lost yours." Her face was suddenly hot, and she just knew it was redder than the sun rising in the distance, seemingly following the cab to the airport. "Alec, I'd be in JAPAN." The decibel level of her voice went up a fraction. "Trust me I'd try not to complain every night about how bored I was all day sitting in the hotel room waiting for you."

"I'm not having this conversation." He turned his head to look out the window, and then, changing the subject, "Pretty sunrise."

She silently scolded herself the rest of the way to the airport, but never let go of his hand. She clung tightly to the fact that she had the pregnancy test stick - positive! - wrapped in foil and carefully tucked in the little red backpack she carried instead of a purse. She'd peed on the stick as Alec was outside the house loading his bags into the cab and when he came back into the house to hug and kiss her goodbye, she announced that she wanted to ride to JFK with him. She wasn't entirely sure he'd be pleased about the pregnancy but hoped beyond hope that maybe, just maybe he might be. In July, after she'd dropped the baby subject completely, he apologized for his outburst and for demeaning her chosen profession and said he would love to try and have another baby. She planned to surprise him with the test strip at the gate, just as he was boarding the plane. She would hand him their foil wrapped fate and ask him not to open it until he was high above the clouds. Now she wished she'd just stayed home.

Baggage check-in was mobbed. By the time Alec's flight appeared on the screen, he had only fifteen minutes to spare. They sprinted through the terminal, and when they got to the gate, the plane was already boarding. He gave her a bear hug and a quick, hard kiss and that was that. She watched as the crowd of people boarding the plane seemed to swallow him. A few minutes later he turned to look at her as he stepped onto the passenger boarding bridge. They locked eyes, he waved and then disappeared.

***

Brenda hailed a cab and luckily didn't have to share it with anyone. It would take a while to get back to Brooklyn this time of day, and the thought of idle chitchat with a stranger unnerved her. She felt an emptiness in her gut that startled her. Two weeks without Alec. Two weeks without his arm around her on the couch. Two Saturday mornings that she didn't get to sleep in because Alec wouldn't be home to take Henry to the park or on errands around town. Two weeks to eat whatever she wanted for dinner - including, but not limited to waffles, cereal, or even scrambled eggs. That was at least one positive thing to look forward to. But mostly she was going to miss him. Even the parts of him she found frustrating, like his compulsion for making lists on any and every available writing surface, including the white tablecloth in a cafe. She was horrified when he did that. He claimed to be so caught up in the moment that he'd forgotten where he was. She shook her head at this memory. They laugh about it now, but at the time, she'd wished she had Harry Potter's Invisibility Cloak.

By the time the cab pulled away from the airport, Brenda was engulfed in loneliness. Rather than give in and wallow, she called her neighbor, Ted, who facilitated an artists' residency program.

He currently had four artists sharing a studio on the ninety-second floor in one of the Twin Towers. A few weeks ago, he invited her and Henry up for a tour. She'd lived in New York most of her life and had never been to the World Trade Center, never eaten at Windows on the World. After their tour, she took Henry there for lunch. She was about to hang up when Ted answered. He was out of breath and explained that he and his partner were on their way out with the dog and he had to run back up the stairs when he heard the phone.

"Could I borrow a corner of your studio for an hour one day soon? Is that even allowed?" And then: "I'd be happy to pay you for the privilege."

"I'll do even better than that. We're all on a field trip in a couple of weeks. I'll give you my key. You can come and go as you please and really have at it. And don't be ridiculous about paying me. Seriously." He laughed.

She pulled a pen and notebook out of her little bag and jotted down the details.

* * *

Brenda had a feeling she'd forgotten something and dumped the contents of her bag on the kitchen table. Yep. In the hullabaloo to get Alec on his plane, she'd completely forgotten about the stick. She carefully unwrapped her prized possession and regarded the pregnant indicator - a thin pink line. Annie. That's what she will call the baby if it's a girl. Annie. She said it out loud. Annie. Like in her favorite movie, *Sleepless in Seattle*. Annie.

"Are you Annie?" In the movie, a million different emotions were evident in the little boy's voice, the most obvious was hope.

Annie had an aura about her, and Jonah noticed it. He had been right in liking her letter best of all. He had been right in wanting her to be his new mother.

"Yes." Annie, standing on top of the Empire State Building, looked straight into the soul of Jonah's dad, Sam, when she confidently said the one word that would change the three lives forever.

"You're Annie?" The puzzled, mesmerized, smitten Sam, mouth agape, asked.

Brenda imagined her daughter holding out a tiny hand and introducing herself to the other children on the playground. I'm Annie. And then someday, hopefully, to her soulmate.

She pulled the address of Alec's hotel off the cork-board and ran down the stairs, out the door, test stick in hand, three blocks to the post office, bought a small express envelope right there at the counter, dropped the stick in with no note, no explanation, just Alec's name and hotel scrawled in her most hurried handwriting.

**

Brenda was excited. The brisk walk, half-jog, half-sprint to the post office left her panting, sweaty, exhausted, and exhilarated. She tried to tone it down a bit on the way home, forcing herself to stroll and let herself recover a bit, but she couldn't. She was excited. She was pregnant! And she had Ted's offer to let her use his art studio!

She filled the tea kettle with water and put it on the stove. A nice cup of tea would settle her down and bring her back to a baseline of normalcy. She couldn't stop smiling as she thought of her baby. Hers and Alec's baby. It seemed forever since she'd had Henry; it was almost like she was pregnant for the first time. She touched her belly and instinctively let her hand wander to her left breast. In her mind, she could see the red splotch. She'd studied it so intently over the past few days that it's color and shape were imprinted in the darkness behind her eyes. It almost looked like Australia. Almost. She willed the thought of her breast away and instead imagined herself standing in front of an easel in Ted's studio, the expanse of the city from the ninety-second floor so close yet so far. What would she paint? Perhaps an abstract of the view. Maybe at dusk or shortly after sunset, when it's dark enough to see windows lit up in the neighboring buildings and blinding red brake lights on the cars below. Or yellow. Yellow light pouring from windows and yellow taxi cabs dotting the street.

She checked the tea kettle. Not boiling yet. She couldn't sit still. She was so excited about Ted's offer and even more excited about Alec getting her package in a few days. She regarded the kitchen table, still laden with piles, but better than before. Her enthusiasm for decluttering had fizzled out sometime in July. By then she had tackled quite a bit and had high hopes that cleaning out her closets would somehow clean out her mind, clean up her marriage, declutter her life. Not that there was anything wrong with her marriage, or her life. It was just that over the past little bit, well, Alec was sulky and quick to lecture and generally unpleasant to be around. Mostly. She mostly tried to ignore it, chalking it up to the stress of dealing with other people's problems all day. Henry escaped in his Legos and video games and books. Alec mostly left Henry alone. Whatever was up with Alec was temporary. It had to be. He was in a pretty good mood last night and this morning before her little meltdown in the cab. It was her mind though, that seemed to need the most decluttering. Sometimes she felt like she was standing in front of a vast display of televisions in a store window. But instead of all the stations looping through the same promo video, they all displayed a different story, a separate thread, a different thought that entered her mind and took her attention away from the idea that was there two seconds before. Soon her head was spinning as she tried to keep track of what she was watching on each TV. She regularly took long walks around their Brooklyn neighborhood and forced herself to just be quiet. No internal dialog. No jumping from one thought to the next. Just be quiet. The first time she tried to do this, it felt like she couldn't breathe. She didn't realize how much of her brain the internal dialog was occupying. Not until she tried to be quiet. It literally took her breath away. Alec sat her down one night and suggested - gently, almost too gently, like he was talking to a child with the kind of feigned calm that preceded a grounding or some other type of disciplinary action - that she be tested for ADHD. He even went so far as to hand her the business card of one of his colleagues.

"But how could I possibly have ADHD?" she'd protested. "Sometimes I can get lost in something for hours and get so focused that the house could catch fire and burn around me and I wouldn't notice that the house was on fire and burning down around me. That doesn't sound like ADHD, Alec."

"Ah, but it does," he said, his voice even gentler and calmer than before. Brenda braced herself - for what, she was unsure. "It's called hyper focusing. People with ADHD have an uncanny ability to hyper-focus on things of great interest to them. Like when you cook. You get that way when you cook. You used to get that way when you painted."

"Well, I think you're wrong. I don't believe I have ADHD."

"Then stop complaining about your 'cluttered mind.' Go ahead and keep cleaning out closets. Let me know if that works."

***

Brenda flitted around the kitchen waiting for her water to boil, taking a pile here, a pile there and making one large pile in the middle of the kitchen island. Earlier in the summer, she'd emptied a cabinet in the corner of the kitchen that wasn't quite large enough to store pots or dishes. There was, however, enough counter space and wall space to make a tiny kitchen command center. And that was her intent when she'd decided to clean out that cabinet. Ah, but she'd gone a step further. She removed the cabinet's two shelves and installed metal brackets that would serve as hanging file holders. When she showed Alec the finished product, well, he seemed genuinely impressed. He squatted and stuck his head in the cabinet to examine the hardware she'd installed. He shook his head and smiled at her. Yes! She'd dazzled him! Maybe he would come out of his funk for a day or two or even an hour. But he didn't, not really. She hadn't really thought about it until now, but the conversation with Alec about having ADHD dampened her enthusiasm.

The whistling tea kettle startled her. She selected a bag of Darjeeling from the jar of tea bags she kept near the stove. The bubbling water she poured over the tea bag made it swell to the point of nearly bursting. She set the pot back down and went into the bedroom to retrieve the box of unopened, multicolored hanging file folders she'd found in the hall closet during the apex of her decluttering season. She had initially wanted to toss it in the bin she'd set aside for donations but decided to hang onto it, suspecting that it might just prove useful someday, violating her own resolve in doing so. She'd started her decluttering venture determined to be brutal with herself when it came to what she should keep and what she should toss. Today she was glad she'd kept it and was reaching for it when she eyed what looked like Alec's small travel bag. She opened it - its contents confirming that indeed he had meant to take it with him. She draped it over her shoulder, grabbed the file folders, and went back to the kitchen to resume her project.

The forgotten tea suddenly beckoned, and she took a long, slow sip, letting its mild flavor and aroma fill her with a sense of calm. She welcomed the peace as she removed, one by one, the contents of Alec's bag. *Men's Health* magazine and an old NYU alumni newsletter. Visine and Afrin. His black leather journal - the one where he keeps his lists - and Laura Hillenbrand's *Seabiscuit*. Oh, and what's this? Another book. A Billy Collins poetry book - *Picnics, Lightning*. She liked Billy Collins and wondered when Alec became interested in poetry. Perhaps he meant to give the book to her. Or he'd planned to memorize a poem or two and recite them to her when he returned. She flipped through the book, wondering if Alec even read it yet. She hated the idea of running back down to the post office, or better yet, FedEx, in an attempt for Alec to have his bag of stuff sometime tomorrow. Brenda picked up his journal and fanned the pages like an animation flip book and watched page after page after page of lists - one or two words per line - flash before her like subliminal messages. She knew how lost he would be without his lists. She set the journal down and picked up Billy Collins again. She skimmed through it, quickly turning the pages, searching for something, some clue she wasn't even sure she wanted or needed.

Frustrated with Billy and what he wasn't revealing, she leaned back in her chair and picked up yesterday's *New York Times* and held it out in front of her, like her father used to do after dinner. The sun pouring through the window above the kitchen sink backlit the paper, overlaying the text on the front page with the writing on the next page, making it hard to read. She was about to fold it back over and turn away from the sun when she saw what appeared to be green ink shining through to the front page. It looked like a circle. So, Alec circled something. She flipped the front page over to reveal a list of ten items that Alec had scribbled in the margin. Item Seven was circled. Alec had scrawled a preliminary list on the newspaper. She opened his journal to see if he'd transcribed it there. He hadn't. Item Seven. Circled like an unintended piece of evidence left behind in one's haste to leave the scene of your yet uncommitted crime. Item Seven. Circled like a whiney taunt, daring Brenda to find it, bullying her to have anything to say about it. Item Seven. Another sense of impending doom - just what she needed, as if the sense of impending doom at having a miniature, red, scaly Australia tattooed on her left breast wasn't enough. She folded up the section of the newspaper and stuck it inside the cover of Alec's journal. Then she threw the journal, Billy Collins, and the rest of Alec's crap across the room.

With a renewed sense of purpose, she opened the box of hanging file folders and stuffed them, one by one, with logically categorized items that had once been random piles. She labeled each folder and placed the folders in alphabetical order inside her DIY file cabinet. When she was finished, she stared at the stark, clean, crisp, decluttered countertops, running her fingers over the granite and noticing - perhaps for the first time - the stone's smoothness. She laid her cheek on it and relished the way it felt cold against her skin. She closed her eyes and tried not to think about anything.

* * *

Brenda was only partially sentient and slightly aware of an ache on the side of her chin when her cell phone startled her awake. She was momentarily unaware of her surroundings and felt as if one side of her face had been pressed flat. She answered the phone and heard what sounded like her son rattling off a list of, oh yes, school stuff: *two pairs of jeans, a New York Giants hoodie, a dozen socks, three green shirts that Aunt Kathy made me get, and a cool backpack lunch thing.*

"Put Aunt Kathy on the phone," she heard herself saying, fully awake now after having fallen asleep at the kitchen counter. She heard Henry's heavy footsteps on her sister's hardwoods.

"You'll never believe what your kid said to the..."

"Are you alone?" Brenda said, interrupting her sister.

"Why are you whispering? Is everything okay?"

"Yes, well no, but yes. Make sure Henry isn't within earshot." She could hear Kathy's muffled voice, her hand obviously over the phone. Then the sliding glass door and the squeak she always talked about fixing but never did. She pictured her sister stepping out onto her little balcony.

"Okay, I'm alone. Now talk."

"I'mpregnantandIthinkAlecissleepingwithJenn." She couldn't believe she got it all out in one breath.

"What was that? Slow down."

"I'm pregnant." She paused, and Kathy squealed. "And Alec's sleeping with Jenn." Silence.

"Who the hell is Jenn?"

"His partner, colleague, or whatever shrinks call each other."

"Jenn with the hair?" Ordinarily, this would have made Brenda laugh. Alec was a self-proclaimed lover of long hair. Brenda hated long hair but wore it well past her shoulders to please him. Jenn had ultra-short, bleached, pixie hair. Right now, there was nothing funny about any of it. "What do you mean he's sleeping with her?" Silence. "Okay. How do you know? Did he tell you? Oh God, you didn't catch them, did you?"

"No. No. No. Please. No. I did not catch them!"

"Then what." Kathy sounded frustrated. "How do you know?"

"Forget it, Kathy." It was Brenda's turn to get frustrated. "I just know, ok?" She started crying, and Kathy let her sob into the phone. It was something Kathy was good at, always had been, probably a product of their age difference - Kathy was always like a little mother - and liked taking charge of things, in a good way, of course. And when she wasn't taking charge of things, she was there. Just there. Like now. Letting her baby sister sob on the phone. Other sisters may have hung up in frustration. Brenda was tempted to hang up on herself. But instead, she got the first of what she expected would be many waves of waterworks out. Then, between sobs: "Alec left his little carry-on travel bag in the closet so I opened it to see what I might need to send him and I found a book of poetry in it."

"Alec reads poetry?"

"This is news to me too."

"So, he reads poetry. So, what?"

"But that book?" She sniffed. "Why would they need to discuss a book of poetry professionally?"

"I have no idea what you're talking about."

"I also found a list. Alec made a list of things to do at the conference. Item seven: Discuss BC book with Jenn. BC stands for Billy Collins. It's a Billy Collins book. He never told me Jenn was going with him. Maybe I should call Rick."

"Who the hell is Rick?"

"Jenn's live-in."

"Did it ever occur to you that Rick might be going on the trip too? By the way, why aren't you on that flight? I would have watched Henry. Anyway, there could be a million reasons he needs to discuss the book with Jenn. Maybe the author is one of their patients. Did you even read the book?"

"Billy Collins couldn't possibly be one of their patients. I read enough of it."

Kathy took an audibly loud, deep breath, doing nothing to hide her exasperation, the compassionate little mother replaced by typical sister-isms. "Who's to say Billy doesn't need therapy? Poets are usually depressed or otherwise tormented souls, right?"

"I'm hanging up now." And Brenda did just that. She was sure her sister was standing on her balcony, phone still in her hand, shaking her head, mumbling something or other about Brenda being crazy for concluding these things based on nothing, really. Nothing but a book of poetry. Poetry! She could understand if it were an academic book on some deep topic about the psyche. Or something that was written by someone within their professional circle - Alec wrote lots of reviews for fellow shrinks throughout the years. But Billy Collins? Poetry? She liked Billy Collins. He was on the radio one afternoon when she just happened to be in the car. He read two or three of his poems on the air. She doesn't remember what they were about, she just remembers that she liked them and could relate to them. They were clear and concise and in plain English. There was nothing depressed or tormented in them. Oh, what were those damned poems about? Billy Collins couldn't possibly be one of Alec's patients.

One by one she picked Alec's things off the floor and stuffed them back into his bag. Brenda was clutching the book when she realized that she and Kathy never did make it back to her other news - her pregnancy.

She opened the book and found it on Page Fifty-one. The little asterisk next to the title of the poem her husband didn't want to forget to discuss with his colleague. Japan. The poem was called Japan. She read the first few lines and quickly closed the book, unable to continue. But her fingers became possessed, and she was unable to control them as they found Page 51 again. She willed her eyes shut, but they were independent of her. The poem started small and benign but ended big. Like a crescendo or Bolero. It got bigger and louder until finally, it ended with the answer to the questions strung across the past few months like clear, plastic beads on a Christmas tree, so subtle that Brenda didn't even know they were there until she plugged in the lights and the beads cast their reflection all over the room.

Pizza Love - Brenda

"MOM, WHAT KIND OF DOCTOR was that?" Henry looked up from his Gameboy long enough to look at the wall behind his mother, then bounced his eyes right back to the tiny screen. "I mean, it wasn't a regular doctor, was it? All the ladies in there had humongous stomachs. Grant's mom is having a baby on Halloween. Are you having a baby mom?"

As if on cue in a stage production, the waiter miraculously arrived with their pizza, half dotted with pepperoni and the other half an orgy of Italian sausage, olives, mushrooms, sweet red peppers, onions, and extra cheese. They were at their favorite pizza place, and Brenda willed the waiter's interruption to avert the conversation long enough to decide what to tell him. Typically, she would schedule her doctor appointments for when Henry was in school, but she noticed some spotting just after Henry got off the bus. Her doctor said she could come right in. Most of Henry's friends' moms worked full time, and Kathy couldn't have gotten there that quickly. So, she left her son in the waiting room with his Gameboy and a bunch of ladies with hu-mongous stomachs.

"Yes, the doctor thinks I'm having a baby, but they need to do another test tomorrow to be absolutely sure." She decided to tell him the truth about the baby, but didn't want to say to him that tomorrow's test had nothing to do with the baby. She didn't want to tell him that her obstetrician noticed the red, scaly patch on her breast and didn't like the looks of it. She especially didn't want to tell him that Liz (yes, her obstetrician insisted on being called by her first name) wanted to send her for a biopsy now. Today. Immediately. Pronto. Without hesitation. What Brenda really wanted was to wait until next week when her schedule could better support it. But Liz alarmed her with her tone when she finally agreed to tomorrow - at the latest. For now, Brenda was trying desperately to put everything in a box - the thing with her breast and the situation with Alec. She talked to Alec Sunday night and told him that he'd left his bag behind but didn't mention the Billy Collins book or Item Seven on his list. She did ask him if Jenn was also at this conference and he got quiet before he said yes. Brenda offered to book a flight and deliver the bag in person, but he grumbled about the cost. *Never mind I'll just mail it*, is what she finally said and thought she heard Alec sigh in relief. She sent it the next day but decided to keep Billy Collins for herself. He should have received the bag and the pregnancy stick by now.

"Cool. I hope it's a girl." His mouth was full of pizza. "Is it a girl? Grant's mom is having a girl."

"It's way too early to tell." Brenda pushed the pizza out of the way and leaned across the table to get closer to Henry's face. She could smell the pepperoni on him and felt a lump rising in her throat. He was dark like Alec. His expressions mimicked his dad's expressions too, like now, with one bushy eyebrow arched all the way up, almost to where it disappeared under his thick bangs. She pushed the bangs out of the way and kissed his forehead.

"You want a girl, don't you? What does Dad want? It will be okay if it's a boy, but a girl would be better." Henry reached for another slice.

"I think we'll all be delighted no matter what it is. And Dad doesn't know yet. I want to surprise him. Maybe I'll call him tonight."

"Just don't tell him we're having his favorite pizza. He's probably eating sushi or something gross like that."

"Dad loves sushi," Brenda said.

"But he loves pizza more."

Brenda couldn't argue with that. When they were first married, Alec was offered a job as an in-house psychologist at a Washington, DC law firm called Martin, Barton, Wilson, and Flynn. She and Alec thought the name, when spoken out loud and in a rather animated way, sounded more like characters in children's rhyme (Martin, Barton, Wilson, and Flynn, sat on a toilet and one fell in). Brenda and Alec soon began a quest for the pizza they both grew up eating. Nothing came close to the kind of pizza you could get in any pizza place in New York or New

Jersey. Brenda's father brought pizza home every Friday, a routine that, when reliving the memories, made her both happy and sad.

"Pops has a meeting every Friday and walks right past Red Moon," Brenda announced this to her sister one day as if revealing a long-held secret she could no longer hold in.

"Well Pops is a drunk, and the meetings are so he can learn how to not be a drunk." Kathy, at age fifteen, didn't mince words.

"What's a drunk?"

"He drinks too much beer and schnapps."

Brenda didn't care. Pops was happy when he had a glass of schnapps or a beer, especially when Uncle Dory was over. When Uncle Dory was over Mommy was a lot nicer to Pops.

One night, Pops came through the door and Mommy yelled something about being able to smell him halfway down the street.

"You stopped at that hell-hole, didn't you?" Mommy whacked Pops with a dish towel.

"I skipped one lousy meeting. So, what? Dory needed to talk, to run a business plan by me. So yeah, we went to Gio's and sat at the bar and talked business. I had a beer."

"He only had one." Uncle Dory walked in and hung his coat and hat on the coat rack.

"Nah, Dor it's okay." Pops looked at Uncle Dory, then at Mommy, then back at Uncle Dory. "I had two. Okay, three. I had three lousy beers." He shoved the pizza box into Mommy's hands. That was the last pizza Pops ever brought home.

Alec's friends at the law firm gave him a list of pizza places to try all over DC, Virginia, and Maryland. Momma Lucia's was pretty good. And Tony's was even better, but it was a bit of a shlep and just wasn't worth the hassle. On a weekend trip back to New York she tried to find Red Moon and take Alec there but after much driving around and then walking in circles around her old neighborhood, a group of old men playing chess said Red Moon had closed a decade ago. Defeated and walking back to the subway, Brenda saw Gio's across the street on the left. It was still there. She crossed the street and walked past the place, pausing to peer in the window, missing her Pops and wondering if maybe, just maybe he was sitting at the bar.

After almost two years of trying to find good pizza in DC (and yes, their standards were perhaps a bit too high) they took to staying in on Sunday nights and making their own pizza. Their first few attempts yielded disastrous results - crusts that were overly soggy or crusts that didn't rise and turned out so thin and crispy that Alec compared them to matzo. They accumulated recipes from newspapers, and spent a rainy Saturday afternoon in Barnes & Nobel, walking out with several authoritative sources on the topic.

The official recipe testing began in their apartment. They invited several friends and opened bottles of red wine. They baked five different crusts and topped them with a tomato sauce recipe they'd found about a year before and liked. A hefty helping of a mozzarella and parmesan combination on each pie and they were ready to be baked. They sampled and rated and by the time they got to Specimen Cinque they were sprawled on the couch and on the floor, swearing up and down that they would never, ever, in this lifetime or the next, eat another slice of pizza. One thing was certain. Specimen Tre was the clear winner. It tasted nothing like Red Moon's signature cheese, which had a subtle, almost burnt quality, and its exquisitely foldable crust. Ah, but Specimen Tre's crust, with its luxurious, yellow sheen, and foldable consistency was the closest they were going to get to Red Moon perfection. Brenda still made this pizza occasionally. The memories it conjured were bittersweet - the version of her beloved Pops that she held close, the fun times with Alec trying to replicate something that really couldn't be replicated, and the darkness that now hung over her broken world and threatened to suffocate her.

The C Word - Brenda

"DO YOU FEEL OKAY? Should I come home? Never mind. I'm on the next flight out of here." Alec sounded sincere, concerned, excited, pathetic, and guilty all in one long, meandering sentence, complete with rising and falling tones and cadence, like the miserable song medleys that pitiable singers spew out in dark, depressing hotel piano bars. *Sing us a song you're the piano man.* Brenda now wished she hadn't mailed the test stick. She almost didn't want him to know. She wanted to keep it to herself for a while longer, get used to the idea of Annie (she felt confident she was carrying a girl). She felt somehow poisoned by Alec and his words and his piano bar tone. She imagined herself telling him about the genuine possibility that she has breast cancer. She imagined him humming another obligatory, dismal medley - Mozart's Requiem came instantly to mind. The hard part was that he would get on a plane and come home. A part of her wanted nothing more than to fall into his arms and sob - just get it all out - and have him tell her that they'd get through the cancer (if it even was cancer) and that nothing was going on with Jenn. It was six in the morning in Tokyo. Alec answered the phone as if he'd been up for hours. She imagined Jenn, freshly showered and wrapped in a thick, white towel, sitting on the edge of the bed. Brenda decided then to keep the cancer news to herself for a while. If she needed to sob so badly, she'd call her sister.

"I'm fine. I'm not even nauseous. Well, maybe a little, but nothing like I was with Henry. I'm fine." She heard him sigh loudly. She couldn't quite make out if it was a sigh of frustration, relief at not having to rush home (leaving Jenn behind), or desire (perhaps Jenn stood up in front of him and let the towel slide to the floor).

***

"Mrs. Arnstein." Brenda jumped. She felt the heat rising from her feet all the way up through her legs. It engulfed her torso and set her neck on fire. She felt like she'd been hit with a blast of steam from an oven filled with Henry's favorite chocolate chip cookies. Only there was no home baked, sweet, buttery aroma wafting through the air. Just the intense heat and all of the fear she stuffed into any and every glass jar she could find.

Until this moment, she had been fine. She'd survived talking to Alec this morning - without anger, tears, or spewing accusations about Jenn. She was able to swallow a multitude of words before they formed, which was extraordinarily rare for her and something she was typically horrible at. She was also pleased with how glib and nonchalant she'd sounded (at least in her own head) when she called Kathy and asked her to come over. She had intended for her to stay with Henry but had forgotten that he would be in school - an indication of how distracted she really was.

Now, at the sound of her name - Mrs. Arnstein - every fear that she'd carefully trapped in the glass jars multiplied and expanded. She willed the jars to not crack by focusing on the fact that she was pregnant. Annie. Annie. Annie. Of course, God wouldn't give her both a blessing and a curse - a baby and cancer. Or would he? It made no sense that God would enable her to conceive and at the same time provide a little bonus gift in the form of a red, scaly patch on her left breast. Although last night she noticed that the skin felt harder than she remembered it feeling before - almost like the growth caused the surrounding tissue to be pulled tight. She willed the thought away. God wouldn't do this. Nope. He simply would not. But the way the nurse spoke her name was almost as if God Himself revealed to her the inevitable truth that the biopsy was merely a formality and that she was as good as gone. It was the nurse's incongruously bouncy, happy vocal quality. Something about that voice caused Brenda's carefully stuffed glass jars to shatter and release all of her fears.

"Should I come in with you?" Kathy's hand was tight around Brenda's arm as if holding her in place, not wanting to let her go in because she might come out a different person. She looked into Kathy's eyes and shook her head. She got up then and let the bouncy nurse lead her to her fate.

***

The three biopsies took less than an hour. Stick. Scrape. Punch. Brenda's breast was now void of the red splotch and sported several stitches. After they stuck a needle into it to extract cells, they scraped some of the surface skin for analysis. Then they punched out a portion of her flesh with what looked like a cookie cutter. She felt sorry for herself and needed Alec. In movies, it was always couples occupying the two chairs in front of the doctor's large mahogany desk. In this particular movie she was alone. The desk was stainless steel - not mahogany. And instead of two chairs directly in front of the desk there was a lime green sofa against the wall. The doctor could wheel her chair around the desk, kitty-corner to the couch, like a living room furniture grouping to encourage intimate conversation. She wasn't a big fan of the color gray, especially on walls, but the gray on the wall behind the couch was a surprisingly warm gray, like the hue the sky sometimes turned on late summer afternoons after a thunderstorm. Gray with a warm yellow glow behind it. She loved how the afternoons that emerged from these short-lived storms were a few degrees cooler and a lot less humid than before. Early in their marriage she and Alec would sit on the front steps and watch the storms. Sometimes a bottle of wine sat between them. Other times they each had a beer. She can't remember the last time they deliberately watched a storm. Back then it was more exciting than going to the movies. She liked this warm gray wall and the way the lime green couch looked against it. She sat down and ran her hand up and down the arm. It was a good, sturdy fabric, almost like denim or canvas. Durable. Gender neutral. Traditional with hints of modern elements. She heard someone come in. Expecting the doctor, she stood up, but it was only Kathy.

Panic set in. Brenda could feel it begin to engulf her. Without her knowledge or consent, her heart rate doubled, and she suddenly felt like she was choking.

"How am I going to tell Henry? What am I going to do?"

"Shush. There may be nothing to tell him. You don't know. Let's wait and see what the doctor says."

Brenda nodded and sat back down, cold and shaking. She forced air into her lungs and held it there, then released it slowly, like Alec told her to do the time they hiked Old Rag Mountain in Virginia and she found herself traversing a boulder that seemed to be suspended in mid-air, a million feet up. Thinking about Alec, she started to panic all over again. He's always wanted to hike Mount Fuji. Ha! It's not that far from Tokyo. She wondered now if he and Jenn were perhaps planning a little excursion there. Breathe. Just breathe. Kathy held her hand and squeezed it hard.

"I'm going to send you for a CT scan today." She hadn't heard the doctor come in, yet there she was in her white coat, notebook in hand, standing in front of the couch. The doctor made her way to her desk, sat down, opened a drawer, pulled out a piece of paper, and started scribbling, never looking at Brenda or Kathy. "No point waiting, since you're already here. They can take you at two o'clock."

"I have to pick up my son at three-fifteen. How am I going to..."

"I'll get him," Kathy interrupted.

"Could we do it earlier, so my sister could come with me?"

The doctor removed her glasses and Brenda was struck with the unusual color of her eyes. Almost a light teal, nearly the color of the Caribbean Sea. Colored contacts. Had to be.

"No, I'm sorry. I'll need to send you down now for your injection. They need to inject the radioactive die three hours before the scan. But listen, this is a piece of cake. And it's routine. I don't want you to think that just because I'm ordering this CT scan that I think you conclusively have cancer. We really won't know that for a couple of days. Like we talked about before, your symptoms present like classic inflammatory breast cancer, but really, it could be anything, maybe even related to your pregnancy."

"Wait a minute, how can you send me for a CT scan if I'm pregnant? How can you even think about sending me for this kind of procedure?" She bounced her head from the doctor to Kathy, then back to the doctor.

"Listen. If you have IBC - and I'm not saying you do - but if you do, there is a chance it has already spread. Typical places are lymph nodes and bones. The sooner we can find these things out, the sooner we can start treating you, the better your prognosis."

"How about this." Kathy jumped into the conversation. "You said the biopsy results will be back when? In a day or two?" The doctor nodded. "Then what difference is a day or two going to make? If the biopsy comes back positive we'll take it from there. If not, then we didn't put my sister's baby in unnecessary danger."

"I'm not the least bit in favor of your approach. As a matter of fact, I think it's the wrong approach. I'll acquiesce, just this one time."

So, her Caribbean blue eyes gave her license to use such words as acquiesce? Like a reproachful parent rolling over after listening to her teenaged daughter beg and plead to be allowed to stay out one-hour past curfew. Alec sometimes used that word. *Okay, I'll acquiesce and do it your way.* He sometimes bowed as he said it. Brenda hated that word. The doctor handed her several sheets of paper.

"Take these with you when you go. And don't worry too much about your pregnancy. "The body scan will check for what we call hot spots. If one is found, then I will schedule another biopsy of that spot."

"How soon would that happen?" Brenda suddenly realized that Kathy's arm was around her. She thought about the night their mother invited them home for dinner. Brenda was still in college and Kathy was a full-fledged adult, complete with her own apartment and a full-time job with benefits. *I have cancer.* Their mother had been matter-of-fact and nonchalant when she told them. She'd been standing at the stove sautéing onions in what seemed like a pound of butter. Brenda and Kathy were deeply engrossed in a conversation about sand. When they didn't respond, their mother repeated, louder, *I have cancer. I'm dying.* To this day, the smell of sautéed onions makes Brenda sick.

"You do understand that IBC is an especially aggressive form of cancer, especially in younger women." Dr. Caribbean Blue Eyes skirted her question.

"Yes, I realize this."

"Good. Because I want to make sure you understand how serious this could be."

* * *

Brenda couldn't recall how she ended up in Times Square, sitting on the red steps behind the statue of Father Duffy. One minute she and Kathy were walking out the door of Brooklyn Hospital Center, and the next minute they were walking across the Brooklyn Bridge. The bridge was notably void of the kinds of crowds you often see on weekends and holidays. This morning it was mostly women pushing kids in strollers, a few joggers, and a group stopping every few minutes to listen to their tour guide and take pictures. There were three men, their suit jackets draped over their shoulders, walking briskly and talking about how they hoped they wouldn't be late for their meeting. She imagined the poor unsuspecting souls, who were probably at this moment sitting around a large conference table, breathing the last particles of clean, unscented air before the three men, glistening with sweat and smelling quite ripe, arrived. She didn't realize how fast she and Kathy were walking until they were well on the other side of the bridge, standing on Canal Street - that precipice where Chinatown meets little Italy. The street was lined with vendors hocking bargains. Brenda stopped to call her friend Wendy to see if Henry could go home with Grant after school. *Of course, Henry is always welcome!* Wendy laughed then about having had false contractions all weekend, and hopefully, Henry and Grant wouldn't end up in the emergency room with her. *Grant was a month early.* Wendy seemed eager to talk and started on about her last doctor appointment and how the baby

- Frisbee is what they were calling her at the moment - had already moved down some.

On the other side of the street, a vendor was selling what had to be counterfeit CDs. She spotted a rack of colorful ties and saw one she thought Alec might like. A hot, silky wind blew her hair out of her eyes and with it, the fact that she had momentarily forgotten that her husband is in Japan with Jenn, instead of with her. Brenda looked away from the ties and thanked Wendy for the help. She shoved the phone into her back pocket and saw Kathy walking toward her with two pretzels. One was slathered with mustard.

"Here." Kathy handed her the mustard drenched pretzel and pulled an ice-cold can of Diet Coke out of her purse. "Water would have been better for you, but I know you like to drink something carbonated with pretzels."

"I've been thinking a lot about mom these past few days." Brenda opened the Diet Coke and took an endless gulp. "I'm wondering if I would even have told her about this."

"This being cancer, or this being Alec?"

"This being Alec. I definitely would have told mom about the cancer. Wait a minute, it's not necessarily cancer. Why do you say cancer like that's what I have? I might not have it."

They walked up Sixth Avenue in silence. Brenda looked at her watch - only twenty minutes or so had elapsed.

"About Alec." Kathy broke the silence as she stopped in front of a sushi place. The thought of sushi caused Brenda to throw up a little in her mouth.

"What about Alec?" She was annoyed, hot, and still thirsty, despite the soda. And somewhat gassy - from the Diet Coke, she guessed. "Could we keep walking please?"

"Why? Where are we going? I thought maybe we could sit somewhere and talk."

"We can sit and talk, okay, but not in this smelly sushi bar." A stout man wearing a brown tee shirt and jeans pushed his way past them to go into the restaurant. Moisture oozed through the sides of his shirt. Subtle hints of garlic mixed with perspiration lingered after the door closed behind him. The pungency he left behind seemed to be having a party at Brenda's expense as it danced around her nose and taunted her. She threw up a little more in her mouth and calmly stepped toward the curb and spit it out. She continued up Sixth Avenue, now with purpose, and didn't turn around to see if Kathy was still with her. Several blocks later she burst through the door of a bodega that was nestled between a cobbler shop, and, horror - another sushi bar. *Gatorade. Where is the Gatorade?*

"Drink up." Kathy handed her a bottle of the yellow kind. As always, her sister was right there, knowing exactly what she needed. Brenda hugged her and reached into her pocket for the five-dollar bill she always carried. Kathy waved it away, walked over to the cashier, and paid.

* * *

Brenda's back ached. She felt foggy and a bit delirious. The walk across the bridge, the walk up Sixth Avenue, the left on Broadway and the right on Seventh Street was a blur. Where did she get this massive bottle of Gatorade? She was hot and sweaty and a little bit confused, but her stomach seemed to have settled down - the gas and cramping she'd felt earlier was gone. Where was Kathy? Oh yes, she was in line attempting to get tickets for today's *Les Misérables* matinee. Brenda was excited to see it, despite having seen it twice. She was grateful for Wendy's willingness to keep Henry for the day. Without warning, she felt an urge to confide in Wendy about what's going on with her health. This was unusual for her - she preferred to keep things private and deal with them herself or with Alec, if necessary. If she were completely honest with herself, she would admit that besides her sister, she didn't have a single, close girlfriend. Today, right now, she regretted this about herself. She imagined herself in bed, ravaged with cancer, bald and emaciated, taking her last few breaths with Alec, Henry, baby Annie, and Kathy at her bedside. Not that this was a bad thing. These were the only people she would care to see in the last seconds before she moved on. She didn't want Henry to see her like that. The way her mother had been at the end of her life. How would he process that? He's only ten. So maybe he'd be older when the time came, like thirteen or fifteen. Those are still impressionable years. Even if he were fresh out of college like she had been when her mother died. It was hard then, even as a young adult. Very hard.

When she and Alec first moved to Brooklyn, Brenda decided to try church and surprised herself by attending faithfully and in earnest, every Sunday. She enjoyed the worship but also wanted to connect with other people. Yet she never seemed able to bond with anyone. Henry wasn't enthusiastic about attending church, and she didn't want to force him. Plus, Alec tried to expose Henry to his Jewish heritage, but even that was sporadic. She joined a bible study group, and one of the women, Lori, was diagnosed with a rare form of liver cancer. Lori was only twenty-eight and had three-year-old twin girls. For the six months or so that Lori lived after her diagnosis, she was surrounded by what appeared to be close friends. Brenda volunteered a few times to bring a meal, and every time, at least a half-dozen women were there, sitting with her on the couch, or later, on the edge of the hospital bed that was set up in the living room. They'd be laughing, telling stories, reminiscing, while the twins, seemingly oblivious, played quietly. She was beginning to think that yes, she wanted these kinds of women in her life, these kinds of friendships. She just had no idea where to start or even if she had enough time for cultivating close friendships. She shook her head as if to shake off these silly aspirations. She had Kathy. It would have to be enough.

She put her hands on the bleacher behind her and stretched, trying to relieve what felt like a ball of knots in her back, or a rubber-band ball like the one Henry worked on every now and again. The last time she saw it, the grapefruit-sized ball of colorful rubber was peeking out from under his bed. She stretched her legs. Her sister seemed to be taking awfully long at the ticket booth. She looked at her watch. If Kathy didn't hurry up, they would miss the overture. She carefully made her way down to the street and wandered to the Father Duffy monument. The inscription on the statue's base read *Chaplain Francis P. Duffy, Fighting 69th Infantry Regiment*. She stood as close as she could and looked up at his grim and scowling face. His fists clenched his coat. Alec did that too - mainly when they were walking, and he was contemplating something serious, either said or unsaid. She imagined that his face will bear a similar scowl when she confronts him over Jenn. And while he may not be wearing a coat this time of year, Brenda imagined that he would clutch something, probably his shirt or the air. She'd had enough of Father Duffy and turned to look at his neighbor, George M. Cohen. Now, George, there was a happy looking fellow, despite being frozen in bronze and unable to move. *Give my regards to Broadway.*

"There you are!" Kathy appeared, breaking Brenda's reverie. She was leaning against the base of George, staring at nothing. Kathy waved two tickets to *Les Misérables* in front of her face.

Brenda took the tickets and nodded in approval. The seats weren't ideal, but it was wonderful to have this diversion. She slid her butt down the statue until she was sitting on the ground, her back resting against it. She put her head in her hands.

"I don't want Henry to see me the way mom was. I can't bear the thought of him seeing me like that."

"First of all, Mom had pancreatic cancer. You know that's a death sentence. But breast cancer, now that's curable. Especially this early."

"But you heard what the doctor said. She said the kind I have is aggressive. If I even have it." She thought about this for a few seconds and panicked. "But what if I do have it? And what if Alec really is running around with Jenn? What do I do then? Introduce Henry to his new mommy? Tell Alec he could sleep with her, move her into our bed while I set up shop in a hospital bed in the living room?"

"Breathe." Kathy sat down on the ground next to her and put her arm around her shoulder, pulling her close.

Brenda tried to take a deep breath and was surprised when the air lodged somewhere between her throat and stomach. Her panic intensified. She stood up and started to walk away, but Kathy was bigger and stronger and walked her to one of the little bistro tables scattered about the square and gently pushed her onto a chair.

"Now breathe."

"What am I going to do?" She felt the tears welling in her eyes for the first time since she and Alec fought over the moths. When was that? Yesterday? The day before? Two days before that? It was a blur, and now the streets of New York were a blur. She blinked, and water rushed from her eyes like a flash flood. "What am I going to do?"

"Breathe."

"Stop saying that! Stop telling me to breathe!" In an instant, the flood receded and gave way to an unexpected, uncontrolled torrent of laughter. Kathy caught the bug, and the two of them laughed so loud people turned to look.

* * *

Brenda was impressed with this Fantine. She flipped through *Playbill* to get a better look at the actress. Her stomach tightened again, this time the pain seemed confined to the area behind her belly button. She abandoned any thought that it was anything other than stress, and with that thought, also abandoned *Playbill*.

Brenda focused on the dying, tuberculosis ravished Fantine. Cosette, the child, dancing before her, but not really there. A man at the root of all the evil who had led the young, vivacious, giddy Fantine down the winding roads where she ultimately made the choices she made. A stranger at the crossroads. The wealthy, young student who wooed her. The backstory that the musical only vaguely addressed. The memory of the kiss that led to more that led to Cosette. A human system - a family - whose primary member abandoned. Did the wealthy young student know he planted a seed? Or did he disappear before even Fantine knew? How could anyone not love her? And then her raw instinct to protect her child, selling her hair, selling her teeth, falling victim to the fraudulent Thénardier - the reason for her martyrdom. How hard must it have been to give up her child to Thenardier's care? Did she expect to ever see her again?

This was the difference between men and women, Brenda thought. The woman has to carry the child and be responsible for the child while the man can disappear. Was it fair to blame a man for leaving if he didn't even know of the child? Brenda wasn't sure. The pain again. She sat still, willing it away. Javert spitting angry, guttural words upon seeing Valjcan. The bass-baritone versus tenor argument that ensued. Brenda slowly raised her body out of her seat, amazed at how badly her lower abdomen hurt. Gas. Had to be.

"Where are you going?" Kathy whispered, never taking her eyes off the stage, perhaps finally becoming a fan.

"To the restroom."

"But this is your favorite part. Can't you wait for intermission?"

"No."

***

The ledge around the giant water tower was narrow. Henry was standing on it, legs spread apart for stability, feet pointed east and west and arms stretched out like a ballerina in the second position. His back was pressed against the cement wall. Brenda, holding her breath, hovered over the top like a ghost. She knew she was dreaming, yet she couldn't wake up. She tried to force herself awake but didn't want to startle Henry. She needed a plan, needed to figure out how she was going to get him down. The water below the ledge was black, rough, and swirling. Suddenly she too was on the ledge, but sitting against the wall, her legs dangling, toes almost touching the water. A little girl - two or three years old - with curly blonde hair and a huge smile leaped over Brenda and ran laps around the ledge. Every few seconds the little girl looked over her shoulder at Brenda and laughed, never stopping, running faster and faster with every lap. In this dream, she somehow knew the little girl was her baby, her Annie. Brenda called out to her, but no sound escaped her mouth. She tried to grab a tiny arm as Annie ran, but she was slippery and wiggly. Brenda tried to fill her lungs with more air and yell again. A squeak. *Annie, stop! You'll fall!* The child ran faster. Curls bouncing, Annie looked over her shoulder one last time, winked, and then jumped into the churning cauldron and was gone. Brenda tried to push herself off the ledge but found herself being held back by Henry.

"Hey. Hey. Shush." Kathy, sitting on the edge of the bed gradually came into focus.

"Annie fell into the water." Brenda tried to sit up but suddenly felt hazy and light headed. She was confused. Where was she? She looked around and saw yellow. Yellow splotches on the wall. Yellow splotches with green stripes. Yellow circles and green lines. No, yellow flowers. Yellow flowers. Daffodils. Bunches and bunches of yellow daffodils. Green stems. Green grass. The nearly wall-sized painting her mother had given her. Her mother had started it when Brenda was in high school and then put it away. She pulled it out again and finished it a few years later - two months before she died. Kathy, being the oldest, got first dibs but didn't want it. Brenda never wanted to part with it. When Brenda and Alec moved into the Brooklyn apartment, the first thing she did was find the perfect wall to hang it. It landed in their bedroom, on the far wall opposite their bed.

"Okay, okay. Whatever you say. Lay back down." Kathy nudged Brenda's head toward the pillow.

"No, Annie fell into the whirlpool." She sat up in a panic and looked around the room. Where is Henry?"

"He's fine. He's in the kitchen doing his homework. He wanted Chinese, so I ordered Chinese. I hope that place down the street is okay. That's where he told me to get it." Kathy took a pillow from Alec's side of the bed and propped it behind Brenda's back. "Don't worry, I didn't tell him what happened."

Luna Moth - Brenda

IN AN ERUPTION OF UNDERSTANDING, Brenda finally realized why she'd felt such a compulsion to declutter and clean during the past few months. She was convinced, finally, that it was because she'd wanted to either prove or disprove to herself that something was up with Alec. At the time, she didn't know what she was looking for, exactly. She didn't even know that she was looking for something. It was as if she were a forensic scientist combing the crime scene for biological, chemical, or physical samples. Samples of what, she didn't know. She found nothing. Nada. Zilch. Zip. Nothing. It wasn't until she stopped looking that it came barreling out of the sky like a meteor and landed in her life, leaving a hole that she doubted could be repaired. The timing was impeccable, really. Couldn't have been better. She could write a sitcom, with each episode reflecting yet one more layer in this cruelly layered comedy routine. The first episode would start with her and Alec arguing about moths on the ceiling. The next would be the pregnancy that Alec really didn't want. Then, a whole episode - maybe even two - on The Discovery. Alec innocently leaving his bag behind in the flail of trying to get to the airport on time. Brenda innocently making The Discovery and finally finding her evidence when she least expected it. Oh, and let's not forget the content of The Discovery - a book of poems. Poems! Alec with a book of poems! If she does a good enough job with her screenwriting and portrays Alec accurately, by the time The Discovery episode airs she will have a cadre of faithful followers, her fans, the ones who relate to and sympathize with "Brenda" would begin to despise Alec. Yes, her audience will know Alec inside and out and will laugh uncontrollably when she discovers the book of poems. Perhaps she will take some artistic license and write a scene where the audience sees her having a nightmare involving Alec, naked on a bed in Japan, reciting poetry to a naked Jenn.

Dammit, she was angry and upset. Simmering with the impossible reality that she has cancer. Stewing in grief about losing the pregnancy. Alec was due home this afternoon, and she had so many things to tell him that she didn't know where to begin. He was coming home, no doubt thinking he was coming back to a healthy and pregnant wife. She'd been two weary in the aftermath to tell him about the miscarriage. How could she say to him that her very short pregnancy abruptly ended in a toilet at the Imperial Theatre, during the confrontation between Valjean and Javert? She was sure it had been a girl. Annie. Even though it was too early to be sure, she was certain nonetheless. She had been thrilled ten years ago when the doctor said the word *boy*. But now she wanted a girl. And now her baby, Annie, was gone. Not only Annie but the thought of a future Annie, or any future baby. Because the doctor with the Caribbean eyes said that at her age and with chemo (yeah reality), well, the baby-making phase of her life was likely over. She ran her hand over her belly and felt the memory of a baby that would never grow inside of her. *This is nature's way*, the emergency room nurse told her as they were scraping out the pregnancy detritus. *The best for who*, Brenda felt like screaming. Kathy squeezed her hand at that moment as if sensing Brenda was about to say something she might later regret. And then there was the oncologist. The one Dr. Caribbean Queen sent her to when her breast biopsy came back positive - the day after the miscarriage! Kathy - leave it to Kathy - mentioned that Brenda had just lost a baby. The oncologist told her the pregnancy loss was for the best. *For the best*. Like hell, it was for the best.

Brenda lifted her shirt and studied herself. She had never particularly liked her breasts. They were on the small side and somewhat asymmetrical. And they weren't as perky as they'd once been. She supposed when she gets them cut off she could have new ones built. Yep, the oncologist recommended hacking them both. She moved in closer to the mirror and examined the spot where the red splotch had been. At some instinctive level, she knew it from the beginning. Knew it wasn't some rash caused by harsh laundry detergent. She'd been using the same soap for years. She fished a folded piece of paper out of her back pocket and checked Alec's itinerary for the fifth time today. He should be home at around eight. When they talked yesterday, he said not to bother with dinner, that he would eat on the plane.

So, she figured she would have wine in the fridge and would just see where things went. Play it by ear her mother used to say. He's going to be pissed that Henry isn't home but when she sits him down and tells him everything, well, he'll understand. Hopefully. Either that or he'll blame her - for the miscarriage and for getting cancer.

* * *

Brenda picked up the phone in the kitchen and dialed the number for the surgical center where she'd had her second biopsy - this time to test a "hot spot" that the CT scan had revealed. The rapidity with which they were able to "squeeze her in" for the procedure was impressive. The spot was at the base of her spine. It was small, they assured her. And it could be anything, really, not necessarily a metastasis from the breast cancer. And that would be the good news. Just chop off her tits, pump a few chemicals into her body, lose her hair, maybe even sign up for one of those three-day walks, grow her hair back, and appreciate the good in everything and everyone and be grateful for every breath. She hung up the phone - the results were not in yet. Definitely by tomorrow. She made sure they had her cell phone number.

Kathy called to check on her, told her that she was helping Henry research green tree frogs for his science report. They were about to head out to the library. Brenda was grateful. Grateful for Kathy taking Henry, even though they hadn't yet worked out whether she would also drop him off at school tomorrow.

She heard herself telling Kathy to just bring Henry home, not school because Alec would want to see him and spend time with him.

"Or not. I don't know. I'm so confused. Alec will be screwed up in the head enough, after spending almost two weeks with the object of his affection, then coming home to my news." She felt her breath catch in her throat. "Oh God, what am I going to do?"

"I'd offer to keep him longer, but you're right, it will be good for Alec to see him. If he is running around - and I'm not convinced he is - well, maybe seeing Henry will make him feel like a complete and utter low-life. And maybe remind him of what's at stake. Plus, I have that thing in the city, with my accountant. I'll take Henry to the diner in my neighborhood for breakfast, he likes that place. I'll drop him off at around eight."

"Thank you." She heard the beep of another call trying to make its way through and was about to tell Kathy she had to go but decided to let the machine get it. She made a mental note to remember to call Henry's school and let them know he will be late tomorrow. "Kathy? I don't know how I could have gotten through the past couple of weeks without you."

"Eh, that's my job. I'll see you tomorrow morning."

"Wait. Kathy? What am I supposed to say to Alec? What am I supposed to tell him? I don't think I could face telling him about the cancer. What if I just tell him about the miscarriage? I think that's what I'll do. Maybe we'll go out on Saturday, and I'll tell him the rest of it then. It's just too much right now."

"What about Jenn?"

"I don't know. I may just play that one by ear. See what kind of mood Alec's in when he gets home. I don't know if I have the strength. Pray for me."

"I don't pray, you know that."

"Pray for me anyway."

***

Brenda hadn't intended to go into Lower Manhattan to check out Ted's art studio this afternoon, but she desperately needed a distraction. She didn't want to think about Alec, cancer, miscarriages, or Jenn. She made a concerted effort to stick all those topics into her glass jars and then put the jars on the highest shelf in her brain. She would leave them there for the time being. They would still be there later. They would still be there when Alec got home. Then she would decide how and when to pull each jar down and begin what was sure to be a few long days of tears, verbal attacks, hugs, more tears, shouting, more hugs, and more tears.

She took a cab to the Twin Towers. It took a few minutes to orient herself and figure out exactly how to get up to and into the studio. But once there she was struck dumb. The view from the ninety-second floor was breathtaking. Brenda could see the dot that was the statue of Liberty, the water, and from another angle, the street below. It was just about three o'clock, and as Ted predicted in the message he'd left on her answering machine, a storm was beginning to roll in. Like a slow-moving train approaching a dusty station, it announced its arrival not with a horn or whistle, but with a loud clap of thunder. She jumped. The studio was quiet and eerie. Half-constructed sculptures, photography equipment, and canvases of varying sizes were stacked against two of the four walls. A long, thin harvest table stood sturdy and proud in the middle of the room. It held tubes of acrylic paint, oils, and watercolors. Jars of brushes and sheets of white paper filled the remaining empty places on the table's surface. She ran her hand over a sheet of watercolor paper, then picked up a tube of alizarin crimson and sniffed. She was suddenly in college again, where every day was filled with the kind of colorful scene and smells that surrounded her now. She looked out the window and saw sepia colored clouds covering part of the giant lady in the harbor. Perhaps she should do a gray on gray, or gray on sepia scene, using the statue as her anchor.

She found the canvas Ted left for her and carried it over to one of the empty easels. It was already covered with Gesso, dried and ready to go. She considered doing an oil painting but decided on acrylic because of its fast-drying properties. She selected tubes of burnt sienna, burnt umber, and ultramarine blue and a picked up a bottle of blending medium. Paper plates stacked on a chair in the corner would make perfect pallets. She grabbed one and squeezed out a glob of each color, then poured a puddle of the thinning compound in the middle. Starting with the blue and layering haphazardly as she went along, she created an ominous scene. She eventually separated sky and water and loosely outlined the Statue of Liberty. She went back to the table and found titanium white, medium cadmium yellow and phthalo blue to use for the statue. A quick glance out the window revealed an entirely different sky than the one that had been present just moments before. It was now darker and was tinged with pink and purple. She grabbed a tube of red to mix with the blue and added a very subtle halo around where she would paint the statue.

Brenda saw the Luna moth - a sudden burst of green, like the green flash she and Alec saw at sunset during a trip to Costa Rica. She glanced around the studio but didn't see where it went. She stood in the middle of the room and spun around, her eyes darting back and forth as she pivoted on one foot, scanning the room, searching for the green flash. She was scanning too fast and forced herself to slow down. She must have imagined the moth, her subconscious mind playing tricks. She hadn't given Billy Collins or the poem much thought in what seemed like weeks, but in reality, it had only been a few days. The poem featured a moth, and was apparently still buried within her - the neon green Luna Moth she'd just imagined a sure sign of that fact.

She scanned the studio again, then stopped herself and squeezed out a bit of green paint for the statue. She added some blue and brown for the statue's patina as if viewed through a hazy scrim. And that's when she saw the Luna moth again. It was glued to the window as if it too enjoyed watching storms. It looked like a dancer on her toes with outstretched arms about to launch into a series of pirouettes. This was nothing at all like the moths hiding in the sticky cocoons that had lined her ceilings just two weeks ago. By now hundreds of plain brown powdery moths would have hatched - the kind that congregate at front doors in summer, waiting for entry and the soft yellow light that they instinctively fly toward.

Ah, but the brilliant green Luna moth. She'd love to have hundreds of them in her apartment, flashing and fluttering and dipping and swooping. What a beautiful sight that would be. She would train them to congregate anytime she needed a splash of color or design. She could have them perch, wing to wing, at the top of her windows, which were dressed in nothing but miniblinds. Or she could teach them to rest at random intervals against the massive white wall in the back of the living room like funky, three-dimensional wallpaper. The possibilities were limitless.

She inched her way as close to the window as possible, trying hard not to disturb the moth and risk it darting away. Its wingspan was huge - maybe four or five inches wide. And at that very moment, against the strange light of the storm, the moth was luminescent. She studied it for several long seconds before gently picking up her easel and moving it back as far away from the window as she could. She furiously started painting the moth, placing it in the lower left corner of the canvas, as if the canvas was the window. The Statue of Liberty was a dot, really, in the opposite corner. She dressed it in the same green as the moth, only more muted, and took a step back to regard her work. She looked out the window, and then it hit her - the canvas was the window, and the view outside of it was from the moth's perspective. She painted furiously for the next two hours and when she was done, signed her name along the edge of the moth's lower left tendril, or what looked like a foot in a ballet slipper.

***

Alec called her cell phone just as she was locking up the studio to tell her that he had landed and would be home at around ten. She looked at her watch. It was nine. So, she had an hour before all hell would potentially break loose. Their conversation on the phone was brief but long enough to for her to lie and tell him she looked forward to seeing him. The only thing she looked forward to was going back to the studio sometime tomorrow to spray the painting with Workable Fixative. She was so excited about her artwork and pleased with how it turned out. It really did look like a window. She even added some realistic looking raindrops on the glass. She was most pleased with the fact that she didn't over think it, she just painted. The brush was in control as it slid effortlessly across the canvas. She thought about maybe doing a series of window pictures from the ninety-second floor of the north tower. Ted said he'd be gone for two weeks - if she were lucky, there would be at least a few different weather perspectives from the same window. Maybe even sunrise. Or sunset. Then she could do a series of windows from her apartment. And then Kathy's apartment in Jersey City. The possibilities were limitless. She was so excited and full of hope that she almost forgot the forest of pain she was sure to be standing on the edge of in a very short while.

* * *

He wanted pancakes. Of all things. Pancakes. Blueberry pancakes! Of course. Nearly midnight. She just happened to have two containers of blueberries, thanks to her dear sister, who picked them up at the farmer's market the other day. So, it was nearly midnight, and she was making blueberry pancakes while

Alec talked nonstop and animatedly about the conference, the connections he made, Japan's beautiful landscape, the pictures he took and can't wait to have printed. And something about a traffic backup leaving the airport.

"Traffic backup my ass," Brenda said under her breath.

"What was that?"

"Traffic backup my ass." She didn't look up from the stove.

"That's what I thought you said." He stood next to her at the stove. "What's going on with you? And why did you ship Henry off to your sister? Where were you when I called?"

"I told you where I was. I was using Ted's studio at The World Trade Center. I was painting. I told you that."

"I don't believe you. Where is the painting?"

"It's still on the easel drying. I need to go back there tomorrow to spray it."

"Who were you with? Ted's not really gay, is he? He was there with you, wasn't he?" Alec looked out the window. "Ah ha! There's a light on across the street. He's home. He's not on some 'field trip.' What adult goes on a 'field trip' anyway. I'm going over there."

"Alec, stop! Donald is home. And I was alone in the studio." She couldn't believe she was allowing herself to get sucked into his tactic. The realization that yes, he had indeed been with Jenn in Japan, in a more than colleague-to-colleague capacity, became radiantly clear. He was twisting things around to avoid a confrontation about his cheating. Slow traffic. Of course. He had to drop her off. Had to say their long goodbyes.

"Why did you have to ship Henry off to your sister's?" Alec's voice was calm, but the left corner of the right eye was twitching ever so subtly. An involuntary peek into his emotions and a precursor to some sort of outburst. Brenda braced herself for either an exaggeratedly calm discussion or him walking away. One or the other was inevitable.

"Please stop it, Alec. Kathy took Henry, to give us time alone on your first night back. Imagine that."

"You're pregnant, you got what you want, so there's no need for a special reunion now, is there?"

"What's wrong with you?" She was yelling now. "I had a miscarriage a few days ago." She sat down on the floor next to the stove. A sob escaped her throat. "Oh, and I have breast cancer. I wanted to share all of that with you alone, without Henry. I haven't told him anything yet."

Another sob escaped. There was no way to stop it now. She was so engrossed in her own emotions and sobbing and sniffling and tears, that she didn't notice the smell of the pancakes until they were burning and the kitchen started to fill with smoke. She calmly turned off the stove, got her oven mitts, picked up the griddle, and carried it to the sink. She ran cold water over the blackened disks and opened the window. Alec was gone. She wasn't surprised that he didn't stick around to comfort her.

Sky Blue - Brenda

BRENDA LIFTED HER HEAD and craned her neck to look over Alec's head at the alarm clock, which was on his nightstand. Almost five. He was snoring beside her, deep asleep and seemingly oblivious to the pain he'd induced just a few hours ago. She lowered her head back down, frustrated and exhausted. She'd gone to bed after she almost burned down the apartment and wasn't surprised that she never fell asleep. And now, if this were a scene in a movie, it would depict an ordinary married couple in bed. She flashed back in her mind: the pancakes, the yelling, the tears - all spoiler alerts to the plot-twist.

Henry would be home in three hours. She wasn't sure she could face her son now, although his presence might be a pleasant diversion. No reason she had to drag her son into her marital problems today. It could wait.

"Something's broken, Brenda." Alec's voice was barely audible. She didn't move. Nor did he move toward her. "Something's really broken with us."

"I know." She held her breath in anticipation of what he would say next.

"I've been stressed." He rolled over to look at her. "I've been living a lie." His eyes were wide open now, incongruent with the sleep still on his face and the aroma of the morning that surrounded him. "I never wanted kids."

"I don't believe you."

"You were the one who wanted kids."

"You were thrilled when Henry was born. You love him, don't you?

"Yes, I do. You know I do."

She slowly peeled the covers down and slipped out of bed. She didn't expect Alec to stop her and she was right, he didn't. She brushed her teeth, splashed some cold water on her face, and tied her hair in a loose knot at the back of her head. She put on the same jeans and sweatshirt she'd worn yesterday. So, this was his way of telling her about Jenn. Every day had been a lie. He never really loved her. Never wanted kids. Living a lie. Lame excuses to justify his actions. She felt rage rising in her throat like bile.

"What are you doing?" Alec was sitting up now.

"I'm going back to the studio to spray my painting."

"Now? It's still dark outside."

"Bye Alec."

"Wait, I'll go with you."

"You need to be here for Henry. Kathy's dropping him off around eight."

"But we need to talk."

"Not now we don't."

"What's this breast cancer business from last night? You were kidding about that, right?"

"Yeah. Right." She shook her head and walked out of the room.

**

The sky was bright blue. Colorado blue. The one and only time she'd ever been to Colorado, this is exactly what the sky looked like. This morning's New York sky was somewhere on the spectrum between cerulean and azure. It was, at once, dark blue and light blue but with no demarcation, just depth. No clouds for miles. The Statue of Liberty shone as if freshly polished. When she arrived at the studio earlier this morning, it was still dark outside. She puttered around for a bit, then sat down on the floor, against the wall, regarding the picture she'd painted yesterday. She found the Workable Fixative and sprayed it over the canvas, letting it dry between coats. She'd been so focused that she didn't notice the dark of pre-dawn turning into full-blown morning. By the time she was finished, the tableau outside the window had completely changed. She needed to capture the color of the sky so she could come back tomorrow and start another painting - one in this very light. She scouted around for tubes of blue paint. She saw a small canvas that had already been covered in Gesso. She tried mixing different proportions of blue and spreading them on the small canvas, but couldn't get it quite right. After several attempts, she gave up and stood at the window in awe of the sky. It was as if last night's storm pushed away the veiled lie that she and Alec had been living. She wasn't even that upset. How could she be upset when she was staring at the most beautiful blue - a blue that filled her inexplicably with joy?

Her cell phone rang and she answered it without looking to see who was calling. She didn't recognize the voice on the other end, but within seconds she was let in on the joke. Her oncologist wanted to see her. Soon. The call was brief. To the point. Direct. Void of emotion. Matter of fact. Abrupt. It was as if someone had just dumped black paint all over her blue sky. She couldn't breathe. She closed the phone and touched her painting. A bit gummy but dry enough. She carried the painting out the door and set it against the wall while she locked up the studio. She carefully took it with her to the elevators and pressed the up button. Why the hell not? She could go the rest of the way up then all the way back down. And that's what she did. The entire evolution - stopping on almost every floor so that the elevator's insatiable mouth could swallow someone whole or spit someone out - seemed to take forever.

It was eight-fifteen when she finally reached the lobby. By then she'd had enough of the elevator and the perfumes and otherwise not so pleasant smells of the hundreds of people she'd shared space with for the past half hour and was glad to be out and on solid ground. She thought back to the phone call: in a single moment, a voice on the other end conveyed her fate.

Instead of caressing her, the sun and blue sky taunted and teased and even roughed her up a bit. The beauty that just a short while ago had filled her with such joy, now threatened to choke her. The sky chanted in an annoying sing-song voice. This is the kind of day poets wrote enchanting and delightful poems about.

The sky was crisp and autumnal and seemed to stretch on forever and back again. Seventy degrees and dry as a bone. Colorado-like through and through. The cancer has spread. The aggressive, fucking, inflammatory breast cancer that manifested itself as a tiny red splotch had been wreaking havoc on her body for what, a month maybe, without her knowledge or consent. Like Alec wreaking havoc on her heart. Only he was a slow cancer, steadily destroying the fabric of her life, one memory at a time. Fuck the blue sky.

In the twelve minutes it took her to exit the north tower and walk to the corner of Battery Place and Greenwich Street she decided that this is the place where the story ends. Her marriage was over. Her life was ending.

A bit farther down the street she saw a group of hippies waving signs at passing cars. Signs that she wanted to yank out of their hands and stomp on. *Honk if you love someone! Smile! Don't be so hard on yourself! Laugh!* How dare they flash those signs at her? She looked at her watch - eight-thirty. Shouldn't these people be at work or in school or at home or at least sitting in a coffee shop somewhere? She kept walking, all the way to the southern tip of Battery Park. She sat on a bench and set the painting down next to her.

Brenda closed her eyes as to not have to look at the glass-like water of the Hudson River. When she opened them a few minutes later, she felt like she was standing on the precipice of a world she didn't know. She saw a yellow sailboat. She closed her eyes again. When she opened them the boat was gone. She wondered if it was ever really there at all.

Foo Fighters - Alec

ALEC COULDN'T THINK OF HIS father's phone number - the one he used in his private office off the mudroom in his Connecticut mansion. Ok, it's not really a mansion, but that's what it had always looked like to Alec. He had seen the house for the very first time at age thirteen when his mother dropped him off after Dad's honeymoon. It was old and scary looking and had what seemed like a million rooms, some massive, but some just the right size for zombies to hide. For weeks that house terrified him. If the house wasn't bad enough, he was horrified by his father's new wife and her stupid, yappy, little dog. Mostly though, he was terrified that his mother would forget to come to get him at the end of the summer. His prophecy came true; on a sweltering day in mid-August, just weeks before starting eighth grade, he stood pacing the sidewalk in front of the house, waiting for his mother to come to get him, the summer vacation - thank God - finally over. His father came out of the house with two iced teas and told him his mother was moving to San Francisco. She would send for him in December - for Hanukkah - but just for a week. He'd be starting school here in two weeks, skipping eighth grade and going straight to high school. He sat down on the grass and sipped his iced tea. Years later in an attempt to make sense of all this, he spent a long night drinking red wine with his father, asking questions, getting answers he didn't like. His father insisted he had come out of the house bearing lemonade, not iced tea. Alec was sure it was iced tea. They argued about this meaningless fact for over an hour, digressing from the original topic. His father got frustrated and retreated from the kitchen table to the couch in the sunroom where he promptly fell asleep. The subject never came up again.

Alec still harbored a small amount of seething anger toward his father over the way he chose to deliver the news that his mother was abandoning him. Apparently, Dad had known about it for weeks and employed a technique that he used in his family therapy practice on kids who were receiving lousy news like a divorce or some other such childhood trauma. Catch them off guard at the last possible moment. Don't give the kid too much time to think about it or avert it. *Kids have a way of dreaming and scheming*, his Dad would say. They use the long weeks or months that it often takes things like divorce to fully materialize to try everything in their power to turn things around. The eventual, inevitable realization that they are powerless is often worse than the original news. If a kid is hit with it head on he goes into survival mode which is the only way to heal and move forward. According to the child psychology maven himself, Dr. Manny Arnstein, Alec was better off spending the summer thinking everything was okay. Then kaboom! There are two things Alec remembers about this particular "kaboom" moment - the iced tea with its perfectly square ice cubes, two of them clumping together at the top like conjoined twins, and his father's matter-of-fact delivery. He might as well have been reporting about the day's weather. His mother never did send for him in December as promised. Logically, Alec knew that she never recovered from Seth's death. Seriously, could he blame her? Could a mother ever get over the death of her second born, her baby? Alec never had been the favorite, but Seth, wow, Seth. He'd walk into a room and Mom would drop whatever she was doing to tend to him. Or laugh at his dumb little antics. Or crouch down on the floor to help him with his block tower or look for a missing stuffed animal. She never laughed at Alec's antics. Never.

And then there was Seth's hair. She was always mooning over his blond curly hair and cried when Dad took him to get his first haircut. In fact, Alec vaguely remembers hearing his mother screaming and yelling over those lost curls. Didn't she realize that hair grows back? Even Alec realized that, and he was only five.

So, his mother was messed up. She was lonely for her baby. He got that. But why couldn't she press on for Alec? Guess there was no point sticking around for the other son when the only one who mattered was gone. Yes, Alec knew what it was like to be lonely. Not the kind of loneliness that was compounded by a child's death. He's had enough training and enough client experience to know what losing a child does to even the strongest marriages. Alec knew his situation was different, but he's been lonely in his marriage for a while now and didn't know why. Maybe he was justifying his feelings for Jenn by blaming Brenda for his loneliness. Or perhaps he wasn't even lonely and was grasping for an excuse - any excuse to give in to his secret longing. What if Jenn had given him the tiniest indication that maybe, just maybe she felt the same way? Would he have considered leaving Brenda? He wished he knew.

He rolled over and pulled the covers around his neck. Brenda must have opened the window last night - a crispy coolness swept in through the screen, bringing with it the first hint of fall, which was technically still about two weeks away. Should he call his father or not? Dr. Manny Arnstein was mostly retired now but still saw a handful of long-term patients - mostly screwed up kids who grew up into screwed up adults. Wasn't that the plan all along? Pretend to help the kids but really feed them just enough bullshit so that they, over time, begin to improve (and just enough bullshit that the parents didn't mind shelling out the big bucks each week). But good ole Dr. Manny always withheld the key, if such a key existed. Withhold just enough, so that over time, the kids ended up more screwed up than before. And by the time they reached adulthood the parents just threw up their hands and blamed the kids for not trying hard enough and saying things like: *If only you listened to Dr. Manny. You still need Dr. Manny. You'll always need Dr. Manny.*

He heard Brenda banging around in the kitchen and abandoned the thought of asking his father for guidance. Or yelling at him yet again for how screwed up his psychologist son really was. Yep. Screwed up. He never bought into many of his father's philosophies or premises. Yet like a defective gene, he inherited them and lived them. So, he'd been infatuated with Jenn for months and crafted a justification for the two of them attending a conference in Japan - a conference that really had not a lot to do with their particular practice. He took money out of his private account to pay for it. He wished he'd been self-aware enough long before Jenn to express to Brenda that something wasn't working in their marriage. That maybe he needed time. Time away from her. Time to figure things out. Why couldn't he have told her that he only married her because it seemed like the next logical step in a perfectly reasonable and perfectly orchestrated relationship? Brenda would have immediately understood and been sympathetic and granted him the space he needed to figure everything out. Yeah right. What the hell was he thinking? His father's ridiculous philosophy was woven throughout his very being: Don't tell her until you're ready to leave her. Kaboom. Don't give her too much time to dream and scheme. Kaboom. Marriage counselors rejoice! The world no longer needs you. Alec's stomach felt knotted at what an asshole he'd become. Or what an asshole he always was. Thanks, Dad. Kaboom.

At the critical moment, as soon as he began baring his soul to Jenn, he'd realized that inviting her to the conference was a mistake. The look on her face before he even got it all out was enough to embarrass a man for life. And this was before his well-rehearsed and oh so very off-key rendition of "Everlong." (*Hello, I've waited here for you everlong.*) What the hell was he thinking? He'd spent the better part of the flight home scripting what he would tell Brenda. He was pretty sure he wanted to ask her for a separation anyway, to give himself time to get back in control of his life. But now, with the crisp fall air bathing his face through the open bedroom window and the familiar sound of his wife up before him and in the kitchen, Alec wasn't so sure anymore. He was pretty sure he wasn't in love with Brenda. But he loved her in the sense that he cared about her very much, how could he not? And Henry. Of course, he loved Henry. He couldn't shake the image of Brenda sitting on the floor crying. Cancer? Does she really have cancer? She couldn't possibly have cancer. She's too young, too healthy. He was sure she threw it in there as a weak attempt at a red herring, or to elicit sympathy. She was desperate, he knew that. How was she so insightful? Could she sense his feelings for Jenn? No matter. All that mattered now was making things right. Yeah. He wanted to make things right with Brenda. This new conviction was sudden and startling. He laughed out loud, sure of himself for the for the first time in *everlong*.

He leaped out of bed and ran down the stairs, taking them three at a time and practically falling and breaking his neck, but by the time he reached the landing, it was too late. He thought he heard the front door close. By the time he got there, opened it, and looked down the street, Brenda was gone.

Alec went about his morning feeling somewhat like Pinocchio. For most of his adult life, he felt like he was locked in a wooden shell, lying to people for the sake of preserving them, like his father had preached. The more he thought about it, the angrier he became. Didn't his schooling, training, and even what he'd learned over the years from his own patients entirely and utterly prove his father wrong? What about Cassie, the sixteen-year-old struggling with eating disorders, stick thin yet recovering nicely. Cassie's mother entered her in a modeling contest - a pageant of sorts with stick-thin girls packed into a Holiday Inn ballroom, each sizing the other up, calculating the averages, feeling obese among the ones who were only a pound or two thinner. The whole idea of it made him sick. The last thing Cassie needed was a venue to feed her obsession with her weight and appearance. He said as much, but Cassie and her mother were adamant. So instead of putting on his professional boxing gloves, Alec spent six weeks coaching Cassie and arming her with various tools and techniques aimed at helping her deal with the attention this would bring to herself and her appearance. Now, standing in the kitchen listening to the gurgle of the coffee maker, he felt he did these people a professional disservice. He did the field of psychology professional disservice. For a wisp of a moment, he considered abandoning counseling altogether.

He caught a glimpse of his reflection in the smoky glass of the oven door on his way to the now full coffee pot. He poured himself a cup and slowly approached the oven again. He regarded his reflection and studied his nose, which was long and hooked downward like his father's. Or, like a parrot's beak. Women he'd known over the years said it was sexy - one of his most elegant features. Apparently, they'd lied. Brenda never mentioned his nose. She never said it was hot. Not when they were dating and not in twelve years of marriage. So, no, his nose was not sexy. Never was, never would be. Okay, so his nose wouldn't suddenly grow smaller if he stopped the lies. But maybe, just maybe he could progress from a wooden puppet to a real boy. Or a man. A real man. He felt too much like a boy most of the time, and that needed to change. He wanted to be a man. A real man. Not a wooden puppet boy.

* * *

It was astounding, the weather, the change. How hot it had been in Tokyo only yesterday. How when he got home last night, he had so many other things on his mind that he didn't notice how chilly it had become. He wasn't dressed quite warm enough but figured after a few minutes of fast jogging he would work up a sweat and let the crisp fall air engulf him. It would be like jumping into an icy pool on a sweltering day. He couldn't believe how clear his head was, how crisp and succinct his thoughts were, how colorful everything suddenly was. Maybe it was just the sky, so rich and blue. The same sky that only yesterday stood between his past and his future. He was determined to make a fresh start, put Jenn behind him and move forward with Brenda.

He ran toward Brooklyn Bridge Park and ran along the edge of the glassy, calm, reflective water. Again, with the dichotomy - he seemed to be full of them this morning. He'd seen this same water spit angry white foam at him. But not today, not this morning. He felt hopeful for the first time in ages. Not like the headiness he'd felt for so long around Jenn. He should have known better. He was a therapist after all. A shrink as his wife and son liked to call him. How could he have been so stupid? Oh, he knew how. All logic evaporates when hormones are involved. Hormones fed by late-night discussions about patients which led to late night discussions about patients over carryout in the office which led to late night discussions about patients over grilled cheese and fries at the diner which led to late night discussions about life.

He liked when the late-night discussions turned to life. They talked about everything from politics to toenails to music to books to offering each other their professional opinions about their flawed significant others. Once or twice he'd noticed a connection, something subtle in Jenn's eyes that said it would be okay to kiss her. But he never did. He didn't want to steal a kiss over a chipped Formica tabletop. Or with curry on his breath. He wanted it to be a kaboom moment and thus was born his convoluted scheme to get her far away from New York and dazzle her with his romantic charm.

Jenn liked the Foo Fighters so Alec painstakingly, for weeks, poured over their songs, listened intently to the lyrics and finally settled on "Everlong." He set it up in his hotel room on a portable boom box. He had it playing loudly - too loudly - when she knocked on his door the second evening to pick him up for the dinner speaker series on Expressive Language Disorder. Ha! He could have been a poster child for this disorder after Jenn failed to pick up on the song he was playing for her. Using a pen for a microphone, he sang to her. And when that didn't work, he tried to pry open the treasure chest in his soul that held the carefully coined words that he'd rehearsed in his mind, the words that were sure to make her fall in love with him. But instead of words, just a few startled moths flew out of his mouth and circled the room, finally coming to rest on a cotton throw that was draped over the room's only chair. The moths made him remember the book and the poem that he was going to read and discuss with her. It was to be Plan B, in the unlikely event that the Foo Fighters failed him.

Big surprise, not only did the Foo Fighters fail him, but Jenn just shook her head the way people do when they witness a pathetic spectacle. Any romantic vibes he'd felt from her all this time were in his head and his head alone. Oh, she was fond of him. She liked him quite a lot. Loved him as a brother, really. But she was in love with Rick. Hopelessly devoted to him. In fact, she planned to bring up the possibility of marriage soon. Hadn't she mentioned any of this during their late-night talks? Evidently, she hadn't. Or surely, she had. Yep, smart people tell it like it is and foolish people have selective hearing. The universe was against him, he knew. Even if he'd had the book or had memorized the poem, the moment that never even really existed in the first place was gone and so was anything coherent he could have possibly said. Classic Expressive Language Disorder: limited amount of speech, limited range of vocabulary, difficulty acquiring new words, word-finding or vocabulary errors. He strongly considered offering himself up at the seminar as a living, breathing example.

He looked at his watch - he'd been running for nearly an hour. That's almost seven miles at his current pace. Where had the time gone? He had about another half hour before he had to be home for Henry and was glad for more time to run. He had long since absorbed the beauty of the blue, fresh, crisp morning and was so high on endorphins that he felt invincible. His thinking was more precise than it had been in months. And while he wanted to keep running, to keep thinking, he knew he had to get home. Plus, Brenda might be there. It was so early when she left the house that he was sure she'd finished doing whatever she needed to do with her painting. He vowed to compliment her on whatever it is she might bring home with her that she called art. He didn't understand her art. It was good, he guessed, by someone's standards. It wasn't necessarily his taste, but if he were honest with himself, he would admit that it was lovely in its own way. Yet he was never able to express that to her. He always thought she could do better if she'd just put in a little more effort, a little more time. He always felt compelled to criticize her and her work and pretty much everything she did, and he wasn't entirely sure why. Just like he wasn't entirely sure why he'd picked a fight with her last night. But she made him so mad. Here he was, trying, in his way, to come clean. And instead of just shutting up and listening, she met him in the ring, poised and ready to throw the first punch. She knocked the breath out of him. He tried quickly to get his balance and throw an equally brutal blow by turning the truth around and making her the bad guy. He was the bad guy, and he knew it. He just couldn't face it. Not like this, not yet. His reflection in the mirror of her eyes blinded him. He saw himself as the asshole he really is. His comments to her this morning about not wanting kids, not being happy, and everything else he said was his half-baked attempt to be honest. He tried to get it all out in the open, explain where he was coming from and all the things that were wrong between them, all the things that annoy him, how very relieved he was to learn of the miscarriage. Now, in the crisp light of day, this new clarity and his genuine desire to make things right, he found himself beginning to feel a long-forgotten tenderness toward his wife.

The apartment building came into view when he turned the corner by the bakery. He sprinted the rest of the way home, reaching the front stoop and flying up the six steps to the door. He nearly tripped over a rope of ivy that had come loose and was strewn across the fourth step like a booby trap. The vine was growing up the side of the stairs, winding its way around the wrought iron rail and up the brownstone. It practically covered the building and was halfway to their apartment on the third floor. He didn't know much about ivy, but he knew enough to know that it tended to eat away at the mortar. Or at least that's what his father always said, and that is why, despite his stepmother's love of ivy, their enormous house in Connecticut never had any. Alec wasn't convinced of ivy's inherent danger. Brenda was always fond of it, and he could care less. A part of him even wanted to prove his father wrong. *Look, Dad, there's been ivy on this building forever, and the bricks are still intact.* He might even be inclined to stick his tongue out too, just for effect - maybe also throw in a *nanny-nanny-boo-boo* or two. Alec stood at the top of the stairs and regarded the ivy. It glistened against the cobalt sky. Brenda was right about the vine. It really did make the place look like it belonged in England.

***

There were two messages on the machine in the kitchen. Alec was relieved to hear Kathy's voice telling him that she'd changed her schedule and would keep Henry for the day. He was grateful that he didn't have to pretend that everything was normal. He

suspected his sister-in-law already knew about the troubles between him and Brenda. She had to. Who else would Brenda
confide in? He couldn't think of a single person she would bare
her soul to except her sister. He wasn't necessarily happy about
Kathy knowing their business, but he was genuinely grateful
that he could focus now on Brenda and not have a fake father-
son jubilee. The second message was Brenda reminding him to
be home by eight for Henry. Why didn't she just call her sister?
Why didn't her sister call her? No matter. He had time now to
shower and get ready. He needed to craft a plan for the afternoon
and evening. He wasn't sure how or where the discussion would
go, but he was determined to spend the day talking and repairing. Maybe he'll leave Brooklyn Behavioral Practice and open his
own practice. It could be his pledge to Brenda. The one way to
show her that he's serious about putting Jenn behind him.

He opened the fridge and guzzled what was left of the orange
juice, then grabbed the first writing surface he could find - a
white napkin out of the napkin holder - and started making a list:

1. *Calculate household budget.*

2. *Patients who would potentially follow him to his new practice.*

3. *Pros/cons of working at home vs. renting office space.*

4. *Timeline for how long they could last financially before he absolutely had to bring in money.*

5. *Brainstorm ways Brenda could make a little extra money to fill
the void.*

He suddenly remembered Brenda's words last night about
having cancer and wondered if she threw it in as a red herring.

Could she have been serious about it? Breast cancer is highly curable if caught early, isn't it? He added another item to his list:

    6. Ask Brenda about cancer.

Part 2 - During

The Attacks - John

IT'S THE KID'S BIRTHDAY TODAY. Two. Or does he turn three? I really don't know. God knows I really don't care either. Except that I do care. I care enough that I've beat myself to death on this day every year. This day. His birthday. And the day the kid was conceived. I'm not sure how many couples know the exact date and time when their kids were conceived. They have a good idea, I'm sure. But the exact date? I'm not so sure. I know when my wife got pregnant, and it isn't even my kid. Nope. The night my wife was raped is the night the kid was conceived. And today is his birthday. A kid that my now ex-wife is gaga over. It pisses me off to the bottom of my feet that she has this kid and it isn't mine. You'd think I'd be over her by now. It's been three years since the divorce. I am over her, I suppose. She betrayed me by having that kid. Keeping the kid that was conceived in rape. Yeah, she betrayed me. I'm still so angry about that. I'd wanted kids. She never did. Now, this. This kid. And his birthday is to-day.

"What are you doing on your boat at this hour?" Shorty saw me as he walked by with his two dogs, just like he does at the ungodliest of hours every day. When I stayed with him after my accident three years ago, Shorty and those damned dogs woke me up every day before the sun.

"I thought I'd go for a sunrise sail. Wanna come?"

"Are you kidding me? I spent half the night dealing with Old Earl. He passed out in the booth again. I hated to do it, but I had to call the cops. I'm going back to bed."

I guess I missed all the fun last night. Since I retired as a cop - medically retired, that is - I've been helping Shorty run his Irish pub, Shorty O'Rourke's. I like it. Who'd have ever thought that I would enjoy running a bar? But I do. I love it. But not as much as I loved being a cop. I was good at being a cop. For a long time, it was the only thing I knew how to be. I think I was a better cop than I was a husband. I hate that about myself, but the fact is that if it hadn't been for the accident that permanently messed up my leg, I'd still be wearing my badge. I'm only fifty-three. I had a lot of cop-years left in me. I miss being a cop more than anything else in this world. I might even miss it more than I miss my wife.

"It's a good thing you gave me the night off. I was in such a pissy mood I would have booted Old Earl out of there before he passed out." I sighed a little too loudly. Shorty knows all my nuances.

"Alright. Out with it. You never take a sunrise sail. Out with it. What's going on."

"It's the kid's birthday."

"Big Deal. The day comes and goes, just like it did the past three years."

He's right of course. It's not just that today is the kid's birthday. That's minor. I reached into my back pocket and pulled out the crumbled, and then re-folded invitation to Dale's wedding. I handed it to him.

"Oh, shit. Sorry man." He handed it back to me.

"Yeah. Came yesterday. My reaction to it stunned me. I don't feel anything for Dale anymore. It's just that I can't picture her married. It's weird. It's messing with my head."

"You always were messed up in the head. It's what I love about you, though." He tugged at both dogs, one of whom was trying to jump off the dock. "You really taking the boat out?"

"Damn straight."

"Let me get these two meatballs home, and I'll come."

* * *

I can't believe Dale invited me to her wedding. What was she thinking? Marina would be there, of course. And Nester. And likely the kid. Well, maybe not the kid. Dale isn't the kind of person to have kids at her wedding. More surprising than Dale inviting me to her wedding is my reaction to Dale inviting me to her wedding. Our little fling three years ago was a whirlwind and fizzled out almost as quickly as it began. I'm happy to say that I have no lingering feelings for her. None. Even when I relive our brief time together and try to remember the feel of her arms around me or the taste of her lips, nothing happens. Not even a blip. It was almost like I had to experience her to highlight the absurdity of my years-long crush. It was almost as if the secrecy of my thoughts held those thoughts captive. It was one of those things that may have haunted me forever had I not experienced being with Dale. Does that make it right? No. Of course not.

I'm wondering now if I would have stayed with Marina or gone back to her even after the kid was born had it not been for Dale clouding my judgment. After Dale and I called a halt to the madness, I finally gave up and found a counselor I could talk to. I spent a lot of money to figure out what should have been obvious: the secret longing for Dale would have lost its power in the light of day if only I'd told someone about it - someone other than Dale, of course. Maybe if I'd confessed to someone - anyone: Nester, my mother, even Marina - the secret longings may have lost their power. Like the squirrel that in the darkness of night looks six feet long but in the daylight is just a squirrel.

**

I love the banter of nothingness. Like *Seinfeld* episodes when the four friends go to the corner restaurant and sit in their booth, talking about nothing. Today, sailing with Shorty - if you can even call what we're doing sailing; there's not much wind - talking about nothing, is doing more for my psyche than any deep conversation about something.

"Hey, does that restaurant on *Seinfeld* actually have a name, or is it just called Restaurant?" This was something I'd wondered about, off and on, for years.

"What the hell brought that to your head?" Shorty was in the cockpit, studying the shape of the jib. He sheeted it in a little bit as we caught a puff of air. We sped up a little bit and then hit another flat spot devoid of any wind. We sat there for a minute not moving.

I saw ripples on the water in the distance. Ignoring Shorty's question, I told him that we need to tack toward the ripples. Fact is, I have no idea what the hell brought the *Seinfeld* restaurant to my head.

"Ready about. Helm's alee." The wind wasn't much better in the new direction.

"It's called Monk's Café," Shorty said.

"What is?"

"The *Seinfeld* restaurant."

"How the hell do you know that? Oh, wait. Someone came into the pub and told you." I laughed.

"It's a long story," he said.

"We have time."

But at that moment, time seemed to all at once stand still and accelerate. It happened in an instant. If I'd have blinked, I'd have missed it.

"Holy shit! Did you see that?" Shorty didn't answer. We stared in disbelief. We'd both seen the fireball on the side of the World Trade Center. The north tower, I think. Yes. The north tower. The cop in me imagined the chaos on the ground. The horns and bells and sirens. The scrambling. The speculation.

"Probably a bomb," Shorty said.

"But why so high up?" Yeah, the cop in me will never die. Not likely a bomb all the way up at the top third of the building.

"They tried it eight years ago - a truck bomb. Maybe the bastards are trying something different. I'm sure it was terrorists."

Well, Shorty certainly had a point. I suppose it could have been a bomb. But not likely.

"I'm not so sure." I turned on the radio and heard the chatter of other skippers out on the water. It was a plane, someone said. A small, commuter plane. I turned up the volume. "You see, it wasn't a terrorist, it was an accident."

"Damn. I sure hope there weren't a ton of people up there in their offices yet. It's still early." Shorty looked at his watch. "Nope. It's not that early. Almost nine. Damn." He shook his head and then made the sign of the cross.

We sat in silence, not moving, as the wind was now nonexistent. There wasn't much point trying to sail. Plus, Shorty would probably want to get back to open the pub. I released the jib halyard, and without having to tell him to do so, Shorty hopped on the foredeck and led the sail down, until it was a crumbled pile of white canvas. He unclipped it from the forestay and then loosely folded it. He carried it aft and then dropped it through the companionway hatch onto the deck in the cabin.

"Is Simon coming in today?" I was no longer sure that I could get us back in time for Shorty to open.

"Yeah, he's opening," Shorty said.

"Good. I'm not sure we'll make it in time, but I'll try to get us back as quickly as I can. We'll need to motor, obviously."

***

Things on the water seemed eerily quiet and normal as we headed back to the marina. Shorty was eerily quiet too, just sitting in the cockpit, eyes glued to the skyline behind him. When he thought I wasn't looking, I saw him cross himself two or three more times. The fact of the kid's birthday and Dale's wedding and my madding inability to move on and just be happy for my ex-wife and her new little family somehow became white noise considering what had just happened. Some hapless pilot, or pilot with a medical emergency, or pilot with a warped sense of suicide, or maybe even someone on the little plane killing the pilot - a crime of passion perhaps. I can only hope that the part of the building he hit wasn't occupied.

"What's the plan for tonight? Do you need me to come in, or am I good until tomorrow?" It was a feeble attempt to distract Shorty, to get him to look at me, not at what was happening in lower Manhattan.

"What? Oh, yeah. Tomorrow. Come in at two." He turned right back around and watched.

"Hey. Leave it alone. Pray about it if you must. I need you to help me tie the boat up when we get back. Maybe you could go down below and get the boat hook. Please?"

He scooted his body off the settee and was about to descend into the cabin when we heard the roar of a jumbo jet. It sounded like it had broken the sound barrier.

"What the fuck?" The plane hit the other tower. A big plane. A commercial flight. I've never been one to panic. Not really. But I can't think of a better way to describe the surge of adrenaline that shot through my veins.

"It's terrorists, man! It's terrorists! I told you. It's terrorists!" Shorty jumped around in the cockpit, and I wondered if he might just leap overboard.

In my panic, I put the motor at full throttle. I couldn't get back to the marina fast enough. Shorty jumped in front of me and grabbed the wheel. "What the hell are you doing?"

"We're not going back," he said. "We're going over there. People need help."

"Have you lost your mind? What, exactly, do you think we, on this fucking little boat, could possibly do to help?" I held tight to the wheel.

"I don't know. But we're going over." And with that, my resolve failed me and my hands went slack. He took the wheel and turned the boat around.

***

It seemed to take forever get to lower Manhattan. I'm not even sure what we were going to do. Other boats were milling about, stuck in purgatory, unsure whether they could dock over there. Several ferry boats were sitting in stunned stillness.

"Look, Shorty, I'm turning around. I'm going back. I don't want to be anywhere near this mess." I lied, of course. After my little bout of panic earlier, I realized that I do want to be there. But not like this. Not in a fucking sailboat. I want to be the cop on the street. The one helping. The one running into the chaos with the firefighters. Shit. Firefighters. Nester's cousin. I'll bet he's on the scene.

"You're right. Turn around. This is nuts. I can't believe this. It's unreal," he said.

"Do you know anyone who works down there," I asked as I took the wheel back and turned the boat around.

"No. You?"

"No. But Nester's cousin, he's FDNY. I'm guessing here's there." Shorty crossed himself again, for perhaps the hundredth time in the last few minutes.

And then we heard the roar. Different from the sound of the second plane. This was different. We instinctively turned toward the noise and saw the south tower crashing down, literally imploding into itself.

"Fuck!" We both just covered our eyes. The skyscraper, gone. Just like that. "All those people! All those people!" I felt hot tears sting my eyes. I couldn't believe it. All those people.

The other boats on the water seemed to scatter like cockroaches. They appeared to be unsure of where to go, what to do. It was chaos on the water. And havoc on the shore. I idled the motor, and we just sat and watched. I don't know how long we sat there before the north tower collapsed.

"That's it. I'm outa here." I lit up the motor and turned the boat around so fast it nearly knocked Shorty down.

"Give me the damned wheel," he said. This time I fought him. We wrestled with the thing, and he won. Once again, we were on our way.

And as if by some sick choreography, all boats were headed toward Lower Manhattan. Tugboats, fishing boats, ferry boats, my little boat. We were all on some sort of mission - a futile one, perhaps, but human instinct wouldn't let us stand by and watch. I wasn't sure what, exactly, our mission was.

Shorty drove, and I listened to the radio for information. Anything to help guide this undefined mission. A command from someone in authority. Something. Anything. But all I heard was speculation, chaos, and the cries of helpless people, probably standing, mouth agape, watching. And finally, a call on the UHF guard channel requesting help to transport people off the island. That was it. Now we had our mission.

The Attacks - Brenda

BRENDA WAS OF A GENERATION, born and raised in America, who lived in a perceived safe and happy bubble. Sure, there were horrible things all around, but as a child, a teenager, a young adult, and now in her late thirties, she'd never experienced the genuine oppression or social hardships that some people have to deal with. She had been too young of a child to be impacted by the Vietnam War. Her father had fought in the Korean War, but that was before she was born. She was less than a year old when President Kennedy was assassinated. She was a preschooler during the Civil Rights movement. Her sister knew someone who knew someone who was killed in the 1983 Beirut bombing, but that was far away and somewhat impersonal. Alec had a colleague whose mother worked at the World Trade Center when it was bombed in 1993. Still, these things seemed like another place and time with zero impact on Brenda's own little slice of life. Alec's great aunt was in a concentration camp during the Holocaust. And his great-great-grandparents fled the pogroms in Russia. Again, long ago and far away. Because she'd never personally experienced these kinds of national tragedies, she arrogantly assumed that no one would ever have the courage or the will to ever try and attack the United States.

She awoke disoriented and confused. She must have fallen asleep on the bench in Battery Park. When she sat down on the bench, her life was a mess. She'd had a miscarriage. Her husband was an ass. And she had an aggressive form of breast cancer. And now, upon waking, she could see and hear that she was in the midst of Armageddon. Something had happened. Something big, something horrible had happened. In her world. In her back-yard. She slapped herself a few times just to be sure she was awake, and that this wasn't her primary state of mind manifest-ing in a very realistic nightmare. Yeah. She was awake.

Brenda ran as fast as she could but didn't know why she was running or where she was headed. Like a lemming, she followed. Or a leaf getting pushed and blown around. Everyone was run-ning. Everyone was yelling and screaming. The Colorado-blue sky was now awash in a suffocating gray. She couldn't breathe.

A hand reached out to her. A hand around her forearm. She was floating through the air, no, being carried, no, lifted. Some-one was lifting her onto a boat. A yellow sailboat. The sailboat she saw earlier? There were other people on this boat, covered in dust like a scene out of a movie. She looked down at her jeans. She was covered in dust too. Her painting. Where was her painting? She must have left it on the bench. She tried to get off the boat, but someone pushed her away from the rail. The boat was mov-ing.

"Everything's gonna be okay." His voice was calm. She stared at his hands. Were those the same long fingers that wrapped all the way around her wrist and pulled her onto the boat? Those were her father's fingers.

"Pops." She tried to touch his face but retracted her hand at the sight of his eyes, which seemed too calm for the situation.

"Try not to talk, okay? Hey, we're gonna be okay. I'm gonna take you to safety. They're not gonna hurt you."

She had no idea what he was talking about, or why she was even on this boat. Who's not going to hurt her? He turned to walk away, then stopped and turned back.

"What's your name?"

"Annie." Before she could stop herself, the name of her lost, unborn baby escaped her lips. He took her hand. Those fingers. They grasped her hand with purpose as if he were willing the chaos away. As disoriented as she was, she felt defeat in his fingers. Her chin dropped to her chest, absorbing the defeat she felt in him. "I'm Annie."

He nodded as if in solidarity, as if this one moment that passed between them was also passing between frightened and confused people all over the city and across the globe. It was the kind of moment that linked souls.

The Attacks - Alec

WAS IT THE APARTMENT vibrating or the phone ringing that jolted Alec out of his hot-shower trance? How long had he been in there? The bathroom was filled with steam, and he was in such a state of deep thought that he wondered if he'd imagined what he'd just heard and felt. He stepped out and quickly wrapped a towel around his waist, but the phone had stopped ringing. His father's voice on the machine soon came into audible range. His father? Had his father read his mind? Could they be that connected that his father sensed Alec's previous contemplation to call? Nah. Not possible. His father was an asshole. And they'd never been close. Still, in some ways, they were simpatico by some unfortunate genetic link.

"Are you okay? Call me," said the voice on the machine. Alec heard someone else in the background, someone with a loud, piercingly high-pitched voice. When he was a kid, that voice frequently made him want to gouge his eardrums out with a pencil. The voice he heard in the background produced the same reaction. Yep, it was his father's wife. He touched his ears. Then his father again: "He's not picking up, Susan. I know. Okay. Sue, enough." His father was yelling. "Sue, I want to..." Click. Dial tone. Silence.

He sat down on the edge of the bed and looked at the caller ID on the phone. He jotted down the number that earlier he couldn't remember and started to dial. Busy signal. He shrugged his shoulders and got up, anxious to put his plan for the day in motion. He jumped when the phone rang again, but this time he could see that it was Kathy. She was the last person he wanted to talk to right now. Especially if she was calling to say that she changed her mind about keeping Henry for the day. He decided to let it ring and make her think he wasn't home. He was grateful that she didn't leave a message.

The sky darkened. Two seconds ago, it seemed, the sun was streaming through tiny cracks between the slats in the blinds. It had been so beautiful outside, not a cloud in sight. It seemed odd that a storm could make its way over the horizon that quickly. He shrugged it off and pulled on a pair of shorts and a tee shirt. Then the vibration again. He went to the window and pushed two of the slats open. Not sure what he was looking at, he yanked on the cord so hard that the blinds didn't open. He tried again, being deliberate and slow, and it worked. The entire south of Manhattan was covered in a thick gray cloud, unlike anything Alec had ever seen. He couldn't see any buildings. He looked down at his street and saw people, his neighbors, running around, embracing, crying. He opened the window and yelled down to anyone who could hear or would dare to answer him.

"What's going on out there?"

"The World Trade Center's south tower just fell," someone yelled back.

"South tower?"

"Turn on the TV."

Turn on the TV. This simple statement jolted Alec into reality. Why hadn't he thought of that?

***

Alec paced the sidewalk in front of the apartment building, determined to not panic. He assured himself that Brenda would be trying to make her way home. She just had to be. She left so early, so long ago. It was still dark when she left. And this time of year, well that's quite early, considering the sun comes up at around six-thirty. He tried to remember why she went over there. Something about a studio? In the north tower? Or was it the south tower? He just could not remember why she went. Ah yes, to paint. No, she did that yesterday. Didn't she say something about spraying her picture or something like that? Okay, that's what she was doing.

"There's no way she would have still been in the building when it happened." He said this out loud to a street full of people who were all lost in their own panicked thoughts. No one responded to his statement, not that he would have wanted anyone to answer. He found himself on the Brooklyn Heights Promenade, his eyes unable to stay focused on any one piece of the gruesome scene that was unfolding across the river. Mostly he kept his head down and paced. Back and forth. Back and forth. Back and forth. Every minute or so, between irrational and rational thoughts, he dialed Brenda's cell. Busy signal. No rolling over to voice mail. Just a busy signal. In his limited knowledge of cell phone technology, he deduced that this meant the cell system was being bombarded with millions of people trying to make millions of calls all at the same millionth of a second.

What time did the news anchors on TV say it happened? Eight-thirty? Nine? He looked at his watch but couldn't make out the numbers. Could it really be ten-fifteen? Why hadn't she contacted him? Even if she had been in there, shit, what tower was she in? No matter. Whichever building she was in - if she was even in one when it happened - statistically she wouldn't have been in precisely the same place the plane hit. Or even on the same floor. Or even several floors above or below. With so many floors in each tower, the chances were damned good that she would have been evacuated out of there. There had been plenty of time for her to get out of there.

Alec felt himself begin to panic, that same sense of impending doom that had enveloped him when Seth fell off the rock. Brenda was okay, she had to be. Seth was okay, he had to be. No matter that Seth was laying on his back with a trickle of red blood, a thin stream really, flowing slowly out of his ear. Alec picked up Seth's yellow pail and started gathering the shells that had spilled out when he fell. He couldn't stop staring at the blood, but it wasn't much blood, no, not much at all. Seth looked perfectly okay lying motionless in the sand. The waves tiptoed closer. One barely touched Seth's cheek, and then another came and washed away the blood. That's when he decided to run to the house and get his grandfather. Brenda was okay. Like Seth had been. But only in Alec's mind. Seth died when he fell off the rock. He died. No matter what Alec told himself, Seth died. Oh God, not Brenda. Please, not Brenda.

He ran down the promenade toward the enormous plumes of smoke, choking on the air he was breathing and the words he was yelling as he ran. The north tower imploded right in front of him in agonizing slow motion - the images searing into his eyes. Straight down. The smoke surged across the river, through the water, and right toward Brooklyn. It seemed to take over the entire sky. The smoke took over everything. He stopped running then. He just stood and watched.

The Attacks - Kathy

KATHY HEARD HENRY BOUNDING through her apartment, the hardwood floors accentuating every foot plant. One after the other. If ever she wished she was a carpet person, it was now. What time was it anyway? She lifted her head from the pillow and peered at the clock on her nightstand. She knew it had to be early - the first light of morning was barely illuminating the edges of her window that the blinds didn't cover. Holy shit. Her downstairs neighbors were going to kill her.

"Henry!" She yelled, the sleep still craggy in her voice. He didn't answer. Of course, he didn't answer. How could he even hear her through the racket he was making. She got up, grabbing her robe that had been tossed on the floor at midnight when she'd finally ushered him to bed.

"Henry!" She was halfway out the door when he nearly collided with her. He made a last-minute change in direction and leaped over her foot. "Henry! It's too damned early to be running around here like a lunatic!"

"You cussed! I'm telling mom you cussed!" He pushed the door all the way open, then hugged her. She was a sucker for his hugs. "I'm kidding. I won't tell. Dad sometimes cusses too. Can we play scrabble again?"

"I'm taking you home today, remember?"

"Can't I stay?"

"You have to go to school."

"I could take a mental health day."

"A mental health day?" Kathy tried hard to suppress the laughter threatening to fill the space. Her nephew, still so baby-like to her, yet, at only ten, quite grown up. His high school graduation flashed before her, and she wondered how she would have ever handled motherhood. Moments like this made it easy to understand parents when they say they wish they could just freeze time. "What, exactly, is a mental health day?" Of course, Kathy knew what it was. She was tempted to take one today herself. But, she had a meeting in the city that she couldn't miss. She'd planned to drop Henry off at school on the way. Still, a mental health day sounded delightful right about now.

"Dad takes a mental health day sometimes. It means he doesn't go to work and he stays home to clear his mind." He flung himself on the bed and turned on the TV. *The Today Show* was serendipitously reporting the weather. Adjectives like *cloudless*, *brilliant*, and *warm* seemed to add fuel to Henry's lobby. "See. It's gonna be a nice day. Life's too short. Please let me stay here today. I promise Mom and Dad will agree that I need a mental health day." At this last plea, Kathy let her laughter rip.

***

Kathy wanted to go outside. It was barely seven-thirty. An endless cutthroat game of Scrabble with Henry was in progress, and it felt like it should be mid-afternoon. She'd decided to keep Henry for the day to give Brenda and Alec more time to be alone and try to sort things out. As much as she was successful focusing on entertaining her nephew, she felt a sense of impending doom. The thought of her beautiful sister with cancer, married to that jerk, made her alternately want to weep and throw things.

She got up from her small kitchen table and went into the living room to look out the window. It was one of the clearest, bluest skies that she could remember. The day simply beckoned.

"What do you say we put this game away, eat some breakfast, and then go outside and get some fresh air. We could go to the park. Or just take a walk by the boats."

"Aw, come on Aunt Kathy. I have good letters."

"You always seem to get the best letters." She looked at the game board and the tiles that were strewn about her table. Last night he'd come up with the word *aecia*. She challenged him when he said it was a fungus. Turns out the kid was correct. Smart kid. "We can leave everything set up and continue the game later. How does that sound?"

"It sounds terrible, but, okay." He leaped from the table and ran into the bedroom, the volume of her TV getting louder, the sound of animated creatures a new white noise.

She sat down and checked her email. She was excited about her mental health day. She cancelled her meeting - consequences be damned. She picked up the phone and dialed her sister's mobile. No answer. She left a voicemail telling her to have a good day with Alec, trying hard to keep the sarcasm out of her voice. She decided she'd better call the house phone too. Again, no answer. She left a similar, albeit more matter-of-fact message there. Next, she called Henry's school, where she was listed as an alternate for drop-offs and pick-ups. *Henry won't be in today. No, he's not sick. Just needs a mental health day.*

* * *

Kathy made pancakes, scrambled eggs, and bacon. She was happily full, and Henry complained that he was unhappily full. He ate four pancakes and his entire plate of eggs and bacon. Impending growth spurt, perhaps.

"Go lay down on my bed - tummy down. That always makes me feel better when my tummy hurts."

"Mom said I should help you clean up when I'm here."

"I got it, dude. Go lay down."

She pushed her chair away from the table, got up, and let the dishes sit, untouched. She had a few emails she needed to send before she could completely lose herself to this beautiful morning. She sat down at the little desk in her living room and opened her laptop. The work-related emails could wait until later. For now, all she could think about was sending a quick email to Robin, the woman she'd recently met, to confirm plans for their date on Friday. She felt a rush of excitement when she clicked on the AOL icon and heard her modem spring to life. Just like in the movie, *You've Got Mail.* She could feel the tension building as she waited for those three magic words. Drumroll. Yes! She had mail! She quickly scanned the list of a dozen or so emails for Robin's name. Yes! Not one, but two emails from her! She would savor the anticipation and decided to open her work emails first. Top of the list: *All Greater New York Area Airports Closed Until Further Notice.* That's interesting. She left it unopened. She wasn't planning to fly anywhere today.

She opened the next email in her queue. A list of alternative dates and times for the meeting she cancelled. She selected the first of three dates and sent her reply. The next email was also about the airports being closed. What was going on? She opened this one, which had a link to a news site. The first image that came up showed the north tower of the World Trade Center with black smoke billowing out of a large hole. She jumped up and went to the window. All she could see was the smoke. So much smoke. What the hell happened? She went back to her laptop and read the article. A plane. Holy shit. A plane. Probably a commuter jet or a private plane. The pilot had a medical emergency? Or maybe this was a suicide? Unbelievable.

Kathy picked up the phone and redialed Brenda's cell. Brenda had been in that building yesterday, not today. Still, her heart pounded with every ring that was not picked up. She dialed the house. Nothing. Maybe Brenda and Alec were outside, watching the events unfold from the front steps of their apartment building. She walked to her bedroom door and peeked in on Henry. He seemed to be engrossed in a cartoon. She left him alone and went back to the window.

She tried to distract herself. She cleaned all the breakfast dishes and tidied up the Scrabble game. Shit. Henry wanted to resume play. She forgot. Hopefully, this will be but a tiny mark against her as being his favorite (and only), auntie. She turned on the small TV she kept on the kitchen counter. Every channel was talking about the plane hitting the north tower. Speculation on the type of aircraft. Horror and wonder at how many injured, how many casualties. She settled on *The Today Show* and listened to Katie Couric and Matt Lauer talking by phone to an eyewitness. Commercial break. And then suddenly there it was. A second plane. The second tower. This was no accident. This had to be an attack, perhaps the work of terrorists. She ran to her bedroom and found Henry, eyes glued to the TV, no longer watching cartoons, trembling.

Lists - Alec

ALEC WAS SITTING IN THE GRASS, his back pressed hard against a tree, when his cell phone vibrated in his hand. "Thank God," he thought and scrambled to flip the top open and hear Brenda's voice. "Where are you?" he said, perhaps a little too loud, a flood of emotions rushing from his heart to his mouth.

"Alec, we're okay, we're home. Where are you? Are you okay?"

Fuck. It wasn't Brenda, it was his father. Alec quickly, in his mind, listed the five things he's most proud of in his life (his writing; his organizational skills; the way he makes pizza crust; his sensitivity; Henry). It's what he does when he's stressed. It's what he does in the middle of the night when he can't sleep. It's what he does when he feels like he's on the verge of losing control of his emotions. It's what he does on the train ride into work sometimes. It's what he does when he feels the first hints of panic welling up in his core. It's what he did several minutes before his pathetic serenade to Jenn in Tokyo. The five things periodically change, depending on the time of year, how he happens to be feeling about himself in general, or what's going on in his life. He learned this trick from Dr. Reeves - his college professor who facilitated a required procrastination prevention workshop for incoming freshmen. Alec didn't think he needed the workshop. He was a classic planner. A classic chiseler of large tasks into manageable chunks. He was a sculptor in that regard. A world famous one at that. His high school yearbook superlative - voted on by the entire student body: *Most likely to drown in a sea of lists*. It was a parody. But not all that untrue. He loved lists. He never hid that fact, and his friends teased him mercilessly. He didn't care. He kept making lists, and his lists helped him get through his honors courses and kept him sane. He had boxes of his old lists in the attic. Someday it might be fun to bring them down and show them to Henry. Perhaps just before he starts high school.

"Alec. Alec? Alec, can you hear me? Answer me. I don't know if I'll be able to get through again. Dammit, Alec. Alec?"

His father hung up. Good. He needed to keep the line open for Brenda. But first, he decided to try calling her again. Nothing. Just a fast-busy signal. He felt the panic start welling up inside of him again. He took a deep breath and tried to remember Dr. Reeve's voice. The man had just a hint of an Irish accent. It almost seemed like an affectation. It seemed that when he said a word that ended in the letter 't' his tongue hit the roof of his mouth in such a way that the sound it produced was a soft, upward trill. Alec could still hear Dr. Reeves, with his pseudo (or so Alec thought) brogue saying: *This is what I do at midnight*. Alec wasn't quite sure why, but this one statement, with the trilling letter 't' at the end, grabbed him and pulled him in. Dr. Reeves proceeded to list the five things he was most proud of in his life at that moment. While this had nothing to do, per se, with overcoming procrastination, Dr. Reeves explained that in a moment of panic, the exercise helped you stay centered and focused. When you have a project or assignment that you're procrastinating on, your body and mind are in a constant state of panic, even if it's just at a low level. And, according to Dr. Reeves, this paralyzes you.

Alec knew he needed to call his father back. He didn't want to but knew he had to. While he never needed to master the art of procrastination avoidance when it came to tasks outside of himself, he had a horrible habit of procrastinating when it came to emotional matters, particularly ones involving his father. Panic began to well up again. Quick, another list of his pride: Henry again; his ability to run outside in winter wearing just shorts and a tee-shirt; his abs; his singing voice; the way he relates to his patients.

He pressed the button on his phone, then wished he hadn't. Before he could slam the damned thing shut, his father's booming voice cut through the chaos. He couldn't believe the call went through.

"Alec."

"Dad." There was what seemed like a long pause, and then, his father's voice sounded like it was being projected away from the phone. "Sue! Susan! I got Alec!" Mouth and phone once again met, this time louder than before. "Alec, where are you? We've been trying to reach you."

"Dad." Alec didn't know where to begin. He hadn't talked to his father in almost a year. "I'm okay. Henry's with Brenda's sister."

"Thank God. Listen. Just stay put. Nobody knows what these bastards are capable of." Alec could hear his stepmother in the background, screeching and babbling. She must be on her cell, talking to someone.

"Dad." He was silent for what seemed like a long time. His father must have sensed something in the silence. Damn, he's good.

"Is Brenda okay?"

"I don't know. She's not here."

"Where is she?"

"I don't know."

"What do you mean you don't know." Again, his father's voice moved away from the phone. This time, though, it was obvious he had his hand over the mouthpiece. "Sue! Hang up, you can call her back later. Sue." Now a whisper. "Brenda is missing."

"Dammit, Dad!" Alec was livid. "She's not missing. She's just not here at this moment."

"Where is here?"

"I'm outside. I'm by the water. Sitting on the grass."

"You're in Brooklyn?"

"Yes Dad, I'm in Brooklyn. Where the hell else would I be?"

"Why are you running around outside? You need to be at home. You need to keep the TV on."

"I need to keep the line open in case Brenda calls."

"She's probably home wondering where the hell you are." Alec hated to admit this, but his father had a point. He got up and started walking. "Alec? Alec, listen to me." Something in his father's voice made him shudder. "Go home."

"I'm going." He took a deep breath and let his body, mind, soul, and voice go soft. "I'm going."

"Call me when you get home. Let me know Brenda's okay." There was a long pause. Alec didn't hang up. For a fleeting second, he felt like he could open up to his father. He wanted to tell him how worried he was. He wanted to tell him about the fight he'd had with Brenda last night; that it was the reason she'd gotten up so early and left the house - to get away from him.

"Brenda was in one of the buildings." He said it quickly and held his breath waiting for his father's response, waiting for whatever opening his father might give him to spill his guts.

"What are you saying? She was in the towers?"

"No. Yes. I don't know. It's complicated. She was borrowing someone's art studio. She went over there very early this morning to work on a painting." He felt himself babbling, missing the point, squandering an opportunity to bare his soul. "She just needed to put a coat of glaze on it or something like that. I'm sure she was out of there before it happened." He took a deep breath and waited for his father to comfort him, to tell him something helpful. To rally around him.

Silence. Then: "You're joking, right?" More silence.

Alec hung up without acknowledging his father's question or answering it. His father's tone - calm and barely a whisper - suggested that it was somehow his fault that Brenda had been in that damned building. Like Alec was supposed to know this was going to happen. Like he was supposed to protect her from something he couldn't have even dreamed up. Some people yelled when they were upset or accusatory. But not Manny Arnstein. He did the opposite of what you would expect. Even after having lived with his father's "technique" for the first eighteen years of his life, it still stung. Manny also used that tone on Alec when he was barely out of toddlerhood like it was his fault Seth fell off that fucking rock. Like it was his fault Seth died. Like it was his fault Brenda was...missing.

He couldn't believe he thought his father would be supportive. What the hell was he thinking? His father would never change. Not even during a tragedy. The great Dr. Manny couldn't comfort a five-year-old who had just lost a brother and was confused and upset because he couldn't quite grasp the concept of what it meant to *lose* a person. At the age of five, Alec had never been lost. Sure, he'd lost a toy or two, but the concept of losing a person didn't make sense. He didn't understand the finality of the words *died*, *dead*, and *gone*. Especially *gone*. When someone was gone, they came back. When Daddy was gone because he was at work, well, he always came home. When Mommy was gone because she went to play Mahjong or went to the store or even when she went out with Daddy, she came back. Although there was that one time, years later, that Mommy left and never came back.

***

Alec's grandmother, Bubbe, bought buckets for sand and shells. A bright red one for Alec and a yellow one for Seth. Seth loved yellow. Alec was indifferent. True, he would have rather had a blue one, but red was okay. He had a red rug in his room that he pretended was hot lava. He'd walk around it and jump onto his bed, being careful to not let his feet get too close to the edge of the rug. Under the bed, he kept several coffee cans filled with plastic army men. The ones that were bent down on one knee pointing a gun lived in an orange Sanka can. He kept the standing men in a blue Maxwell House can. All of his random and mismatched men lived in a yellow Chock Full o'Nuts can. But the best - the paratroopers - stayed in the castle, which was an old Eight O'Clock coffee can - a square one that Mommy said came from when she was a little girl. Alec loved the paratroopers. And he loved the square castle-can. Every night when Mommy was tucking Seth in, Alec played hot lava on his bed with the army men. Whenever one of the men fell into the lava, he threw a paratrooper down to save him. Sometimes the little parachutes opened. Most of the time they didn't.

Alec decided he liked the red bucket better than he would have liked a blue one or even a green one. He would use it in his hot lava game. It would make a good volcano. Because that's where hot lava comes from - volcanos. He learned that from watching *Mr. Rogers' Neighborhood*. Their grandfather, who they called Joe, said he and Seth could take the buckets down to the water and collect shells. But they had to stay where Bubbe and Joe could see them. And they couldn't climb on the rocks.

First, they ate lunch on the picnic table. It was a hot, sunny day and Bubbe made them wear their white sailor hats. Alec helped Bubbe bring the hot dogs out, and Joe let him taste a little bit of his big-man juice. It made Alec shudder. He was happy to be a kid because kids got to drink Kool-Aide. He didn't want to grow up. And he didn't ever want to drink big-man juice.

***

Come on Brenda, where are you?" Alec looked at his phone for what seemed like the millionth time in the past several minutes. No missed calls. He decided to try his office. Nothing. Just a fast busy. Desperate to talk to someone, anyone, he tried Kathy next. More nothing. How the hell did his father get through? Of all the ironic things. The one person who got through was the one person who was able to offer him the least comfort, the least help. He shook his head, shoved the phone into his back pocket, and started running toward home.

***

"You're to hold your brother's hand by the water." Joe walked Alec and Seth down the patio steps and all the way to the gate at the back of the yard. He carefully opened the gate, revealing the expanse of soft sand - wet sand by the ocean where all the shells were, and off to the right by the shore at the end of the sand, the big rocks. The sun was so bright it made him squint. He remembered his mother telling him not to look directly into the sun, so he looked at the sand instead.

***

For the first time all morning, Alec noticed the smell. It smelled almost like newspapers. Moldy, musty papers. Smoldering newspapers. Smoldering, dank, musty newspapers. He knew this smell. His father used to burn newspapers. He'd kept them in a pile next to the chain link fence. He'd collect several weeks' worth, tie them with twine, then toss the pile out the back door with perfect aim. Alec watched this evolution many times during his childhood. The papers would sit outside by the fence for weeks. They'd get wet. Then they'd dry. Manny always waited until they were good and dry before tossing them into a metal trashcan and lighting them with a match or two. Sometimes it took several tries, but the flames would soar, then eventually die down, and the papers would smolder for what seemed like hours. The smell of the smoldering newspapers was not pleasant. And today, Alec's world smelled just like he remembered the smoldering, moldy, musty newspapers.

Things were beginning to come into focus, one by one it seemed, almost like it was happening in slow motion, like scenes in a movie. He didn't notice the sirens before, but he was confident they'd been howling minutes after the first plane hit. But it was only now that Alec heard them. Howling. Wailing. Screaming. He's wasn't sure if it was just sirens he heard or if there were human cries mixed in. He also became aware of a sort of scything roar - military jets flying overhead at regular intervals. A tragic symphony. He looked out toward Manhattan to where the towers once stood and saw only dust and smoke. He couldn't imagine how anyone in those buildings could have possibly survived.

The Brooklyn Bridge. Of course! The Brooklyn Bridge. Brenda was probably on the Brooklyn Bridge, trying to make her way home. Even from this far away he could see that the bridge was jammed with people, creating an eerie pedestrian rush hour. They looked like they all just emerged after having jumped into a vat of flour. If only it were that simple, that fun. White ash. Try to make a cake out of that. More emergency vehicles. Everywhere. Hardly any regular cars on the streets at this point. And the ferries. The ferries seemed to appear from out of nowhere, emerging from the Manhattan smoke. There was an armada of boats everywhere.

"My God." He saw his apartment building in the distance. But instead of running toward home, he ran toward the bridge. He was confident Brenda was among the ash covered zombies. It's something she would do. She would try to walk home.

* * *

Alec and Seth walked hand in hand toward the water. He looked back at the gate and saw Joe leaning against the pole. He could see Bubbe walking toward them with the hats she'd bought the day before at the little drugstore down the street. Alec stopped and told Seth to wait right there and ran to get the hats. He kissed Bubbe on the cheek and ran back.

Seth didn't want to wear his hat. It was one of those classic mid-century white sailor hats for kids. They were adorned with *Be Happy* embroidery in cheerful multi-colored letters

"You have to wear it, or you can't come with me to find shells," Alec said with the authority of a big brother. Seth started crying.

"Come on. Stop crying, or Joe will hear you. He'll make you go to the house. You don't want to go into the house, do you?" Seth shook his head and reluctantly put on his *Be Happy* hat.

Alec held onto Seth's hand just like Joe told him to. They walked along the edge of the water and picked up shell after shell after shell. Seth broke loose and ran toward the rocks, leaving his bucket on the sand near Alec who was too focused on picking up shells to notice anything else. He carefully rinsed each one in the waves before placing them in his bucket. He kept the curly, horn shells on one side of the bucket separate from all the other shells. When he had enough of them, he drew a circle in the wet sand with his finger and pressed the curly, horn shells into the groove. Then, with the regular white shells, he built a tower right in the middle of the circle. That's when he heard a noise and remembered that he was supposed to hold Seth's hand.

***

Alec didn't remember his grandfather Joe taking the picture. It looked like it could have been taken that day. Or maybe it was taken some other day at Bubbe and Joe's beach house. Brenda had found the picture a few months ago when she was in the throes of her decluttering project. He had to give her credit for knowing it was something he wouldn't want to see. She'd slipped it into a magazine and left the magazine on the coffee table. He found it a few days later when he was sitting on the couch in the living room contemplating how he was going to make Jenn fall in love with him.

Like the slow motion they sometimes use in crappy movies to emphasize a point, the three-by-five-inch black and white photograph seemed to fly out of the magazine and then deliberately float back and forth as it made its way down to the floor. He picked it up and studied it. There they were - two brothers sitting on a New England jetty. They looked happy in their cute little matching sailor hats. They were wearing their swim trunks and had huge smiles. The black and white of the photo seemed to emphasize the blinding sun and how hot it had been that day. Was it hot the day of the accident? Alec couldn't remember. Nor did he remember climbing on those rocks that day. His grandfather had told him not to climb on them. He was a good boy and obeyed his elders. Okay, he was a pretty good boy and mostly obeyed his elders. Okay, he obeyed his elders most of the time. Dammit. He was a mostly good boy who obeyed his elders some of the time. So, he didn't hold Seth's hand. But really, how could he? They'd been collecting shells. They needed both hands - one to hold the bucket and the other to pick up shells. But what about the rocks? He remembers Seth disappearing. He remembers Seth whimpering. He remembers finding Seth laying in the sand. He doesn't remember being on the rocks with Seth. But those sailor hats. He's pretty sure Bubbe bought them during that trip. And that was the only day he remembered wearing the hat. So, the picture had to have been taken the day Seth died. Didn't it?

Brenda was horrified that day when she came into the living room and saw Alec with the picture in his hand. He told her not to worry. He said he was okay. He even hugged her and encouraged her to go back to whatever she had been doing. She must have sensed that he wanted to be left alone because she complied without asking him fifty-thousand times if he was okay. She's come a long way since they were first married. This both pleased him and made him feel just a little bit guilty.

Two seconds before the picture unlocked a part of Alec's heart that he rarely opened, he had been plotting and planning his big reveal to Jenn. He was so grateful now for whatever Brenda had gone back to doing at that moment that kept her out of his hair. But two seconds later, after studying the picture, looking for clues, scanning the rocks for something, anything, he needed Brenda near him. He almost wanted her to ask him if he was okay. Because a small part of him wanted to tell her about his being tormented by his feelings for Jenn. He willed Brenda to open the dialog by asking him if he was okay. He wanted her to come back into the living room.

They'd broken bread recently as a foursome - he, Brenda, Jenn, and Rick. There were no overtones then. None. At least he was cautious along those lines. He wondered if Brenda had read between those lines. He didn't think so.

He got up and started pacing the living room. Back and forth. With the black and white photo still in his hand, he scripted in his mind what he would tell Brenda. He decided to be straight with her. He felt being honest with Brenda would vindicate him of any wrongdoing, even though he hadn't done anything wrong. But you see, he wanted to do something wrong. He wanted to so badly. And he had done these wrong things in his mind more times than he would ever be willing to admit. But he was also quite aware of the potential consequences of taking this thing with Jenn to another level. The fallout of a full-blown affair with her would be unrecoverable. He knew this. He knew he needed to be prepared to leave Brenda in the event he succumbed to his feelings for Jenn. He felt that all it would take was one touch. One thoughtful and reciprocated touch. Just one touch and there would be no rewind, no turning back. Forward would be the only option. Most of the time the thought of leaving Brenda and all that was familiar with her and with their life sent him into a panic. There were other times, though, when the thought of leaving her didn't send him into a panic. During those times, the idea of leaving her made him happy. These were the times when he laid in bed, wide awake in the middle of the night, well after he'd made his lists. Well after he'd exhausted every psychological tool and trick in his repertoire of devices and methods to quiet his mind and find slumber. It was at those times when he let his mind drift, ever so gingerly, into a series of complex scenarios where he and Jenn were together - legitimately together - making a home, making a life, maybe even making a brother or sister for Henry.

He walked into the kitchen looking for Brenda the day he found the photo, but ended up looking out the window instead. The sun came forcefully through the glass and created a beam so bright that he almost closed the blinds. Then he remembered his mother's words. The ones she used to say whenever they visited Bubbe and Joe at the beach. The ones about not looking directly at the sun. The song "Blinded by the Light" began circling in his head. He sang out loud: *Momma always told me not to look into the eyes of the sun.* Alec never listened to what his mother told him. He stared at the sun as it pierced his eyes. *But momma, that's where the fun is.*

***

The sunlight in Alec's face as he inched his way toward the Brooklyn Bridge was an insult and belied his mood. The sky was so blue and the sun so bright. It was as if the sun and sky hadn't a clue what was happening beneath the smoke that so deliberately covered it. Or that the sun and sky broke a promise they had made when they decided, early this morning, to work together and produce one of the most beautiful days in recent memory. When you woke up to a sky like today's sky, you believed the entire city would whistle a happy tune. You couldn't help but feel that during the whole day the sky would remain blue, the sun would remain bright, and the air would remain crisp enough to remind you that the humidity of summer was over and the promise of fall was lurking. Not only had the promise of a continued, beautiful, sing-song day been broken, but also the sign of a typical fall. Falling buildings. The fall of life before. Falling bodies. Falling hearts. Fall and everything Alec loved about it was now stained. This year and forever. The blue sky was gone.

He worked his way onto the bridge, heading into the crowd of zombies trudging toward him. Going against the flow. Swimming upstream. The refugees exiting Manhattan seemed oblivious to the clean man, the only man (it seemed) not draped in the dust and debris of what once was. The only man walking toward Manhattan instead of away from it. Yep, the blue sky was gone. A broken promise. Perhaps it wasn't really gone. Maybe it was hiding. Maybe it was frightened like everyone else and pulled a blanket of dust over its eyes to not have to look at the scene below. Alec wasn't religious, nor could he remember the last time he set foot in a synagogue or even had a heart-to-heart talk with God. Still, he couldn't help but think of all the people in those buildings, pieces of their bodies, lives, even the vapors of their souls mingling to form what was now this horrible gray screen covering the bright blue sky.

"Please God, let me find her. Please God, let me find her. Please God, let me find her." Alec mumbled this prayerful plea, half to himself, half out loud, over and over again as he walked. Is that how you're supposed to pray? Alec didn't know. He didn't think so. It didn't sound authentic in his own head, so how could it sound authentic to God? It wasn't even unique. Alec imagined every person on this bridge saying some version of the same prayer. Could God hear all of it? Or in a situation like this, when just about everyone, everywhere was praying, did God have to be selective? Was it like an essay contest? He only listens to and answers the good ones? What about the ones uttered by assholes like himself, assholes who, just two days ago were contemplating leaving their wives? What about assholes who walked away when their wives told them they have cancer?

Alec kept praying his dull, repetitive prayer as he walked across the bridge. He tried to scan every zombie, every expressionless face, for a sign of his wife. He glanced at every person he came face-to-face with and then beyond them, several rows of people deep, to see if he could see her in the distance. He'd know her gait. He'd know it anywhere. She had a perpetual saunter. He doubted that she'd be sauntering today. She would more than likely be running, or at least jogging, bobbing and weaving her way through and around the zombies. She'd be on a mission to get home. To at least let Henry know she was okay. Even if she didn't want to talk to her asshole husband. Even if she gave her asshole husband nothing but silence for the rest of his life, all he wanted was her body next to him in bed every night. Even if he did all the talking from this moment on. Her asshole husband would spend the rest of his life apologizing.

**

Alec didn't remember promising to hold Seth's hand on the beach. But that's what his father kept saying, over and over at Bubbe and Joe's house later that day. He remembered very little about the blur of activity that occurred immediately following the accident. It seemed that everything happened on the periphery of his tiny existence. He remembered the waves washing the blood off Seth's face. He remembered thinking that Seth was just sleeping. He recalled a primal fear that Seth was badly hurt - a kind of fear he didn't remember experiencing before or since. Except for maybe today. Maybe today. But he wasn't sure. Today was all about focus. Today was all about finding Brenda and making sure she knew he was sorry for all the broken promises.

Nope, he didn't remember promising to hold Seth's hand on the beach. He remembered holding his hand for a little while. And he remembered running back to the house to get Joe. He remembered Joe sprinting down the sand toward the rocks. He remembered Joe tripping in the sand, falling flat on his belly, scrambling to get up - the attempt was unsuccessful the first time - finally getting up, and then running back to the house with Seth in his arms. He remembered Bubbe in the house. She was sitting in a chair fanning herself with a magazine. Her bouffant hairdo was a frizzy mess. Her hair terrified him. Bubbe was always immaculately put together. The woman with the frizzy mess of a coif was not his Bubbe. That's when he started crying.

Silently at first, then big, heaving sobs. Nobody noticed. Nobody put their arm around him. Nobody scooped him up in their lap. The ambulance came and went. And his father told him to go to his room. It seemed like forever before anyone came to check on him. He was sitting on the bed, still in his bathing suit, the silly sailor hat on the floor.

"I want my shells. I want my bucket." Alec's eyes were swollen and red, his nose a mess.

"You promised to hold Seth's hand." His father, standing in the doorway, had a look in his eyes that frightened Alec almost more than Bubbe's crazy hair had frightened him. "You promised to hold Seth's hand." He took a few steps into the room. Alec turned and rolled into a tight ball, like those little rolly-polly bugs. "You promised to hold Seth's hand" He turned and walked out of the room, slamming the door behind him.

"I want my shells!" Alec yelled at the closed door. "I want my bucket!"

He didn't remember promising to hold Seth's hand. A promise not made is a promise not broken, right? He remembered reading something in college, some epic poem about a guy named Sam McGee. There was a line in that poem, a line that said something like *a promise made is a debt unpaid*. So that's it then. If he really did promise to hold Seth's hand and he really did indeed break that promise, well, there was a debt that's gone unpaid for thirty-five years. Not a damned thing he could do about it. Not now, not ever. But if a promise made really was a debt unpaid, then he had an entire lifetime to repay Brenda for breaking his promises.

Alec didn't remember anyone coming into his room again that night. He remembered hearing his mother yelling at his father, his father screaming at Joe, Joe yelling at everyone, and Bubbe crying. The next day, Alec's father told him that Seth died. Nothing was ever the same after that.

* * *

Refugees. That's what the zombies on the Brooklyn Bridge looked like. Every last one of them. Like the people leaving Anatevka in *Fiddler on the Roof.* The only difference being that the people of Anatevka were pushing, pulling, and dragging their essential belongings. The zombies on the Brooklyn Bridge were dragging their souls. Alec had walked the entire length of the bridge. He was officially in Manhattan now - a place he didn't want to be. On his journey across, he looked at every soot-covered face, studied every head. Looked through the people. Looked beyond the people. He knew that his wife was not among them. He just knew. He and Brenda never really had one of those elusive soul connections he'd always dreamed of having with someone. Yet despite the lack of a spiritual bond, he always felt her presence. You just don't live with someone for as long as they've been together and not be able to feel or sense their presence, even in their absence.

Refugees. Where were all these people going? He wondered. He suddenly felt sorry for them. He suddenly wanted to take them all in and feed them. Not that he even knew if there was any food in the house. He sat down on the curb and pulled a white piece of paper and a pen out of his back pocket. He always carried a blank piece of paper and a pen. Always. Because one never knew when one was going to need to make a list. Sometimes these pieces of paper and pens ended up in the washing machine with his jeans. This drove Brenda crazy. The last time it happened, oh, two years ago or something, she declared from that moment on he was doing his own laundry. The decree lasted a week. At most.

Alec grew frantic with the thought of never seeing Brenda again. He looked at the screen of smoke and oriented himself with the bridge and its relationship to his house in Brooklyn. He drew a simple map. Wrote his address at the top. Put the pen back in his pocket and started walking in the other direction - toward home. He held onto the map until some pathetic looking refugee inspired him. The inspiration came much quicker than he expected. He handed it to an older woman who appeared to be alone and was holding a sweater over her nose and mouth. Her gray hair looked nicely done yet undone at the same time. Not scary like Bubbe's had been all those years ago. But similar. He tapped her on the shoulder.

"Here." He placed the paper in her hand. "This is a map to where I live." They locked eyes. "If you need anything." He walked quickly away, leaving the older woman and all the other zombie-refugees in the wake of the dust.

***

Two blocks from home, Alec mentally wrote a list of the five things he's most proud of in his life: the fact that he's always prepared with paper and pen; the map he gave to the old woman; his resolve to be a better husband; his will to not give up until he finds Brenda; his ability to think clearly at a time like this. It's what he does in the middle of the night when he can't sleep. It's what he does on the train ride into work sometimes. It's what he did several minutes before his pathetic serenade to Jenn in Tokyo. It's what he's doing now to maintain his sanity.

If Brenda was in the house when he got there, he would tell her everything. First, of course, he'd hug her until she turned blue. Then he'd tell her he was sorry. Then he'd bare his soul. Where would he begin? He wasn't sure. Maybe he'd just come out with it. Perhaps he should just make a list:

1. *Yesterday I had feelings for Jenn.*

2. *Yesterday I took her to Tokyo for a reason.*

3. *Yesterday nothing happened.*

4. *Yesterday I loved you.*

5. *Today I love you.*

6. *Yesterday I walked away from her.*

7. *Today I won't ever see her again.*

8. *Yesterday I loved Henry.*

9. *Today I love Henry.*

10. *If you have cancer today, I'll take care of you today and tomorrow.*

11. *Tomorrow, when the dust settles, let's have another baby.*

One block from his house, Alec panicked. What if she's not there? What if she's never there again? What if he never has the chance to tell her that he's sorry? Alec had the sudden desire to stare at the sun. He looked up at the sky and heard his mother's words from so long ago. He heard the song. *Momma always told me not to look into the eyes of the sun. But momma, that's where the fun is.* Only this time it wasn't fun he was seeking. He wanted to be blinded by the light. He didn't want to see what he feared he would see when he crossed the threshold into his apartment - the threshold between yesterday and today. He didn't want to see what he already knew. That his wife wasn't home.

Confusion - Brenda

ARE SPACE ALIENS AND UFO'S real or imagined? Brenda had always brushed them off as being imagined, but now she supposed they could be real. Who was she to know? Who was she to discount the possibility of life outside of our planetary eco-system? Whether or not space aliens were real or imagined, there was no question in her mind that UFO's were real. After all, isn't that what happened today? Two unidentified flying objects flew into two very much identified non-flying buildings?

She felt like Rip Van Winkle, waking up from a hundred-year nap. There were a few other people on the boat, all of them cov-ered and caked in a thick layer of white and gray. Forget waking from a hundred-year nap, this was more like she and everyone around her had awakened from the dead. Zombies were what they looked like. A zombie was what she felt like. What was she doing on this little boat in the middle of the Hudson River any-way? The Hudson River, that thin blue line on the map that bisects New York and New Jersey, two places so close in proximity yet so different in every possible way. Just like now. The two UFO's did their best to bisect yesterday and today in a way that a bright rising sun cannot. Because you expect the sun to come up. You hope today to be somewhat of a repeat of yesterday. Same actors in many cases. Same stage. Same scenery. Sometimes the scenery changes. Often new actors and extras enter and exit. Mostly though, yesterday flows into today smoothly and seamlessly. Unless yesterday you were blindly healthy and today someone flicked the lights on, and you realize you're not. How could you possibly see cancer in the dark? Unless yesterday you were comfortably (if not happily) married and today you know your marriage will never be the same. Again, in the dark. Happily, in the dark. Then a discovery that falls into your lap when your husband brushes against the wall on his way to meet his lover and accidentally hits the light switch with his arm, illuminating a world you never knew you were inhabiting.

Brenda tried to remember the last time she was on a boat. The cruise she and Alec took the winter before she got pregnant with Henry didn't count. That was more like a floating city than a boat. Nope. She couldn't recall ever being on a boat like this - a sailboat with the sails down. Or even a sailboat with the sails up. She might have been on a small powerboat once. Yes. In college. Her roommate's father had one of those fast powerboats. She remembered going out on that boat and clutching the seat, fearful of the speed yet invigorated by the wind in her face. So that was it. The last time she'd been on a boat. All those years ago. Henry went on a fishing trip just a few months ago with the scouts. He wasn't sure that he even wanted to be a scout. She didn't push him. All she wanted was for him to have a nice childhood - a simple childhood. One made up of imagination and friends and coloring and making up stupid games and riding bikes around the neighborhood and yes, watching a little TV now and then. Kind of like the simple childhood she and Kathy had before their dad died. Henry came home from the fishing trip a bit nonplused. When she picked him up at the pier, the troop leader took her aside and said Henry had been a bit fearful on the boat. In the car on the way home, she tried to draw out of him how he felt, but she couldn't get him to open up or to talk to her about it. She suspected he might be embarrassed. What he said was that he wasn't sure about being a scout. That the kids were annoying. She let it go and never mentioned it again. He never mentioned it again either.

Sitting on this little sailboat, motoring, not sailing, she wished she had seen the planes. She never saw them. She only saw their aftermath. Had she seen them, would she even have recognized them as planes? Or would she have mistaken them for shooting stars? The ones she could wish upon. Like in the song. Like in that Disney film. Which one was it? Ah, Pinocchio. That was it. Jiminy Cricket. *Like a bolt out of the blue, fate steps in and sees you through.* Isn't that what the lyric promises? A flash out of the blue. Cancer. Infidelity. She looked up at the sky. This. Two flashes out of the blue. Two planes. Two stars. Two wishes. None granted. Life changed forever for her yesterday. Today is just the reinforcement. Damn. She looked up. The sky was void. Except for the occasional military jet. Shooting stars indeed. Cutting through the blue, blue sky. And the smoke. The smoke like an inky black Rorschach test. It looked a lot like a cluster of cancer cells. No. Not cancer cells. It seemed more like an intertwined couple, their bodies stretching and rising to the heavens. No. Not an intertwined couple. It just looked like a massive, black cloud. That's all. A black stain on crisp blue table linens. Dried blood. No hidden messages. Just one big, black, evil blob of dried blood. How could the sky be so damned blue today? It was an insult. A slap across the cheek. A black bloodstain on the world. Jiminy Cricket. What was he talking about? *Like a bolt out of the blue, fate steps in and sees you through.* Sees you through to what? Certain death? A crumbling marriage? A ten-year-old boy who was likely running up and down the street in front of a Brooklyn apartment building wondering why his mother isn't home. Henry. What was she going to do about Henry? She felt panic well up inside of her. He's with Kathy. He loves his Aunt Kathy. Her sister will comfort him today. Her sister will take care of him until he is re-united with Alec. Brenda started to relax a bit. Henry would be okay. She just needed to figure out how she was going to get home. She opened her cell phone to call Alec. No signal. Nothing. She looked up at the blue sky again, but this time she turned her back to the inkblot, the blood stain.

She noticed a teenaged boy sitting on the deck at the front of the boat, his back against the mast. The boy made her think of *Oliver Twist,* and suddenly tunes from the musical were floating around in her head, like a mantra, a distraction.

"Who will buy my sweet red roses, two blooms for a penny?" Brenda's voice was barely a whisper, her pitch nearly perfect, her accent almost identical to the woman selling her wares in a nineteenth-century London street market. "Who will buy my sweet red roses, two blooms for a penny?" She imagined Oliver watching with wonder from his window above the market. "Will you buy any milk today, mistress, any milk today mistress?" She kept singing. "Ripe strawberries ripe! Ripe strawberries ripe!" Slow and steady. "Any milk today mistress?" She drew her knees up to her chest and buried her chin. "Who will buy?"

"Who will buy this wonderful morning? Such a sky you never did see. Who will tie it up with a ribbon, and put it in a box for me?" She looked up to see an elderly man, covered in dust, a zombie like everyone else, come to life. His voice was craggy and soft, much lower pitched than Oliver's pre-pubescent choir-boy voice. But he knew the lyrics. Perfectly. His inflection was a bit melancholy.

She continued with the next lyric. "So I could see it at my leisure whenever things go wrong. And I would keep it as a treasure to last my whole life long."

A young woman on the opposite side of the boat piped in, a bit louder than Brenda and the elderly man had been. "Who will buy this wonderful feeling? I'm so high I swear I could fly. Me-oh-my I don't want to lose it so what am I to do to keep the sky so blue there must be someone who will buy."

The trio looked at each other briefly. Three pairs of eyes looking at the same sky, pretending the ugly black ink blot wasn't there. Three pairs of eyes, in a split-second flash, sharing the same grief, understanding, indescribable sadness of the moment. They nodded and tried to smile. Brenda willed herself to smile, but her mouth didn't seem to move. It appeared singing had used up what little will she had left, what little muscle strength she possessed. Now all she wanted to do was roll up into a tight little ball. Then someone could pick her up and toss her into the water. That would be that. Done and done.

"We're here." The voice from behind made her jump.

She was aware of people talking, people moving about. She sat still, her gaze fixed again on the black ink blot. It wasn't as black as it had earlier been. There were browns and grays mixed in. It was bigger.

They'd apparently reached their destination, wherever that was, on the other side of the Hudson. She had no idea where she was or where she was to go. She supposed could try to walk to Kathy's apartment. It couldn't be too far away from where they were. That would be good, that's what she would do. She opened her phone and called Kathy. No signal. Nothing. She tried Alec again. Same. Nothing. She closed her phone and decided to wait until everyone else was off the boat, then she'd walk to Kathy's. She couldn't take her eyes off the smoke, the ghosts of the towers, or better yet, the souls of the towers, rising to meet God. She tried to remember what floor she had been on. Would she have been able to get out? Would she have been killed instantly? Maybe that would have been better, given the grim prognosis she received yesterday? Today? It was all a blur.

"Annie, we're here."

Brenda tried to think about Alec, tried to wonder if he even realized or made the connection that she might be among today's casualties.

"Annie."

She turned around to see a tall man standing over her. He looked familiar. He put his hand on her shoulder.

"Annie, we're here."

She slowly turned her head toward the hand that was still on her shoulder. Long fingers. Why was he calling her Annie? Long fingers. Long fingers. Pops. His hands were just like her father's hands. She suddenly remembered. When he helped her onto the boat, he asked her name. She told him her name was Annie. Why did she do that? Her painting! She suddenly remembered her painting. She'd left it on the park bench. A new wave of panic washed over her. That painting was all she had left of her life before today.

"I can't." She stood up and looked at his face. His face looked nothing like her father's. Only his hands and his height. "I can't get off the boat. I left something in New York. Could you take me back?"

"I don't think so."

"Please, I beg you."

"I know you want to get home. I know all the phone lines are screwed up. I wish I could help you. I'm sorry that I can't."

"I left something that's very important to me on a bench in Battery Park. I need to go get it." She paused. "I need to go home."

"I'm so sorry. I understand. But I'm low on fuel." He left her and took a few steps toward the back of the boat. She watched him look at some instruments, then stick his head inside the cabin. He yelled something that she couldn't quite make out. The guy who had been driving the boat most of the time - a stout little man - climbed out.

"I'm Shorty O'Rourke," the stout little man said. "Where do you need to go?"

"I left something on a bench near the towers."

"Nothing's left over there. You might as well forget about it."

"No. Not right near the towers. I was sitting, well sleeping on a bench when I heard an explosion. I started running. I'm pretty sure one or both of the towers were gone by then. I was in Battery Park."

"Right. Okay. Right." Shorty took her hands. "I'm sorry, but we don't have enough fuel to make it back over there. I could try to make my way over to the fuel dock, but as you can see, there are a million boats lined up for fuel. It could take hours. And this little boat isn't legal at night. Doesn't have a working mast light. It would be too dangerous in the low visibility and with the amount of other boat traffic. I can't take that chance." She let her hands slip out of his. To her complete and utter embarrassment, she started crying. She plopped down on one of the settees in the cockpit, and she just sat there and cried. And cried. And cried.

"Hey." The man with hands like Pops had his arm around her. How long had she been sitting like this? Had she laid her head on his shoulder? "I put the boat away in her slip. She's tied up good and tight for the night. If you want, I could see if there's another boat going back. Or, you can spend the night here."

Brenda was confused. She had no idea what time it was and couldn't even think straight enough to look at her watch. The thought finally registered, and she brushed off the dust so she could see the numbers. A bit before seven. She could see a golden beam dancing across a mostly calm Hudson, likely a reflection from one of the mirrored glass buildings still standing. A thick screen of smoke mostly masked the colors of sunset, although some color seeped through its thinning, outer edges.

"The marina has a pretty decent shower facility. Shorty's girlfriend is about your size. She brought you a change of clothes, just in case you decide to stay. He has a pub just down there." The man pointed in the direction away from the sun. She could barely make it out, but she thought she could see the name Shorty O'Rourke's painted above a green awning. "The clothes and some towels are down below. We'll take you across in the morning."

* * *

Always be prepared. Isn't that the wisdom of the scout motto? Isn't that what she strived to instill in Henry? Even though he would likely decide not to become a scout, the mantra was fresh in her mind. Always be prepared. Scouts or no scouts, she was always on Henry, and Alec too, for being ill-prepared for everyday situations. For example, Brenda rarely left the house without some sort of snack in her bag. Snicker's bars, trail mix, roasted almonds. And a bottle of water. Always a bottle of water. How many times has she had to hand over her treasures to Henry or Alec? A delayed subway ride. She'd tell Henry to eat as discretely as possible because you weren't really supposed to eat on the subway, even though many people did. She knew she wasn't setting a good example when she would pop a candy in her mouth. She'd just brush it off and justify that she wasn't littering and she wasn't obnoxious about it. Countless other times she'd had to part with her treasures because she was the only person in their little family to prepare for the unexpected.

Always be prepared. Isn't that the wisdom of the scout motto? What about being emotionally prepared? What about not loving someone too much - holding back just a tiny bit? Holding back just enough so that when you find a book of poetry that your husband was going to "discuss" with his female colleague in Japan you will be prepared to handle it with grace and wisdom. Anger yes. Anger would certainly be justified. But wasn't there a way to get angry and a way not to get angry. She looked back now - what was that, two days ago, three, a week - and wished she had confronted him head-on. She wished she had just asked him about the damn book and listened to what he had to say. She could have done this if she had been prepared.

What about being equipped to handle the inevitability that your health will someday fail? Being prepared, as in not taking for granted that you will always be healthy. Doing away with the notion that cancer happens to everyone in the world except for you. The irony is that she felt young and physically resilient. Except for her lower back, which was a bit sore from time to time due to the cancer's desire to plant itself there. With that one tiny exception, she felt great. Physically great. The pain in her lower back was nothing, really. Just a localized tender spot. Nothing more. She put her hand where the rough, scaly spot on her left breast had been. How long had it been since the biopsy? This had to be a mistake. The doctor was wrong. The tests were false. Had to be.

Always be prepared. Brenda stood in the marina's shower - a surprisingly lovely, private shower - and let the hot water pound on her chest. The last bit of soot had long since disappeared down the drain, and she had rinsed the last bit of shampoo out of her tangled hair. She didn't expect the man with the long fingers to have conditioner on his boat. Perhaps she should teach him the motto - always be prepared. Surely, he could have anticipated a national tragedy and a strange woman spending the night his boat. He could have been prepared and had a bottle of conditioner tucked away in a rarely-opened drawer.

* * *

Brenda's wet hair was one big tangled ball of yellow string, knotted and matted, and impossible to decipher. She twisted it as best she could and secured it with a hairband that she'd just happened to have been wearing around her wrist. She'd tried several more times to reach Kathy and Alec - on their cell phones and on the house phones. She gave up the idea of trying to walk to Kathy's. Her sense of direction was bad and it was already dark.

She walked the few yards to the pub the man with the long fingers had told her about, and stopped in front of the double doors. She stood frozen, unable to put her hand on the door handle. She turned around and started walking back to the boat, unable to fathom eating, as her stomach was in worse shape and had more knots than her hair. She didn't think she'd be able to eat. But she was thirsty. Quite thirsty. In fact, a cold beer sounded good. She turned around and once again found herself standing in front of the door. Two men came out, talking. One of them said, *my dog ate it,* and the door closed behind them. She watched them walk up the street. She took a deep breath and went in.

The place was full. Loud. Solemn. Full of nervous energy. People were talking, debating, crying. They were watching CNN on a TV above the bar. There was no music. No laughter. She turned to walk right back out, but the aroma of onions and peppers and grease begged her to stay. Despite the chaos in her gut, she realized she was hungry. Starved in fact.

Shorty saw her and motioned for her to sit at the bar. He had apparently reserved a place for her. She ordered a cheeseburger and a beer. She watched with horror as CNN played the footage of the towers being hit, then collapsing, over and over. All those people. She could have easily been one of them. She began to panic and couldn't remember which tower she had been in or even what floor she had been on. She didn't remember. She started shaking and tried hard to look and act as normal as possible. She didn't have the gumption to talk to Shorty or anyone else and was grateful that everyone else, including Shorty, seemed to have someone to else to talk to.

Two women a few seats down were talking loudly about a funeral one of them had attended a few weeks ago. Leo. Someone named Leo. One of the women said she was glad Leo wasn't alive to see what had happened today. That he wouldn't have been able to handle it. Brenda would give anything right now to know more about Leo and his story. She was grateful for the distraction, listening to the two women talk. She tried to focus on pleasant things. Her painting. That was pleasant. Although she had given up the hope of ever seeing it again. And the cheese-burger. That was extremely pleasant. As was the beer. She thought about Leo and his funeral and wondered if the woman was right - that Leo would rather be dead than have witnessed what happened today. If only Leo could have decided for himself. Funeral. How many funerals will there be after what happened today?

And now this - the reality of her own impending funeral. She ordered another beer. She knew she needed to go home. If not to see Alec, then to let Henry and Kathy know she was alive and okay. She was sure they all thought she was dead. She looked around for a pay phone. Where was the tall man? Why hadn't he come by to check on her? Why would she even think it was his duty to check on her?

"John told me to tell you he'd be by in the morning to see how you're doing." Brenda looked up at Shorty in disbelief. It was as if he'd read her mind. He handed her a fresh beer, and she drank half of it in one, long, slow, gulp. So that was his name. John.

"Thanks. I don't see a pay phone anywhere. Do you have one?"

"Yeah. We have one. In the hall by the rest rooms." He gestured with his head toward the back of the pub. Brenda started to get up. "It's out of order." He looked at her. "Yeah, I know. All the lines are busy or no signal. I wish I could help you. I'm sorry."

"It's okay."

"Don't worry too much. John will take you home in the morning. He'll take you wherever you need to go."

Relief washed over her. She'd be home tomorrow. But the thought of going home suddenly made her panic with all of the problems that awaited her there. Home. She really did need to go home, didn't she? Or did she? Maybe she could disappear and die from cancer without dragging her family into it. Perhaps it would be easier for Henry to think she died heroically in a terrorist attack than to watch her shrivel away from cancer over the next few months or year. She knew that it would get progressively worse. She would probably lose her hair and much of the meat on her already lean body. She would become haggard and exhausted and would likely just want to be left alone. Seeing her like that would have a long-lasting negative impact on Henry. He would probably need therapy for years after watching his mother slowly die before his eyes. If she didn't go home, chances are he'd remember her exactly the way she was yesterday. If she didn't go home, then maybe, just maybe she would always remain, in her son's eyes, his hero.

Spilled Milk - Kathy

KATHY RAN UP THE STEPS to Brenda and Alec's building - keys in one hand and the cuff of Henry's sleeve in the other. Henry broke loose and ran ahead of her, squeezing through the door just as another tenant came out. He ran into the foyer and up the three flights to their apartment. Kathy entered, climbed the stairs in a deliberately calm manner, and found her nephew standing in front of the door, out of breath, already having run through the entire apartment, having opened it with his own key.

"They're not here."

"What do you mean, they're not here?" She caught herself asking this ridiculous question. She hated when people said things like that. Asking what you mean when what you mean was clearly stated. Concise. Succinct. Concrete. They're not here means only one thing in the context of a little boy running through an empty house looking for his parents. They're not here means, simply, that they're not here. "I'm sorry, Henry." She hugged him. "Okay. They're not here. They're probably on their way to my house, to get you." She pulled her cell phone out of the back pocket of her jeans. "I'll try calling again."

"They won't answer." Henry tried to yank the phone out of Kathy's hand.

"Maybe they won't. But I'll try. I'll keep trying until I get them." She gripped the phone tighter. "Let's get something to drink first. I'm thirsty."

Henry ran into the kitchen and pulled a container of milk out of the fridge. He looked at Kathy. She shook her head. She would rather drink warm bile than a glass of cold milk. She considered having a beer, but quickly washed that thought away with a glass of water from the tap. There was a small TV sitting on the kitchen counter. She turned it on, then quickly turned it off again. She didn't want Henry watching airplanes flying into buildings and the buildings crumbling and falling. He'd watched enough of it earlier, at her house. She caught herself being ridiculous again. The damned buildings were across the river. Henry saw the smoke. He heard the sirens. He knows what's going on. She couldn't protect him. He's ten, not four. She turned on the TV. Then turned it off. Better to watch this on the bigger TV in the living room. Great minds think alike. He was sitting on the floor in front of it, his milk untouched on the coffee table.

"You okay sweetie?"

He nodded.

"I'll keep trying to call your mom and dad."

He nodded again, never taking his eyes off the TV. Kathy went back into the kitchen and sat down at the old picnic table that Brenda and Alec used as their main dining table. She and Brenda had found it two or three years ago at a flea market, and for whatever crazy reason, Brenda had to have it. The benches were attached to the table, like the picnic tables you might see in a park. The thing had been in horrible shape, painted green on top of red on top of yellow on top of some indescribable color on top of the original wood. It seemed like it had taken them a month to remove all that damn paint. They sanded it and let it sit, untouched, for what seemed like a very long time. Then one day when the absolute last thing on Kathy's mind was this damn table, Brenda called and said she wanted to paint the top white, with black, yellow, and lime green stripes. And for the benches, well, she would somehow incorporate the black, yellow, and lime green. Kathy wasn't a huge fan of the colors her sister had selected, but Brenda was the artist in the family, after all. A bit quirky, yes. Always. Even as a kid. Looking back, she had always been ahead of her time. The way she dressed. The colors she loved. Even the colors on this table. Kathy had never seen colors like that used together in quite that way. But, she would never have bought such a table in the first place, and if she did, she would have made it rustic. Kathy would have stripped the paint, but then the similarities would have ended right there. She would have stained it a dark chestnut or walnut.

She ran her hand across the length of the tabletop and thought about Robin, wondering if she would like this table, or if she was more the rustic, simplistic type. She wanted to call her but hesitated in the name of not wanting to be a pest or seem clingy so soon. She looked out the window and saw the smoke that would define this day forever. She had no idea where Robin was or if she was even okay. Impulsively, she dialed Robin's number. Nothing. It didn't ring. Went right to voice mail.

Kathy promised Henry she would keep trying to get his parents, so she phoned - again and again. Right to voice mail each time. It was useless. She felt a pang of guilt for feeling more of an urgency to reach Robin. She knew Brenda and Alec were okay. Likely just stuck in traffic. A modified Gift of the Magi, only in this case the gift was Henry, and the medium was delivery. The more she thought about it, the more confident she became that Brenda and Alec were on their way to her apartment in Jersey City to pick up their son. Now she wishes she had just stayed put. Maybe then Robin would have stopped by, just to give her a hug. Just to tell her she was thinking of her. Perhaps they could have sat on the couch together and watched this whole ugly mess unfold. Maybe they would have ended up in bed together. Shit. Henry. Not with Henry there.

* * *

"Dad! Dad!" A blur flashed in front of Kathy's face, like the light that lingers after a photo is snapped. When her father was sober, which wasn't often, he took photos. Of everything. Blades of grass in summer. She and Brenda sitting on the floor with a pile of blocks between them, building a tower to the moon. Uncle Dory brandishing a Thanksgiving turkey leg like Henry VIII. *Hold still! Smile! Say turkey!* Snap. Flash. Lingering light. Blur. If she didn't know it was Henry running through the kitchen to the front door, she wouldn't have known it was Henry. It happened that fast. She didn't hear anyone come through the door until

Henry was already in motion. It was as if he sensed Alec and Brenda's return, long before the return occurred.

"Alec." Kathy was standing in the threshold between the living room and the kitchen. He hugged her. Hard. Quite hard. Hard enough that she knew something terrible had to have happened. Of course, something terrible had happened. Someone had flown planes into buildings. But there was something else. One doesn't hug one's sister-in-law like that without reason. He was beginning to smother her. She wiggled free and then looked at him.

"Where's Brenda?" Kathy tried to keep her voice calm.

"Where's Mom?" Henry clutched Alec's arm.

"I think she's at work. I think she said she had an art therapy session."

"But she won't answer her phone."

"She always turns her phone off when she's at work. Plus, all the phone lines are messed up right now. She should be home in a bit. But until then, we'll keep trying to call her."

Kathy knew Alec was lying. Now she wondered if Brenda left him or if he asked her for a divorce so he could chase that woman, whatever the hell her name was. She suddenly felt sick. She suddenly wished she'd been honest with Brenda a long time ago - that there was something about Alec that she just didn't care for. Something she couldn't define. Damn, she wished she'd spoken up. May not have made one bit of difference. Or may have. She sighed loudly and shot Alec a look that would confirm in her mind his incompetence as a man if he didn't immediately tell her the truth. And he didn't. He walked into the living room with Henry. Case closed.

"Let's change this channel."

Kathy could hear Alec getting Henry settled down in front of the TV. Okay, perhaps she misread his motives when he ignored her death stare. Maybe he wasn't really walking away from her. Maybe he just needed to occupy his son with mindless entertainment on TV, if there even was such a thing during an action disaster movie that wasn't really a movie at all, but sure looked like one. She could hear the remote magically spooling through whatever brilliant list the networks and cable channels had built for this day. Most were news type shows. Keywords jumped out like people jumping from burning buildings. *Terrorist. Awful. Tragedy. Pentagon. New York. Flight 11. Flight 175. Flight 77. American. United. NYPD. FDNY. Death Toll. Dust. Debris. Collapse.*

"That one!" Henry yelled a little too loud.

Kathy peaked into the living room. *Sleepless in Seattle.* Brenda's favorite movie. It was just starting. Alec sat down on the couch with Henry and put his arm around him. They sat there for what seemed like a long time. Finally, Alec stirred, and Kathy quietly retreated into the kitchen. She didn't want Alec to see the ice cubes in her eyes melting.

"Here." Alec handed Kathy a beer. Great. Just what she needed this early in the day. She'd pretended to not hear his footsteps on the kitchen floor. She pretended not to listen to the fridge open and close. In her best Oscar-winning performance, she feigned complete surprise at his presence.

He popped open a beer for himself and sat down across from her. And as if having heard her earlier thoughts, mumbled something about hating the table and wishing he'd put his foot down when Brenda brought it home. *It should have gone straight back to the flea market. Or to the dumpster.* He ran his hand along its colorful surface.

"But you know what?" Alec's eyes grew distant. "It's grown on me. Just in the last thirty seconds. I'm looking at it now, and it's her. It's Brenda. I see her face in it."

"Why are you talking like this Alec?" Her internal alarms and antennae went up several notches. She didn't want to hear what she already, somehow knew. "She's not really at work, is she?" She lowered her voice as to not attract Henry's attention.

"You know, a few weeks ago we were at the grocery store." He spoke to some invisible person at the table, not to Kathy. He didn't even glance in her direction. He took a sip of beer. "I forget exactly what we were buying. Something for dinner. Henry was at a friend's, and we were going to cook a romantic meal together." As if he suddenly realized Kathy was there, he turned and looked at her. "We got home and ended up fighting about something stupid. Something that meant little then and means nothing now."

She reached across the table and rested her hand on top of his. "It's okay, you don't have to tell me all this."

"We ended up throwing the food out about a week later. We never even cooked it. Look, I know you probably think I'm an ass."

Alec was right. She did think he was an ass. But his ass-ness was beginning to flake off him like dead skin cells. She wondered if there was a pile forming near his feet.

"I don't know what she told you." He held the beer bottle to the light and twirled it, then chugged the small amount that remained. He got up and helped himself to another. "I don't really want to know what she told you. And I know you're not going to believe me, but I do love her. I want to do right by her. I want things to be better. I don't want to lose her."

They sat without talking. Kathy went to the fridge and got her own second beer. She sat back down. Alec was staring at the corner of the kitchen, with eyes that appeared to be looking at the wall, but upon further examination, were wholly inward bound, as if he were working a complicated math problem in his head. As if he were one equation away from solving the world's problems. It occurred to Kathy that the topic of her sister's cancer didn't surface. Maybe she never got around to telling him about it. The miscarriage didn't come up either. She decided now wasn't the time to talk about those things, so she continued sitting with Alec, not talking, not really thinking much about anything, except, maybe, Robin.

She didn't know how long they sat there, but she was suddenly aware that Henry had barely moved from his spot in front of the TV. She and Alec had earlier agreed that they'd tell Henry something, anything once the movie was over. Kathy kept tabs on how much time they had based on Tom Hanks' voice. When the Empire State Building scene arrived, she knew they had to get their game faces on. Alec told Kathy about Ted, the studio, the damned painting, and that Brenda went there early this morning. They knew they couldn't say these things to Henry, so they concocted a lie. They hated doing it but agreed that at least for now, it would be best. They decided they would tell him that Alec finally reached Brenda and that she couldn't talk because her cell phone battery was very low. She was at work and would have to stay with her students until each of them could get home. She had three students left and had to wait for them to be picked up. They would tell Henry that Alec would try to call again in a little while, for a status update.

"Mom's not coming home, is she?"

Kathy and Alec both jumped as Henry sliced open their individual reveries with a jagged blade. Alex looked at the clock on the wall. "It's dinner time. Let's go get something to eat."

"I'm not hungry." Henry walked to the phone. "I'm calling Mom." He dialed and hung up, repeating the sequence at least twenty-seven times. Kathy knew he was getting a fast-busy signal. He finally gave up and buried his head in Alec's chest.

"Look. We're going to find your mother." Kathy peppered the air with a voice barely above a whisper, the convoluted lie long forgotten. Henry broke free of Alec and listened. "We'll find her. I'm sure she's okay. She's probably looking for us. She didn't realize I was going to bring you home as early as I did."

"She was there, wasn't she?" Henry's voice was a whimper.

"What makes you think that?" Alec and Kathy said in unison. And as if carefully choreographed, both placed a hand on his shoulder.

"I know she was there. She told me that's where she was going."

"That was yesterday, buddy," Alec said.

Alec seemed relieved to be able to tell Henry the truth, at least about that one minor detail. Kathy figured that Henry didn't need to know the specific details. She was convinced Brenda was okay. That she just wasn't home yet and would walk through the door soon. Brenda probably left the building long before anything happened and took a long walk to clear her head and now couldn't get back, or didn't want to get back because she didn't want to face Alec and his infidelity or show Henry how upset she was. And she was sure that her sister didn't know how to tell Henry about losing the baby or about being very sick. Complete and utter avoidance seemed plausible. Very. Or not.

***

The World Trade Center was not visible from the Brooklyn Heights Promenade anymore. Gone. Poof. Just like that. All that was left of the once beautiful view was an eerie trace in the form of the smoke that still lingered and would likely linger for days. People wandered aimlessly. Somberly held each other. There were none of the joggers, cyclists, or power-walkers you would often see on a beautiful late-afternoon fall day. It was almost as if people couldn't bring themselves to engage in their daily routines. It was more than that. If you weren't out searching for a loved one, then you were wandering aimlessly, experiencing the pain of those who were. Everyone was affected. There was no escaping this horrific reality.

Despite the horror. Despite the smell. Despite the uncertainty of Brenda's whereabouts, she was filled with something she hadn't been filled with in years. Not since her last relationship, the one that lasted for almost a decade. The one where they tried to start a family. After the third round of treatments failed, Lydia decided she didn't want to be a mother after all. And then the coup de grace: Lydia decided she didn't want to be in a long-term relationship after all. Basically, she no longer wanted to be with Kathy.

Yes. Kathy was filled with something that hinted at hope. The dream of something new. She'd finally gotten through to Robin, and was buoyant as a result. Even better than getting through to Robin was the fact that Robin seemed genuinely worried about her and had been trying to call her too! Her relief and utter joy stunned her. She put thoughts of Robin aside so she could focus on looking for Brenda. She was determined to find her. Alec was convinced Brenda was either dead or trapped in the rubble. Kathy didn't believe it. Nope. She sensed her sister was out there somewhere. Yep, Brenda was out there, wandering around, thinking about her crumbling marriage. Thinking about her son. Thinking about the fact that she has cancer. She would walk through the door soon. Okay, maybe not soon, but before dark. She would. Kathy just knew it.

Robin offered to come over and help look for Brenda. Kathy smiled at the thought. It would be too distracting, but that's not what she said on the phone. It would just be too hard to get to Brooklyn, too much traffic, too much, too soon. Yes, too much too soon. Who wanted to be thrown into such a thing during the early - pre-early phase, really - of a potentially budding relationship? Yes. This one had potential. Robin said she'd poke around Manhattan, around the park, and around Wall Street. She would just walk and look at people. What did Brenda look like? *Brenda is beautiful*, she wanted to say. Long, blond hair. Slender. She could be describing a million women in New York. Then she remembered Henry's movie. *Brenda looks like Meg Ryan*. Meg Ryan in *Sleepless in Seattle*.

The dust would settle soon. Kathy cringed at the pun. A pang of guilt flitted through her body. Guilt that she could be giddy with the buoyancy of potential new love as she scanned the landscape for her missing sister. She smelled something burning. Something other than the death smell of the day. It was a grill. A young couple had a small grill set up on their stoop and were grilling what smelled like brats and peppers. Her mouth watered. She suddenly realized it had been quite some time since she'd eaten anything. In fact, the last thing she ate today was a handful of Goldfish crackers in the kitchen with Alec. She found herself fantasizing about steak. Her mother's steak. Marinated with soy sauce and onion salt. The result was something grand. No matter who you were or whether you even liked steak, the smell of her mother's steak on the grill made your mouth water. It smelled so good that it could make you sell your soul to eat one of those sizzling, tender slabs. The incredible thing about it was that the steak didn't taste like soy sauce or onion salt. It was just beautifully tender and delicious. Of course, using a nice cut of beef helped. And her mother always used nice cuts of beef, which was why they didn't have steak very often. Mom never told any-one about the soy sauce and onion salt. Only her daughters.

Yeah, the dust would settle soon. And when it did, Kathy would marinate a couple of steaks in soy sauce and onion salt. She would pull out her hibachi grill and set it up on the balcony. She would get a couple of boxes of those paper lanterns - maybe red ones - and string them along the rail. And candles. She would get candles of varying shapes and sizes and place them on every available surface. She'd set up her little CD player in the corner and have soft music playing while she grilled. She imagined Robin leaning against the rail, sipping wine. Or did Robin prefer beer? Kathy didn't know. They barely knew each other. They'd been out twice, during the day, at coffee shops. That was it. No dinner yet, no drinks. Wow, she didn't even know if Robin imbibed. Or ate meat. These were the things that Kathy would get to the bottom of, once the dust settles.

* * *

If today were yesterday, dusk would be beautiful. Clear. Crisp. Sure, today there are elements of beauty - bits and pieces of clear sky, hints of sunset colors reflected in the water, the way strangers suddenly sought one another out, if for nothing else but to exchange a knowing glance and a knowing shake of the head. But the elements of beauty were marred by a gap in the skyline, from which smoke billowed upward. How long, Kathy wondered, would there be smoke? Hours? Days? Weeks?

She found Alec sitting on the stoop, with the same blank stare that he'd worn earlier at the kitchen table.

"I don't even have to ask, do I?" She sat down next to him, sure that Brenda hadn't materialized during the last few hours.

"Henry fell asleep on the floor in the living room. I see no point in waking him." Alec examined the laces on his running shoe. He pulled one side loose and fiddled with it for a few seconds, then tied it. "You obviously didn't find anything, did you?"

"Nope. Nothing. Look, Alec." He looked up at her, and she hesitated. She didn't know how or where to begin. "Alec, I spent a lot of time with her while you were gone. She thinks you're cheating and are about to leave her. She had a miscarriage. She was diagnosed with inflammatory breast cancer." She took a deep breath and paused, waiting for him to chime in or become defensive. To her surprise, he sat silent. "That's a lot for someone to digest and carry around by herself."

Alec was quiet. He looked back down at his shoes and began fiddling with the other lace as if it had been feeling left out and wanted to be tied and untied, just like its friend on the opposite shoe had been. Only Alec would do this. He was so damn anal. She wondered how Brenda could live with a person like that. She couldn't do it. It would drive her crazy.

"You're asleep, you're not at home." Alec was barely audible and seemed to be talking to his shoe. "You know what I'm talking about?" He finally looked up and into Kathy's face with an intensity that, for a fleeting second, frightened her. Her instinct dictated that she nod in agreement, even though she had no idea what he was talking about. "So, I'm asleep in Japan," he continued, "and all I could think about is how much I wanted this one thing, this one person when I have this dream about spilled milk.

There was spilled milk all over the floor in my room, in the hall-way, in the elevator, in the lobby. There was even a stream of spilled milk trickling under the front door, down two marble steps, and into the street below. Only the stream flowed left, not right. In fact, it flowed into a river as far as I could see if I looked left. If I looked right, well, everything was dry as a bone." He looked at his feet again. "I woke up in a cold sweat. I have no idea what time it was, three in the morning, maybe."

"She was right about you." Kathy couldn't bring herself to look at him. "You were cheating."

"That's the point. I wanted to cheat. Then I had the dream." He paused. "I woke up. It freaked me out. The meaning was ob-vious. Spilled milk. As in, don't cry over spilled milk. Or once the milk spills you can't un-spill it."

"What are you getting at?"

"The dream was a warning. Yet the next day I tried to ro-mance Jenn, sweep her off her feet. That's her name. Jenn didn't want anything to do with me." He stood up and walked down the steps, walked a few paces in front of the building, walked back up, and sat down at the top. "When Jenn rejected me, well, it was like getting a bucket of cold water dumped over my head. I was shocked. I honestly thought we were both on the same page."

"I can't listen to any more of this." Kathy got up and put her hand on the front door. She wasn't entirely sure why, but she felt herself hesitating. She let her hand drop. She sat back down.

"I had incredible clarity on the flight home yesterday. God. It seems like a year ago. How could that have been yesterday? Any-way, I figure the spilled milk in my dream represented what a lousy husband I've been over the last little bit. Or longer. On that flight, I committed myself to do better by Brenda." He shook his head as if in disgust. "But then she started harping on me the minute I walked through the door."

"You bastard." She glared at him. "You have no idea what she's been going through." Kathy was neither sympathetic or the least bit moved by Alec's dream or his epiphany. He indeed was a bona fide ass.

"She never gave me a chance. She just started harping. And she was cold. Icy cold. Glaringly cold. Filled with a sort of hatred."

"How can you sit here and make this about you? Or her reaction to you? You call yourself a Licensed Clinical Psychologist? You should know better. You should have at least anticipated that she would be less than jovial. Less than welcoming."

"I had no idea she has cancer. Not until very late last night. And I didn't believe her. I thought she was making it up."

"Why the hell would she tell you she had cancer if she didn't, in fact, have cancer?" Kathy was incredulous. "You knew about the miscarriage?"

"That baby was nothing."

"That baby was everything." Kathy got up and went back into the building, slamming the door behind her.

* * *

Henry was sprawled out on the living room floor snoring. He sounded more like a little old man than a little kid. Kathy was amused and stood to watch him. Had she and Lydia been successful in motherhood, their child would be about Henry's age. She couldn't help but think that had they been successful, she and Lydia would likely still be together. It's been ten years, and she still imagines Lydia coming to her senses and walking through the door. But Lidia's in Portland. Kathy had heard through a friend of a mutual friend that Lydia has been in a relationship with someone for a while now. What is a while? A year? A week? A decade? Kathy still tells herself that Lydia had been confused. That if they hadn't ridden the roller coaster of IVF, then she and Lydia might still be together. The hormones associated with the IVF treatments could cause the most even-tempered soul to display a raging sea of emotions. Kathy knew she, herself, couldn't have handled it. She was older, but that wasn't it. She was a coward when it came to that. She loved kids but never had the instinct or the desire to have one living inside of her. And Lydia did. Or so she said. She remembered that stupid little exercise they did early in their relationship. They'd gone to a friend's house for Thanksgiving. It was a relatively small group - six or seven of them. The host handed each person an index card. Everyone had to write what their favorite activity was at whatever age was printed on the card. Then the cards got shuffled, the host read each one, and everyone else had to guess whose card it was. The age written on Lydia's card was five. And she wrote that her favorite activity was holding and taking care of a collection of baby dolls. They'd never talked about their childhoods before, not really. Oh sure, they covered the big stuff early on. Her alcoholic father. Her mother's death. Lydia's older brother going missing in Vietnam. But not the stuff daily life is made of. Not the stuff that shapes you and gets you from Point

A to Point B. They spent the next day talking about baby dolls and real babies and life and love.

They saw a reproductive endocrinologist that came highly recommended by an older couple who'd gone through it and had two kids. The initial meeting was grueling. Medical history. Fertility history. Family history. Relationship history. History of the country. History of the world. Who would be the donor? Kathy and Lydia looked at each other and thus began a laughing fit that went on for what seemed like forever. Who would be the donor? It was the one detail they'd failed to discuss.

Attempt 1: Lydia got pregnant right away. Well, right away is relative, given the fertility drugs, the daily injections, the hormones, the mood swings. She had good quality eggs. That's what the doctor had told her. Good quality? Like a carton of Grade A eggs. Scrambled eggs. Omelets. Eggs Benedict. Poached eggs. Hard-boiled eggs. *Green Eggs and Ham.* They laughed about this at the time. Mostly though, they were happy that Lydia had good quality eggs and that they would soon be fertilized with what they hoped was good quality sperm. The eggs were harvested, fertilized, and transferred into Lydia's womb. Everything looked good. The doctor said so. They believed him. They trusted him. They looked up to him. They followed his instructions religiously. When Lydia started spotting at around four weeks, they were unprepared for the clump of cells that materialized a few days later. Kathy thought it looked like a massive blackberry. But really, it was their baby. They sensed it was a boy and named him Benny.

Attempt 2: They froze six viable eggs, so about six months later they tried again. This time, Lydia never became pregnant.

Attempt 3: This time everything really did look good. They rejoiced when they made it to the twelve-week milestone, and with the doctor's well wishes, they threw a big party and announced that they were expecting. Two months later they delivered a dead baby boy. This one they got to see. It was a baby. Not that Benny wasn't. Not that they felt less devastated at Benny's loss. It's just that they never saw Benny through the big blackberry clump, which had happened at home, in the toilet. The attending doctor at the hospital washed the baby. Kathy and Lydia took turns holding him and saying goodbye. It was surreal. They never even named him. Six months later, after a futile attempt at normalcy and a brief discussion about adopting, Lydia left.

**

Kathy sat cross-legged on the floor next to Henry, stroking his hair. The back of his neck was sweaty, and his snoring was light and rhythmic. She imagined that he was in the type of deep sleep that befalls people who have experienced something traumatic. The kind of sleep that is so deep that upon waking you don't quite know who or where you are, and for a blissful moment until you are fully awake, you have forgotten whatever you had wanted to forget. She imagined that a lot of people were going to fall into this type of sleep in the days and weeks ahead.

"Don't worry," she heard herself whispering - half to Henry, half to herself, "your mother is okay. She's alive. She's out there. She's wandering around. She needs time to think. She doesn't want to scare you with everything that's going on in her life right now. She loves you. She will come home. I can't really say when. But she will come home. I can almost promise that she will. Almost." Her barely audible whisper began a decrescendo until she couldn't even hear herself.

"Do you really believe that?" Alec crouched down on the floor next to her.

"Yeah. I do." She hadn't heard him come in and wondered how long he'd been there.

"But it's nearly dark outside. Where will she sleep?"

"I have no idea. She'll be okay. I know she will." She stood up slowly. "If you don't mind, I'd like to sleep on your couch tonight. I'd like to be here when Henry wakes up."

"That's fine. Actually, yes, please. In the morning we could divide and conquer. I'm determined to find her."

Alec took her hands, and she immediately pulled away from him. And as soon as she did, she regretted it. He looked anguished, and she suddenly felt a twinge of compassion for him. "I'm sorry about what I said, you know when I said the miscarriage meant nothing. I wasn't thinking. I'm sorry."

"Peace."

Signs - Annie

HOW DID I MISS THE SIGNS? How did I miss the signals? Annie repeated these two questions to herself over and over. They became somewhat of a mantra, and she wondered if the repetitive nature of saying them, asking them, mouthing them and, most importantly, not answering them would lull her to sleep. She had been too upset to sleep several hours ago, when it was normal for a person to grow tired, lay their head down, and drift into the land of Nod. Nothing was normal, though. Take away all that had transpired in the past twenty-odd hours - all that had crashed and exploded and burned and crumbled. Take away all that, and still, nothing would ever be normal in anyone's life again. Normal was a word that didn't exist in this new world. Would there ever be a normal again? What about a new normal? A new normal of burying Brenda and creating Annie. Annie Wells. Yes, she would use her maiden name. How could she do this? Was it even legal? She had no idea. Nor did she care. She would merely be Annie Wells for the foreseeable future.

It was incredulous that she was sitting in the cockpit of a sailboat at five o'clock in the morning, alone, thinking about these things. She was cold. So cold. She pulled her knees up to her chest and tented them with the wool sweater that she'd found balled up between the cabin wall and the mattress, in that triangular place in the boat where she'd slept. She guessed it was John's sweater. It smelled faintly of sky and salt and maybe a little bit musty, like an attic. She looked up at the sky. Pitch black. No hint of the coming dawn. Dead quiet except for the sounds of clanking sailboat halyards coming from other boats in the marina. The clanking soothed her soul, kind of like wind chimes but without the kaleidoscope of notes and tones. This was more like a percussion that provided a rhythm to her repetitive questions: *How did I miss the signs? How did I miss the signals?* She was, of course, asking these things about her marriage, yet she had to believe that somewhere - probably in Washington, DC - someone was asking these very same questions about what happened yesterday.

She looked out beyond the other sailboats, beyond the marina, beyond the bridge, and searched for the smoke that had come to define yesterday. The crisp air was acrid - it contradicted the quiet of the still night, ensuring that anyone awake and outside remember that the gaping hole in the ground was smoldering and would likely smolder for many days yet. Had there been anything to contradict the slow and steady dissolving of her marriage? What masked the smoldering hole in her heart? Was there even a smoldering hole it her heart? Or was Alec the one with a hole in his heart? She could have easily gone off and had an affair over the years. Why hadn't she? She could have found opportunities if she'd looked for them. *Guard your heart?* Isn't that what the Bible says? A few years ago, when she'd tried church, that was one of the messages that stuck with her. What was that from? Psalms? Proverbs? She was pretty sure it was Proverbs. *Above all else, guard your heart.* That's all she remembers. *Above all else, guard your heart.* She didn't actively or consciously guard her heart, but looking back over the twelve years of her marriage, she never once let anyone else into her heart. It was guarded for Alec. And Henry, but that was a different part of her heart. Sadly, she guarded her heart so tightly that she didn't even leave room for close relationships with other women. Or perhaps that wasn't so much heart-guarding as it was time-guarding. Although her father died when she was quite young, she'd over the years gained much insight into the relationship between her parents - her father's love of beer that drove him to be out with "the boys" almost all the time. Doesn't everyone need other people in their life to completely fill it? Isn't it a recipe for danger when you tie all your happiness and emotional nourishment to your spouse? Alec had routinely encouraged her to go out with "the girls." What girls? She had no girls. She didn't know how to make friends with girls. Sure, she had her sister. But now she feared it wasn't enough. It would never be enough. She suddenly felt more alone than she ever had. She sat, looking at the dark sky, trying to see the smoke, failing to see the smoke, trying anything to fill the well of sadness that she didn't think she could ever even begin to describe.

Sitting alone at the pub last night, it struck her that everyone in there had someone. Everyone had someone to comfort them. She could have leaned on Shorty if she'd wanted to. She could have opened a conversation with him. They didn't lack for a topic. She could have talked to anyone about what had happened. She may not have made a friend, but for the minutes that the two or three or more were engaged, they would have had an instant bond. Like yesterday on the boat when she started singing, and the others joined in. That scene - that emotional bonding - would be with her for life. In her current despair, this made her smile.

She should call her sister - she figured phone service was restored by now. She should let Kathy know she's okay. She could explain what she's doing and why. She could tell Kathy she's paralyzed - a deer in headlights - and just can't go home yet. Kathy could concoct an excuse for Henry. She would need no explanation for Alec because he would know. But didn't she need Alec? How would she get through the next few months of chemo and whatever else her decaying body would bring? She needed him. She couldn't do this alone. How could she possibly do this without Alec's help and support? She was in a dark tunnel. An endless, dark tunnel. There was no looking forward to that first glimpse of light that, under normal circumstances would appear within a few minutes. There was no light, no end to her tunnel. She was so cold, so alone. The thought of going home suddenly looked good, felt good. She wanted the warmth of her own bed. She wanted to hug Henry and tell Alec that she'd put their marital problems in a box until she could get her health back to some stable baseline. Mostly though, she wanted yesterday back. No, not yesterday. She wanted the day before yesterday back. No, not even that. She wanted however many days before yesterday back - however many days it was before she began missing the signs and signals.

How did I miss the signs? How did I miss the signals? Her mantra continued. She and Alec were not newlyweds. Things stopped being new long before their most recent, silk and linens anniversary. Things stopped being new even before they were married. Things stopped being new the moment they let their individual lives intertwine to make one big, wet, messy life together. Isn't that what marriage is all about? Isn't that part of the fun, the joy, the things you look back on and relish? The tedious nights of a daddy walking his colicky baby up and down the hall, the colicky baby's chubby cheek resting on the exhausted daddy's shoulder - a routine that had presented itself quite by accident and worked without fail and without consideration for the exhausted daddy's aching shoulder. They even joked about those days recently. Joked - well, sort of joked - about those being some of the best days. And missing them. There had been something different in Alec's voice when he said he missed those days. It seemed filled with melancholy and regret. She had been afraid to ask him about it. Afraid of hearing the answer. Fearful of the floodgates she might open with such a question. She now wondered if this was a sign or a signal of the beginning of his pushing her away and pulling Jenn close. She wondered.

For twelve years she created her own picture of their world and who they were in it. She was sure there had been other signs and other signals. Certain. She just didn't have the mental capacity to dig for them now, although she suspected that over the next few days or weeks she wouldn't need to dig at all - they would just float up to the surface like putrefying bodies on a lake. Then she'd be able to put random samples under a microscope. The patterns would later emerge. In many ways, it would be so much easier to just forgive Alec and then crawl into a protective shell where she could stay until she dies.

The light was beginning to protrude from the horizon. Civil twilight rolling in like a charcoal pencil sketch of distant images. Annie could see the smoke now. It was lighter than it had been. Sepia. The whole scene was in sepia. Like the rows of brownstones and apartment buildings lining her street and other parts of her neighborhood just before the sun rises - during that time of neither darkness nor light. So many different shades of brown. Brown. A simple mixture of orange and black, or, yellow, red, and black. It has always been Annie's feeling that brown doesn't get nearly the respect that it should. Mousey brown. Is there really such a thing? According to her sister, there is. Even a brown field mouse is a beautiful shade of brown. Her sister's hair was nothing of the sort, it was more of a light brown, a crisp brown. Nothing at all mousey about it.

Annie closed her eyes as she imagined walking the streets of her neighborhood at dawn like she frequently did in the late stages of her pregnancy with Henry. Her street was a pallet of brown. And if you looked at it carefully enough and with an open mind, you would be amazed at all the different nuances and variations of brown that exist. On her side of the street alone: pale brown, medium brown, dark brown, chestnut, khaki, raw umber, and rosy brown. Around the corner, there was tan, taupe, burnt umber, and sandy brown. And then there was the apartment building with the fire escape - the one across the street that Ted and Donald lived in. The bricks, once red, had over the decades turned russet. The color of a baked potato or extra crispy, hand-cut French fries. There was enough red left in some of the bricks that certain light made the building sparkle like it was adorned with old rubies. Fragments of the bricks could often be found on the sidewalk under the fire escape. Annie habitually picked them up and stuck them in her pocket. And if she remembered to empty her pockets, which was often not the case, she tossed them into a glass bowl that sat on the windowsill in her kitchen. Maybe someday she'd make a mosaic of the fragments.

Sometimes during those dawn walks, she saw a light in Ted's kitchen window. He had a small table pushed against the window and two chairs side-by-side. One for Ted, the other for Donald. They were her age but seemed more like an old married couple than she and Alec. At least to her. Sometimes she and Ted caught each other's eye - both voyeuristic in their own ways. Wasn't everyone somewhat of a voyeur? Rather than pretend, they'd both smile and wave, Annie trying hard to suppress a solo laugh out on the dawn street, and Ted, stifling his own, trying to not wake Donald. One morning Ted came down in a plaid bathrobe wearing fuzzy green dinosaur slippers and carrying two mugs of steaming coffee. They sat together on the front steps of his building. She pointed at the slippers, and all the laughter that they'd ever held in came tumbling out.

She wondered what Ted was doing right now. Was he at his little table with the *Times* spread open? She could almost hear the dripping of the coffee maker and smell the freshly ground dark roast that she knew filled his tiny kitchen. She'd sat at that little kitchen table with him every afternoon for almost two weeks when he and Donald had called it quits. One day she was out pushing Henry in a stroller and found Ted was sitting on the bottom step of the fire escape looking, well, looking like someone had died. She walked past and waved, kept going, and on a whim, turned around and asked him if he was okay. That's when he broke down. That's when he told her, between sobs, that Donald had packed a duffle bag and stormed out the door the night before. She took him by the hand and led him across the street to her apartment. This was the first time he had been inside, and when she took him back into the kitchen, he stopped crying long enough to marvel at the size. She was sure she'd heard him mumble something about how expensive the neighborhood is and how could she and her husband afford what was essentially an apartment-sized mansion. He eventually sat down at the kitchen table, and she turned to the stove to put on a pot of tea. She could hear him sobbing again.

"We were in a café," she remembered him saying. "Some guy wearing running shorts and a ratty sweatshirt comes sauntering in, beads of sweat on his forehead, legs pink from the cold. He and Donald exchange a look. I know that look." Annie was still reeling from his comment about their apartment and his assumption that at their age, they couldn't possibly afford it.

"So, Donald cheated on you?"

Ted laid his head down on the table. "Yeah. He did."

Annie went into the living room and lowered Henry into his playpen. She watched him squirm a bit and then quickly fall asleep. Ted was right where she'd left him, frozen in time, frozen in grief. She poured two cups of tea and set one down beside him.

"We didn't actually buy this apartment, Ted," she heard herself saying, angry at herself for feeling the need to justify. Like it was any of his business. Sure, they were neighbors, they were friends, sort of friends. Still, she continued. "Alec's dad bought it. Not for us, though. He bought it as an investment. When Alec and I moved here from DC and needed a place, well, he offered it to us with the agreement that we'd pay a nominal amount toward the mortgage and all taxes, utilities, etc. Not sure now what the long-term plan is." She wasn't sure he was listening. She didn't really care whether he was listening or not. She was surprised by how good it felt to get that out. To tell someone that she isn't really who she appeared to be. It was liberating.

Ted eventually lifted his head off the table, took a few sips of tea that had long since lost its soothing heat, and thanked her profusely for listening. He laughed when she reminded him that he didn't talk. He laughed for what seemed like a long time. He sobbed again, laughed again, then whimpered for long minutes. When he was finished, she walked with him to the door. He hugged her and left. Donald eventually came home. All these years later they're still together.

***

The darkness of the long night faded, and the smoke across the river came into view. She realized that no, Ted couldn't possibly be at his kitchen table because he was traveling with his art fellows. She panicked again. Her painting. Her first real painting in ages - born of raw emotion and strange weather - was likely trampled on, covered in mud, possibly floating in the Hudson. It was the only tangible evidence she had of the day before the world changed. She imagined that other such art, mostly tourists' photos, would emerge over the coming days, weeks, and months. She felt like she was about to lose control. She closed her eyes and forced herself to breathe.

**

A breeze brushed her cheek, caressing it like she used to caress Henry's cheek when she'd put him in his crib to sleep. Usually, by the fourth or fifth stroke, he was snoring in that precious, gentle way that babies do. Annie became aware of something wet on her chin - tears that had rolled down? Semi-awake she touched her chin, then her eyes. Her eyes were dry and sleep caked, so she hadn't been crying. Her forehead was wet too. She was hot. She was sweating. She sat up, aware now that the morning was in full swing. The sun was beating down on her, and she felt like she was cooking from the inside - like she was in a microwave oven.

She pulled the wool sweater over her head and tossed it across the cockpit, toward the opposite bench. It missed the seat but landed on something that was leaning against it. Funny, she didn't notice anything there last night or earlier this morning. The weight of the heavy sweater made this thing fall. It hit the deck face up. She stared at it in disbelief. She was confident she knew what it was but hesitated before crouching down beside it to get a better look. The fear that she was wrong momentarily paralyzed her. She got up and went down into the cabin, careful to not let her eyes meet this thing. She found a roll of paper towels and grabbed a wad. After moistening half of it with water, she climbed back into the cockpit and carefully let her eyes pour over it. She wiped it clean. Annie Wells. She doesn't remember signing it at all. But she did. And she used her maiden name.

Lost - Alec

ALEC FELT LIKE A HORRIBLE father for allowing his ten-year-old son to watch the terror attacks play out over and over on the news. He imagined parents all over the country shielding their cherubs from all that was bad, all that was evil. He'd tried last night twice to coax Henry away from the TV. This morning, his sister-in-law had better luck. She'd seen a goldfinch - Henry's favorite bird, apparently - on the ledge outside the kitchen window. Henry reluctantly and with feigned interest got up and looked at it. He flicked the window with his thumb and forefinger, scaring the bird away. Then Kathy tried to entice him with homemade oatmeal muffins which he picked at but didn't eat.

He knew he should do something, anything to distract his son. Henry had fallen asleep for a few hours yesterday afternoon watching *Sleepless in Seattle*, and then, at nearly midnight was wide awake, watching CNN the way he used to watch *The Brave Little Toaster*. Henry used to watch that silly animated movie to the point that Alec knew the entire script - word for word. And last night, over and over again, the same images of the planes hitting the towers and Pentagon. The fireballs. The smoke. People running from a tidal wave of thick soot.

He still hadn't heard from Brenda, couldn't even get an open line to her cell phone. It didn't help calm him that he was able to make and receive other calls, both on the landline and on the mobile. Two therapists from his office had called to see if he'd made it back from Japan and if he was okay. He never mentioned Brenda, because by not mentioning her, by not acknowledging to people outside his immediate circle that his wife had been in that fucking building and hadn't come home yet, well, by not uttering those words or any variation of those words, well, it gave him hope.

Jenn called him too. His reaction at the sight of her number on the caller ID troubled him. He was happy to see it. He let it go. No way was he about to answer a call from Jenn. Then something bubbled inside him, and he grabbed at the phone. The complete and utter relief he felt upon hearing her voice unnerved him. He broke down and sobbed when he told her about Brenda. She offered to come over. He wanted her to come over. He longed for the comfort of her presence, her perspective, her laughter even. He would have gladly welcomed it. It was almost as if Japan never happened. Jenn's verbal countenance on the phone suggested that Japan was behind them. But, were his feelings for Jenn behind him too? Had they never happened? He was so damned confused. Mostly though, he was grateful that she seemed to not hate him. They were still friends. The relief he felt was immense. She had, over time, become his best friend and he didn't understand until now how hard it would have been to give that up. He was about to tell her yes, come over when she made the decision for him: coming over would probably be a terrible idea. A terrible idea indeed. He hung up the phone disappointed but at the same time, a tiny bit relieved.

"Hey, Buddy. Come here and eat some breakfast. Frosted Flakes." Henry had fallen asleep on the couch after Kathy's failed goldfinch and oatmeal muffin attempt.

For the rest of the morning, Alec and Kathy politely danced around each other, trying hard not to talk in front of Henry, working hard not to lose control. For all his education and training, he felt like he was walking blindfolded with nothing to grab onto of for support. In the back of his mind, there was an endless abyss that threatened to swallow him. He couldn't see, but was too afraid to remove the blindfold, too fearful of what it might reveal. He needed to be in control of his household. Today more than ever. He couldn't lose control like he'd lost control of Seth's well-being out on the beach so long ago. He couldn't lose control like he did in Japan. Being in control was as vital to him as breathing. Even when it had become clear that his mother was never coming back for him, he maintained control in a way that he now knows was far beyond his thirteen years. But today, now, this morning, this moment, well, control was not a word in his vocabulary.

The clock on the wall above the kitchen sink was loud. Brenda found it at a yard sale a few years ago. The thing was vintage seventies, complete with unnaturally large, lime green and fuchsia daisies harassing the bubble-shaped numbers. She'd hung it up while he was out running. The thing was so damned loud. He'd teased Brenda that it sounded like a ticking time bomb. How ironic. A bomb. Today. He gradually grew accustomed to the ticking, a sort of metronome. He often found himself making his lists in rhythm with that damned ugly - oh so ugly - clock. And when the battery died and it took a week to finally replace it, he almost couldn't think straight in the silence that was louder than the ticking had ever been.

"Come on Henry. Have some breakfast."

The clock ticked in time with his heart. The clock ticked in time with the pounding in his head. He felt like he was rapidly losing his remaining thread of control. If he could just focus on the clock, the one-second ticks. If he could just focus on that, then externally at least, he could function. But he couldn't even get his son to eat breakfast. He couldn't get his son to step away from the TV. He couldn't get his son to buy into the lie that his mother was okay and would walk through the door soon. He had to keep reminding himself that he was the father. All he needed to do was walk into the living room and turn off the TV. That's all. Henry was still little enough to pick up and carry. Alec could do that. He could pick his son up and carry him into the kitchen and make him sit there, listening to the clock, until he consumed the entire box of Frosted Flakes. Alec was the father. Alec says what will and will not go on in his home from now until when-ever.

"Dammit." He sat down at the table and ate a spoonful of the cereal he'd laid out for his son. He pushed the bowl away and sat listening to the clock and trying to define the sick, heavy feeling in his gut. Was it the physical manifestation of having been up all night? Or the raw, emotional fatigue from desperately gripping the reigns and realizing that he just could not hold on any longer? He was not in control. He was helpless. He felt like a horrible, sorry excuse for a father. Maybe if he just sat down on the couch next to his son. Perhaps just sitting together would bring them both some semblance of comfort. Perhaps it would distract him - even for a few minutes - from how utterly out of control he felt.

Alec rose from the table determined. But instead of heading into the living room and plopping himself into the cushions, he just stood there - his toe on the precipice of his inability to just go in and sit with his son. Yeah, he screwed up as a father more times than he could count. He screwed up as a husband. He was at least willing to admit these things to himself. All he needed to do now was to sit on the couch and reassure Henry. It wouldn't erase his mistakes - nothing would - but it might at least put him one baby step closer to being a better father and maybe, down the road, a better husband. If only he would be given a chance to make things right by Brenda. If only. He pushed thoughts of her whereabouts out of his mind and took one step toward the couch. He couldn't do it. He couldn't close the gap that was growing between father and son. All he had to do was hop over the hole and land on the couch. He stood frozen, wanting nothing more than to flee. In fact, if he didn't escape, and soon, he would fall right into the gap and be swallowed whole.

He retreated out of the living room through the kitchen, down the stairs, and out the front door. He was halfway down the street when he saw three pumpkins sitting on the second step of a brownstone on his side of the street. He didn't know the people who lived in that house. He'd seen them many times but never took the time to meet them. He wondered now if Brenda knew them. She probably knew a lot of people that he never even noticed. Wasn't it a bit early for pumpkins? Pumpkin Month, as Brenda liked to call October, was still a few weeks away. He could almost hear her saying that anyone who would put pumpkins out before then was not worth knowing. He felt suddenly justified in never having associated with these heathens who would dare mess with the Pumpkin gods. Brenda never, ever took Henry to get pumpkins before the First of October. Never. She'd be horrified if she'd seen this. Maybe she had seen it. He'd been too busy trying to have an affair to even notice. He felt like scum.

Alec stood on the sidewalk and regarded the medium sized orange gourds. Oh, what the hell. Why not? He picked one up and tucked it under his arm and without another thought, continued walking. By the time he reached the first intersection his resolve to be a better father and a better husband was back. He considered crossing the street but then turned around. He couldn't steal a pumpkin. Nope. Not Alec. Adulterer, maybe (he'd have to work on making sure he never actually became one). But pumpkin thief? No way in hell. He made his way back to the second step of the fourth house on his side of the street where the other two pumpkins sat patiently awaiting their orange friend's return. He put the pumpkin back on the stoop. As he walked home, he could almost feel the three pumpkins scowling at him.

He opened the door to his apartment, and a low murmur of voices coming from the kitchen caused him to wonder if he'd opened the wrong door. He couldn't possibly be standing in the wrong apartment, could he? He looked around. His eyes fixed on the coat closet - one of Brenda's brilliant ideas. Remove the door and install cubby holes and hooks. She kept it neat and tidy, but it still drove him crazy that it didn't have a door. Every time he came home from the office and kicked off his shoes, he hated it. God how he hated that damned thing. The very thought of it made him want to throw things. Today, he kept his shoes on.

The low murmur was comprised of the scholarly sounds of people engaged in hard and serious work on what seemed to be a critical project. A study group, like the ones he led during grad school. Before he could sharpen his focus so that he could make out individual voices, the murmur subsided, leaving only the punctuation marks - the shuffling of feet, the rustling of paper, a drawer opening and closing, and the occasional rap of a utensil or some other such implement hitting the table. This couldn't be his apartment. He heard a man's voice that he couldn't quite place. Who else's house though, would have a ridiculous, coat closet without a door? A quick glance at the opposite wall provided a comforting confirmation that he was, indeed home. While it was highly unlikely, there was a small hint of the possibility that he may not be the only loser in Brooklyn with a perpetually open coat closet. He did know, however, that he was probably the only loser in Brooklyn with a signed and numbered Katz's Delicatessen print. *Send a salami to your boy in the Army.* He'd nabbed it from his grandparents' estate before his father could get his grubby hands on it. Yes. Alec was now quite confident that he was indeed in his own apartment.

The low murmur of voices continued. Alec tilted his head to better hear it. *Ishkabosh*. There was only one person who ever said that. *Ishkabosh. Ishkabosh.* Noted in an exaggerated, agitated way. Hit your toe on the coffee table? *Ishkabosh!* Open your credit card bill in January, after the holidays? *Ishkabosh!* He couldn't believe it. It was as if his father knew how to push him over the edge. Knew how to push all of his trigger buttons. It was as if Dr. Manny Arnstein knew how annoyed his son would be at the thought of a visit - any visit - let alone a surprise visit. Alec imagined that this realization alone was enough to get Manny in the car, fighting whatever obstacles needed fighting, jumping whatever hurdles needed jumping. Yep. Just to infuriate him. Just to show him - no - to prove to him just how incompetent he was as a shrink, as a son, as a husband, as a father.

Alec tiptoed up the half-staircase leading to the living room. When he reached the last step before the landing, he braced himself for a superficial round of greetings and an accusatory round of inquiry. The low murmur of voices he had been hearing came into more precise focus. *Ishkabosh.* Yep. Unmistakable. His father's voice, giving orders, making decisions, handing Henry a stack of papers. Wait a minute. Handing Henry a stack of papers? He waited until he saw his son disappear down the hall, the stack of papers in hand, before making his own presence known.

"What the hell are you doing here?" His voice was barely a whisper.

Manny turned away from his task, glanced at Alec, and did his signature simultaneous nod of the head and wave that meant: *Yeah, I'm aware of you, but you're not important enough for me to stop what I'm doing.* Alec had cowered in his father's dismissive body language all his life. Not today.

"I asked you a question." He grabbed his father's arm, midair, and forced him to turn around and look at him. Manny's eyes looked tired. Old. Droopy. He never really thought of his father as being old. Manny always seemed younger than his counterparts. Yet his eyes belied all the years of keeping himself fit. All the years of running. Didn't he just complete a half-marathon last year? Or was it the year before? Alec didn't know, didn't care really. Or did he? Did he care? Did he care that his father had the eyes of an elderly man? The fleshy pads beneath his eyes were swollen, as if competing with the puffy cheeks he'd always had. Where had the tiny moles dotting the skin just under his eyebrows come from? When had a colony of gnats landed on his father's face? Manny's eyes locked on Alec's and seemed to plead - for what, Alec didn't care. He was uninspired to fall for any of his father's affectations. That's what this whole thing was, wasn't it? An affectation. A big, ugly affectation of feigning concern. He stood frozen, disgusted by the feel of his father's arm, yet not wanting to let go. Because by releasing the stronghold he had on Manny's arm would be conceding to his presence in his home, in his world. Arms still midair, he glared at his father, boring into those tired eyes, trying desperately to penetrate the white film that made his father's brown eyes murky like clumps of mud on the floor of a dried-up swamp.

Alec suddenly became weary of the impasse and released the grip on his father's arm. It fell quickly as if made of lead, hitting his thigh with a loud thump. As if on cue, Henry sauntered into the room with a happy bounciness Alec hadn't seen since this whole crazy, bloody mess became their new reality. He swallowed the words he was about to spit at his father.

"Grandpa is helping us find mom." Henry beamed. "Look, he brought these posters. We're gonna go hang them around the city."

Alec took one from the pile. Of course. Very professional. Almost too perfect. On TV he'd seen posters on virtually every surface in lower Manhattan. Light posts, sides of buildings, telephone poles, store windows. The thing that stuck in his mind whenever he saw the TV camera pan on the wall near Ground Zero or zoom onto a random poster nailed to a tree was that they all seemed to have been made quickly and with purpose and intent. Not to wow anyone with the best graphic art but merely to put a face out there - usually smiling - in the hope that someone, anyone might know something, anything. The childlike quality of those posters touched him. The crayons, markers, and blue ballpoint pens even suggested that the signs had been made with the raw emotion that comes with fully loving someone.

Alec looked at his father. "These are too good. They're too perfect. Too professional." He handed the glossy fliers back to Henry.

"Susan made them."

Of course. Susan. His stepmother. Manny's wife. High-pitched squeaky mouse voice. A perfectionist in every way.

"They look great." His vitriol was evaporating, against his will and consent. He wasn't emotionally capable of a paradigm shift. Not now. He was just too damned exhausted to continue fighting. "Don't you think it's a bit premature to write Brenda off as 'missing'?"

"What would you call it then? She's not here now, is she? If she's not missing, that what is she? Where is she? She went out for a stroll and will walk through that door at any second?"

"Dad." Alec's vitriol returned. He willed himself to remain calm and gentle. If he was on his game, he could pull this off. And when he was on his game, unless you knew him very well or were close enough to see the corner of his left eye twitching ever so subtly, you wouldn't guess him to be angry or upset. Today he was not on his game, but he took a deep breath and continued. He would go for an Oscar nomination today. "I don't think this is good for Henry." He lowered his voice even more and looked around, but Henry had disappeared.

"Actually, if I may, I think the posters are a good idea," Kathy said as she emerged from the kitchen with three beers. She handed one each to Alec and Manny. "If nothing else, it's making Henry feel like he can do something or exercise some sort of control over his fate." She lightly clinked her beer bottle against Manny's. "It's good to see you, Dr. Arnstein. It's been a long time."

"Excuse me." Manny looked at Kathy, then looked inquisitively at Alec, then back at Kathy. "Do I know you?"

"That's it." Alec would not be getting that Oscar nomination after all. His vitriol broke free. "That's it. I'm done. I've had enough. You can leave now." He took a long, slow swig of his beer and stood eye to eye with his father, incredulous.

"I'm just asking a question." Manny took several steps backward. "Your wife is gone, and another woman is walking around here like she belongs. Like she owns the place." He turned to Kathy. "I just want to know who you are."

"I'm Kathy. Brenda's older sister. I met you at the wedding. We talked about your work?"

"Oh. Well. Then. Um. Okay."

"Dad, please leave. I beg you."

"I'm just trying to help."

"Kathy came to Joe's funeral. And she was at Bubbe's too." Alec shook his head. "Don't you remember?"

"I care about you and especially my grandson. I want to help." Manny ignored Alec's question.

"Yeah, I know. You care about us but not Brenda. She's not Jewish. You never got over that, did you? She didn't go to the right school either. Oh, and guess what? You'll love this." He raised his glass to Kathy. "Kathy here, well she's a lesbian! How about that!" Alec guzzled what was left in his bottle.

Manny ignored him and set his bottle down on the coffee table untouched.

"Enough. Let's collect Henry and get these posters out there. Susan spent a lot of time making them." And then to Kathy: "Please excuse me for not remembering you. Your hair must be different or something. It's been a rough couple of days."

Alec sighed and turned toward Kathy, mouthing "I'm sorry." She winked at him and shrugged. She was so thick skinned. It was one of the things Alec liked best about her. Too bad she liked women.

* * *

"Hey Buddy, what are you working on?" Alec wasn't exactly sure how he extracted himself from the hullabaloo in his living room or how he mustered the gumption to go to Henry. Standing face to face with his father - remembering all that he hated about him - made him feel like he wasn't such a failure after all. Alec was just doing the best he could. The best he knew how. It was all he could offer at this point in time. It was an easy choice - acting like a real father by meeting Henry right here, right now, in his ten-year-old boy world or getting the life squeezed out of him in the vice that was his father. Well. An easy choice. He silently thanked Manny. Dr. Manny. Fantastic, marvelous Dr. Manny. Without knowing it, this might very well be Dr. Manny Arnstein's best work.

Henry was lying on his stomach on his bedroom floor. He had a street map of New York City spread out before him. It was a map Alec didn't remember ever having seen before. Yet it didn't look new. Is this what his life had become? He hardly knew anything about his son.

"I'm mapping out where to put Mom's posters." He had a green marker in his hand and, without looking up, slid it along a small stretch of the Brooklyn Bridge.

"The Brooklyn Bridge. That's an interesting place to hang posters. But do you think enough people will see them there?"

"Dad, everyone will see them there. Plus, I could hand them out to people walking."

Alec considered this for a minute. "You do have a point. Yep. The Brooklyn Bridge is an excellent place." He wanted to tell Henry to stop. That it was premature to consider his mother missing. But with every hour, with every second really, with every loud tick of Brenda's ugly wall clock, the possibility that she had, indeed, been in one of those buildings became that much more real. He sat down on the floor next to Henry and just stared into the void that so many years of being disconnected and self-centered had created. When he looked back down at the map, Henry had circled Grand Central and Penn Stations in red and purple respectively.

Sailing - Annie

JUST THREE MONTHS AGO, Henry wanted a bow tie, so Alec took him to Barneys to let him pick one out himself. It had to be a man bow tie, is how Henry put it. And it had to be the kind that you tie, not the kind with the clips. Alec had tried to talk him out of a bow tie. But Henry was adamant. Alec argued - in that infuriatingly, patronizingly, mesmerizing way that is pretty much Alec's signature style - that you don't wear a bow tie to a summer birthday party. *What if you want to swim in the pool?* But Henry didn't want to swim in the pool. He just wanted to wear a bow tie. Because Sarah liked bow ties. This had been the first time Henry's olive complexion turned shades of red when talking about a girl. He was only ten! But, looking back, Annie remembered having a crush on a boy named Scott sometime around the third or fourth grade. She remembered pulling Alec aside then and telling him to just take Henry to Barneys, or she'd do it herself. He'd shot her his *I'm not happy about this* look, and in response, she shot him one right back that said *don't make him feel silly, just let him get a damned bow tie.* Alec volleyed the ball right back at her with the final look between them that day, the look that silently screamed *we'll talk about this later.*

When was all that with the bow tie? Could it really have been as recent as this past summer? June, just a week after school ended. Just this summer. How could things have changed so much in only three short months? Her health, her marriage. The world as she once knew it. Her world. But also everyone else's world. She wondered how many people would take a serious inventory of their lives after all that had happened. For how many poor souls would Tuesday be the catalyst for change? She looked around the boat. Her temporary home. What the hell did "home" mean anymore? She didn't feel like she could go home yet. Perhaps she would ask John if she could stay on his boat until she dies. Because die was what she was going to do. Probably sooner rather than later.

At least Henry would have a bow tie to wear to her funeral. She pictured him peering over her open casket in his black suit and his bow tie, impeccably tied all by himself. He would want no help from his dad, this she knew. The bow tie he'd selected at Barney's had Pac-Man characters on it.

Annie mindlessly fiddled with her cell phone, tossing it from one hand to the other. When it vibrated earlier this morning, she didn't even look at it. There was no one she wanted to talk to. Not Alec. Not her sister. Not even Henry. The longer she stayed away, the harder it would be for her to explain to her little boy why she didn't come home. She had already stayed away too long. She knew that whoever called had left a voice mail. She knew this by the telltale second set of rings, and then the beep. She figured it had to be Alec. He was only calling about a million times an hour. Her sister too. Maybe even a little bit more frequently. Annie had long since turned the thing off. At some point, she had turned it back on. She wished she hadn't.

A quick glance at the missed call log revealed that the caller was none of the above. It was her oncologist. She'd sat on the voicemail for about an hour and when she finally listened to it she deleted it quickly as if removing it would also eliminate the reality of what the doctor said. *It is urgent that you come in today.* As if terrorists hadn't attacked our nation two days ago! As if there wasn't the possibility that she was already dead or trapped under a pile of metal and concrete. As if, after Tuesday, her cancer was even that important to her. Maybe she'd lost a loved one. Perhaps she didn't want to live anymore. Maybe she just wanted to die. She continued turning the phone over and over in her hand. Again and again. And then she tossed her damned phone across the boat. It brushed the mast, halfway up, then hit the foredeck with a thud, bounced back toward the cockpit, and slid toward a pair of brown Dock Siders. Fixated on the shoes, she watched a set of newly familiar long fingers wrap themselves around the battered phone. Her eyes met the top of John's head, his strands of grayish-brownish hair blowing wildly in a wind that seemed to have arrived with him. He was still holding the phone as he looked up at her.

"Not sure what the phone did to deserve such abuse, but here you go." He handed it to her.

"How long have you been here?"

"Long enough to now know this key thing about you - that you're a violent phone abuser." He smiled. "You know, if I were still a cop, I could arrest you for this horrible act."

"Maybe getting arrested wouldn't be such a bad thing. Then I'd have an excuse to not have to go home again." She didn't mean to hand him such an open-ended statement, but she did. It was her heavy heart speaking. Her mouth had little to do with it.

"I know. It's hard to go home after something like this." He pointed at what was now a gaping hole in the Manhattan skyline. And as if sensing that she'd revealed just a little too much, he stopped talking and sat down on the bench, directly opposite her. "That's quite the painting, by the way."

John's eyes were fixed on the canvas. She was sitting cross-legged on the bench and holding the painting tightly against her chest. She looked away from him. The tears rolled down her cheeks like a rushing river. She watched, as if in slow motion, teardrop after teardrop slip off her chin and land on her jeans. This man, this stranger seemed eerily perceptive. He sat quietly and let her weep.

"Take me somewhere." She finally lifted her head and looked at him. He was still staring at the painting. "Please. There's wind. We're on a boat." The tears threatened her again. If she could just swallow them even for a minute, she'd be okay. Yesterday, John offered to drive her home or pay for a cab. She'd told him that she didn't want to go home yet, that she didn't want to be alone. It was a lie. She wouldn't have been alone at home. She just wasn't ready to face the things that awaited her there. She'd expected him to ask about a husband or whether or not she had children. But he didn't. And she didn't know what to make of that. "I need a distraction."

John kept his eyes fixed on the painting. He finally looked at her. "It's not that simple." He took a deep breath as if considering his options. "I'm not sure the waters are navigable yet. Maybe in a day or so. I've seen ferries come and go, but no pleasure boats. No private vessels. Definitely no yellow sailboats." He was quiet again. He reached into his back pocket and pulled out his wallet. He looked inside then set it down on the small table between them. "If you need a distraction, I could show you around Jersey City. Have you ever been here before?"

"Yep, my sister, uh. Yeah. I've been here." Too much. Too much. The last thing she needed was for this man to get all high-horsey on her and encourage her to call home. To demand it even. To make it a condition for using his precious boat as temporary quarters. She braced herself. The tears came without her consent. Damned tears.

"Let me go talk to the dock master. He'll know if it's okay to sail." He looked at her as if he couldn't quite figure her out. She suddenly felt self-conscious and exposed, not to mention she more than likely looked like one of the street urchins in Oliver. "You're right. There is wind, and we're on a boat." He smiled then. A little.

***

They sailed in silence. Upper Bay. Lower Bay. Sandy Hook Bay. All day, or so it seemed. They sailed in the kind of silence she was grateful for, the type of silence that included sporadic words here and there - words focused on sailing. Words that didn't draw attention to the reality of her situation. Because it was the reality of her life that she wanted to forget, at least for a sliver of time. He asked her no personal questions. For this she was grateful. And she asked him none in return. He taught her how to helm the boat - or more simply, how to steer. How to trim the sails. How to feel the wind. The difference between port and starboard. How to navigate the waters and how to remember that the red buoys were to be on the right (starboard) when coming back from the sea, which put the green buoys on the left (port). And an easy way to remember: *Red Right Returning.*

The first hints of dusk appeared on the horizon as John backed *Thee-Ring Circus* into her slip. A chill washed over Annie, and she shivered. He took off the flannel shirt he'd been wearing and tossed it to her. She studied the police tee he had on underneath. She remembered him mentioning that he had been a cop. She tucked her arms into the shirt, backward so that the front covered her like a blanket. The shivering was slow to subside and was an abrupt reminder that she was a very sick woman, with probably less than a year to live. She began to panic and started pacing the boat frantically. She climbed over the lifeline and stepped onto the dock. She was suddenly overcome with heat and tore the flannel shirt off as quickly as she'd put it on. She ran toward the boatyard where many boats were already out of the water and on stilts in preparation for winter.

"Hey. Annie. Are you okay?"

She crouched in the gravel, leaning on one of four stands holding up a sailboat much larger than *Three-Ring Circus.* She looked at John but didn't answer. He sat down beside her. He was holding the flannel shirt that she had thrown on the ground in her panicked attempt to flee the world. He leaned toward her and draped it across her body. He stared at her for a few seconds before moving a respectable distance away.

"I guess that was a dumb question. Of course, you're not okay. Look what happened two days ago. Nobody is okay. Nobody will be okay for a very long time."

He stood up and held out his hand, just like he had two days ago when she was a soot-covered mess. Today she wasn't covered in soot, but she was still a mess. She let her hand slowly meet his, and in a gently powerful way, he pulled her to her feet.

Disclosures - Annie

"TELL ME ABOUT YOUR PAINGING."

Annie opened her mouth as if to answer, but instead just looked down at her plate of fried rice that she'd been playing with for the past few minutes. She'd asked for chopsticks, and when they arrived, she wasted no time moving globs of rice from one side of the plate to the other. By now she had a small pile in the center, surrounded by smaller piles. It looked like a flower.

"You were there, weren't you," he said, changing the subject.

She nodded. She needed no explanation, no clarification. She knew John meant in one of the towers.

"I'm sorry, I'm just not hungry after all." It was the first thing she'd said, other than ordering the fried rice and asking for the chopsticks. John had managed to coax her out of the boatyard. She'd thought she was hungry. It was getting dark. He'd heard her stomach rumble and suggested they grab a bite. They'd walked away from the marina and into a small Chinese restaurant. John knew the owner - a woman named Lil - and chatted with her for a few minutes before sitting down in a booth near the window. She pushed the plate away and put her head down on the table, like a kindergartener during rest time.

"If I had a camera I'd take a picture of your plate. I could see it on the cover of *Food and Wine*," he said, obviously trying to lighten the mood.

She lifted her head and felt her face changing. She didn't need a mirror to tell her that it had turned into a melancholy contortion of squinty eyes and, more than likely, a frown.

"I have cancer." She blurted it out without thinking and wished she could shove it back in. She looked at him, really looked at him, for the first time. His eyes never left hers. She thought she saw a firefly but knew that was impossible. For the strangest second, she saw her future flash in the light from his eyes. She knew this was crazy. She had no future. She pushed her plate away and got up to leave.

"Please don't go. Please." He smiled a little but looked sad at the same time. He pulled the plate of uneaten fried rice toward him. He took small bits of colorful vegetables and placed one on each mound of rice. If nothing else, it made her laugh a little. She sat back down.

"I'm sorry, I didn't mean to dump that on you. I just found out. It's still raw. You're only the second person I've told. My sister knows - inflammatory breast cancer is what they're calling it - but not that I'm dying. Yeah. I'm basically dying. They didn't say as much, but I'm not stupid. Oh, and it's in my spine too. Just a tiny spot, but it's there. My oncologist called a few days ago with the happy news. He called again this morning."

"Ah. So that's what the phone toss was about. I just figured you were practicing to pitch at Yankee Stadium." His eyes fell in line with hers again. "I'm so sorry. You can't be dying though. You seem too healthy."

She just sighed. She looked out the window and tried to remember Alec's face, but his face was blurry in her mind - the man he had become was so different from the man she thought she knew. She wondered now if she ever really loved him. She cared about him. Even now, even in her anger she cared about him. But did she love him? She wasn't so sure anymore. It was comforting to sit in the booth with John and his unconditional kindness, his gentleness, and his respect for her privacy. Even in his bluntness she sensed he wouldn't push her. Yet, he wasn't going to ignore this disclosure or shy away from it. Her mind sprinted up and down the streets of this horrific time in her life and brought everything to the surface. Her breath caught in the back of her throat and tears sprang out of each eye in an almost projectile sort of way. She quickly wiped them, but they kept coming. She plugged what she could, and despite the streaky face, turned from the window and looked at John, who never took his eyes off of her. Lil walked by the table and handed Annie a wad of napkins. By the time she stopped crying, every napkin was a wet, crumpled ball, lying on top of the table between them.

"I really am dying. I'm guessing I have maybe a year. If I'm lucky, two or three years. I don't know. I really don't know." She felt strangely calm. Saying these words out loud seemed to make them less frightening, less real, even. It was like she was talking about someone other than herself, and she basked in this fantasy.

"So, tell me about your painting."

And that was the end of that. John wasn't going to bombard her with questions about her health. Nor was he going to offer her pity - phony or otherwise. To him, she was a runaway - someone he picked up during a national tragedy - living on his boat. Why even care whether she will be alive on the first anniversary of this horrible time in history? She was in awe of this. Most people would feel obligated to offer pity. They would tsk-tsk and shake their heads and offer platitudes until they could run as fast as they could to get away and escape into whatever diversions help them forget the reality that they too, will someday die.

"There's not much to tell." She shrugged. "My neighbor has studio space in the north tower." As she listened to herself talk, she was struck by the fact that Ted's studio was gone. As well as all the works in progress that will never be recovered. Compared to the lives lost, the art was nothing. "My God. His studio is gone." She put her head down.

"I know. It's hard to believe. I haven't even begun to process the whole thing." He touched her arm, and she sat up again. "You've noticed that I walk with a limp, right?" Annie nodded. "I told you I was a cop, right? A few years ago, I got into a fight with some guys at the boatyard. One of them pulled a gun. Long story. Fell wrong and broke my leg in a bunch of places. Like Joe Theismann. Remember that? They medically retired me."

"Sorry." It was all she could think to say. Then: "I was at that game."

"Wow. You'll have to tell me about that sometime. Anyway, what's really killing me is that...um." He looked at her. "Yikes, that's not how I meant it."

Annie laughed at this. And laughed. And laughed. Genuinely laughed, in a way she hadn't laughed in weeks. Months? Maybe even longer. It took a while, but John apparently wasn't appropriately inoculated and caught the bug. They were both hysterical.

"Let me guess," she finally said. "It's killing you that..." She started again, this time, snorting. He shook his head and started again too.

"It's killing me that I wasn't there." He was finally able to squeak the words out. "It's killing me that I couldn't help, you know, as a cop." He wasn't laughing anymore. "I should have been able to be a cop on the front lines that day."

"But you were there. You did help. How many people did you transport? How many trips did you make, back and forth?"

"Not that many. My former partner on the force, his cousin died. A firefighter. I just found out last night." His eyes took on a glassy, watery look - the precursor to tears. Annie didn't know if she could handle seeing him cry. She offered him one of her own, tear-stained, crumpled napkins. He took it and put it right back down on the table without dabbing his eyes. He sighed and looked at her.

"My neighbor let me use his studio," she said. "I've been itching to paint something, anything. I went over on Monday. I didn't have a plan. Then I saw this moth sitting on the window. Ted's studio is on the ninety-second floor and had a fabulous view of the Statue of Liberty. It looked like the moth was looking out the window, contemplating life. Then the storm. I just started painting. God, it felt good to paint." She pulled the plate of now cold rice back toward her side of the booth and mindlessly picked up one of the little mounds and popped it in her mouth. She chewed slowly and then took a sip of water. "I used acrylics - they dry quickly. I went back early Tuesday morning to spray it with this clear spray that protects the painting. I'm not sure what time I walked out of there. It was a beautiful morning and I had a lot on my mind so I wandered around and eventually sat down on a bench in Battery Park. I must have fallen asleep because when I woke up, it was like I was an extra in a movie. A horrible, horrible movie."

"Where's home?"

"Brooklyn. I live in Brooklyn." She looked down at her left hand. She'd taken her ring off when Alec left her crying in the kitchen. She'd placed it on top of the stack of burned, blueberry pancakes that were probably still sitting on the stove where she'd left them.

"It's okay. You can stay on the boat as long as you need to."

***

They'd moved from the Chinese place to Shorty's because Annie feigned a desire for fries. She didn't really want fries, she just didn't want to go back to the boat. She didn't want to be alone. She didn't tell him any of this, of course. She just said she wanted fries.

"Hold on, I'll be right back." John got up and went behind the bar, grabbed a CD out of a cabinet, and slid it into a slot in the wall. Within a few seconds, Beatles music seeped through a set of speakers on a shelf above the rows of Irish whiskey. "Shorty's gone for the night which means I have dominion over the music." He sat back down across from her in the booth. It was after nine, and the place was nearly empty.

John stood Annie's moth painting against the wall next to photos of some of Shorty's customers' missing loved ones. A place of honor, he'd told her, and a centerpiece of hope in the midst of tragedy. She didn't like the idea. Not at all. But what else was she going to do with the painting? After the flail and panic when she'd realized she'd left it in the park, she wasn't sure she wanted it anymore, with all the bad memories surrounding its creation. Right now, however, she could care less about the painting, as she tried to focus - really focus - on the plate of fries she didn't have any desire to eat. She thought about what John told her as they walked from the Chinese place, back to the boat to get the painting, and then to Shorty's: that his wife was brutally raped three years ago. After the rape, while fighting to get away, she struck the rapist in the neck with her elbow, killing him. The rape left her pregnant. She decided to keep the baby. John couldn't deal with it, so he left. They had been married twenty years. He said they tried to make it work. He lived on the boat for a while when they first separated, then he started helping Shorty at the pub. He bought a small fixer-upper not too far from the boatyard last year.

This disclosure was more personal - more than she wanted or needed to know about him. They're strangers, aren't they? Why did he feel it was important to tell her these things? He seemed like a logical person, and logic dictates that if you have a runaway living on your sailboat, particularly one who would soon die, you didn't owe them any meaningful insight into your life.

She stole glances at the tiny squares of yellow that the dim light in the pub cast on his brown eyes. She looked away from him then and peeked through a small opening in the window blinds. It was darker than it seemed it should be, even at this hour. Darker than the way she was feeling. She wished it would get even more dismal. Because if it were darker, then maybe, just maybe she could remember how dire her situation - the whole situation - really was and muster up the courage to tell him the rest of her story. Her real name. She held the blinds open just wide enough so she could press her cheek against the window.

"My ex-wife is an artist," he said, breaking her reverie.

"What's her name? I wonder if I've ever heard of her or seen her work."

"Marina. Marina Butterfield. She does mostly birds. Sells them locally."

"No, I've never heard of her, but I will look her up." Then: "Don't you wonder who I am?" The question flew out of her mouth and she was horrified that she'd asked it. But really, the guy found her standing on a pier acting like a dementia patient and covered in soot. She was clearly shell-shocked and somehow damaged in the head. Everyone was shell-shocked that day. Weren't they? Yes, of course, they were. Suddenly though, she was yearning to open up and share. Maybe she just needed a stranger to spill her guts to. He made her laugh tonight. He made her laugh in a visceral, gut-wrenching, sort of way. It was the kind of laughter that caused everything else in the world to fade. She wondered about this now. During what was undoubtedly the low point of her life - she had terminal cancer! - she relished the laughter. It made her forget who she really was. For precious moments she could pretend to be someone else. Someone who didn't have the proverbial weight of the world on her shoulders. She wanted to tell him about Henry. who was probably devastated that his mother was presumed dead. She wanted to tell him about Kathy - her only real friend in the world - and how determined she would likely be to find her. Kathy was probably still searching the streets. She wanted to tell him about Alec and how their marriage was crumbling. She wondered if Alec was looking for her. She figured he was with Jenn, playing the martyr, playing the part of the devastated husband.

She looked out the window again. Clouds punctuated the ambient light of the marina. She didn't want to spoil the laughter. They could talk about the attacks, and still laugh. They could talk about the fact that she's dying and laugh.

"Yes, I do wonder who you are. I've been wondering who you are ever since I helped you onto the boat, actually." He looked serious.

"I look for my mother's face in the clouds sometimes." She said, changing the subject. The look in his eyes scared her. "She died of pancreatic cancer when I was in college. She was a teacher, and she died in June, two days after school ended. She talked a lot about how she felt she was abandoning her students. Nobody was surprised that she died in June." She quickly pulled a thin thread from that thought and shifted the conversation just enough to take some of the serious edges back out. "In some parts of the world, children are taught that it's a rabbit in the moon, not a man."

"I've heard that too." He grew quiet. Then: "I tell myself I didn't see it coming, that I never thought Marina would want to keep that baby. The truth is, deep down I knew. I knew she would keep it. I think I knew it even before she did."

"Do you ever think you could have learned to love the baby?" It wasn't like his wife had an affair and then became pregnant. She was raped. It was different. Wasn't it? She wanted to know the details of his despair, what it was like to be the husband of a rape victim. It was something she'd never thought about, never considered. She looked past him, but without warning, he came back into focus. She realized with a heart-thud that his eyes had a tiny bit of sadness in them. She previously associated the little lines jutting out from the corners of his eyes with his laughter. Now, upon closer examination, the lines suggested a man who laughed a lot but cried some too.

"I don't know. Sometimes I think yes, maybe. I've asked myself that very question many times. Everyone asks me that question." The corners of his mouth crinkled and within seconds he was laughing. "I don't mean to laugh. It's just that I'm still working through this. I really am."

"I'm sorry." She didn't laugh with him this time.

"Look, I'm doing better. Marina's doing better. I think she somehow felt that having the baby assuaged her of the guilt she felt for killing Riley. Phil Riley. The bastard who raped her. He'd been my partner on the force for a while. We were good friends. Anyway, she killed him in self-defense - he had a gun - but she was adamant that she could have helped him after she struck him. Or at least called for help. She felt that she let him die." He took a deep breath. "Plus, she carries around guilt for the death of her little sister when they were kids." He looked pained as he talked. "It's a long story. Let's just say she had nothing to do with her sister's death, but she doesn't want to hear it." He sighed and rubbed his forehead. "Anyway, now she's in a relationship with my best friend. He loves her. He loves the kid. He takes good care of them both."

"I know someone who had a similar experience with the death of a sibling. They were two and five. The five-year-old was supposed to be watching the two-year-old. Their grandparents were there, but couldn't get to him in time. The two-year-old climbed on the jetty at the beach and fell. Hit his head on a rock and died." She looked out the window again and noticed big raindrops that almost seemed like they were floating, almost like snowflakes. She should have just told him it was her husband's brother. Her husband. There was no reason to withhold her marital status. Yet she couldn't bring herself to utter the word *husband*. "The raindrops look like little parachutes," she said, again changing the subject.

He smiled and nodded his head in agreement. He got up from his bench and walked over to the side of the booth where she was sitting. She got up too, and they walked out of the pub and into the rain, down the central pier, then a left at the C Dock and back to *Three-Ring Circus*. He waited until she was safely on the boat before leaving. He hesitated, started walking, and then hesitated again.

"You don't have to tell me anything," he called to her from the dock. "You don't have to tell me your story." He stood for a second, then smiled a little and turned away from her.

The rain stopped and, in its place, came a heavy mist. She stood in the cockpit watching John disappear down the pier. She knew she would never forget the image of the mist swallowing him whole - hands deep in his pants pockets and head tilted to avoid the mist. The curve of his body as he got farther and farther away made him look like a question mark.

Searching - Alec

TO APPEASE HIS FATHER, Alec put his stepmother's professional looking 'missing persons' glossies in a manila folder, then
placed the folder in a small backpack along with a roll of duct
tape and two bottles of water. He headed out the door with
Henry. First stop: Staples to make copies of the poster that
Henry had spent several hours creating. Alec was touched and
moved by Henry's work. He'd selected a picture of the three of
them on the beach at Sandy Hook, taken last summer. It had
been one of those rare moments when Brenda seemed genuinely
happy. Her hair was wet from the ocean, and she had sand caked
on her shoulders. Henry was sitting at her feet and Alec, well,
Alec seemed far away. Sure, he was right there with them. But
his eyes were looking out at the horizon, and while his mouth
formed the shape of a smile, it looked forced and artificial. One
more reason for him to feel like a complete and utter asshole.
One more reason for his resolve to make it up to Brenda. He was
determined. Above the picture, in bubble letters colored with a

myriad of Sharpie hues: Brenda Wells Arnstein. On either side of the picture in red and ten-year-old boy handwriting were the specifics: age, hair color, eye color, and Henry's perceived notion of his mother's height and weight. What really got him, though, was what Henry wrote under the picture, covering the entire bottom half of the poster: PLEASE HELP FIND BRENDA ARNSTEIN. She is an AWESOME mom. She is the BEST mom in the UNIVERSE.

Alec handed Henry's poster to the woman behind the counter at Staples. When she started to cry, he distracted Henry by sending him to look for a heavy-duty staple gun and some heavy-duty staples. For the telephone poles and wooden fences, he told him. They'd save the duct tape for anything glass, metal, or plastic. Henry seemed satisfied with this explanation, and off he went.

"Please stop," he pleaded with the woman. "I beg you. My son will freak out if he sees you crying."

"I can't help it. You're not the first person to come in here today, for this reason."

"Look. My wife is neither missing nor dead." He looked around to make sure Henry wasn't within earshot. "I think she's just disoriented and wandering around. She was only supposed to be at the Trade Center for a little while. She left before dawn. I'm certain she was out of there before the planes hit or the towers fell." To his own ears, he sounded like he was trying to convince himself more than he was trying to convince anyone else. "I'm certain of it." He softened a bit and took the pile of posters. "We had a fight the night before. I'm guessing she's wandering around trying to clear her head." He choked on the words. For the first time since this happened, he allowed himself to breathe in the genuine possibility that Brenda was gone. Really gone.

Henry appeared with the goods, and Alec willed his inevitable breakdown to stay put for a few more hours. Long enough to be strong and brave for Henry while they hung thirty posters. Long enough for him to manage the day until he could lock himself in the bedroom that he and Brenda shared, bury his face in her pillow, and release all the pent-up guilt, fear, grief, and a thousand other emotions that he'd been choking back for the past few days.

* * *

They looked like obituaries. Big, bold obituaries. Obituaries written with resignation, yet with a small, beautiful sentence or two of hope. *He was always smiling. She was a terrific cook. He loved fishing and beer. She was a wine guru.* Was. Was. Was. Only Henry's posters used the word "is" in describing his mother.

Areas outside of the major hospitals were mosaics of these oversized obituaries. Henry seemed oblivious to Alec's observations, which was a good thing. Henry said he didn't want to put Brenda's among the hundreds outside of Saint Vincent's Hospital. There were just too many, and he wanted theirs to stand out; he wanted people to see them. He wanted his mother to see it if she walked by. They retraced her steps, or what they believed her steps to be. Alec knew she loved Battery Park, so they went there and hung posters on trees and benches. They took a taxi to the

Manhattan side of the Brooklyn Bridge, and went to work hanging the remaining posters.

"Are you sure you want to hang these here Buddy?" He still wasn't convinced this was a good use of their resources.

"Yeah, I'm sure Dad." He hung the first one and framed the entire thing with duct tape. "There." He stepped back to admire his work. "There's no way someone won't see this and stop."

"There aren't a lot of people walking the bridge these last few days. Yeah, on the first day. But now, not so much." He took in the expanse of the bridge with his arm.

"We'll just make more if we have to." Henry folded one up and put it in his pocket. "We can make more copies of this one, but I don't think we'll have to. Mom will see this. Someone will see this and go get her."

"So, you're convinced she might just come walking down this path?"

"Yes. Mom walked across it with Aunt Kathy when you were in Japan. She loves this bridge."

"Indeed, she does."

* * *

Back at home, Alec pretended to need a shower and left Henry in the living room with Manny, Kathy a friend of Kathy's. He exchanged pleasantries for a few seconds but knew he was running out of time. He hurried to his bedroom, locked the door, turned on the shower partly to support his story, but mostly to mask the sound of his sobs

Elephants - Alec

ALEC WOKE IN A PANIC. He'd been dreaming about elephants. Dancing elephants. Hundreds of them. In varying shades of blue. Dancing. Pounding. Jitterbug. Rumba. The jumpy, odd dancing of the early Eighty's. Elephants. Stomping. Pounding. Banging.

His head felt like it could explode. It was dark and icy cold in his bedroom, yet hot sweat rolled down the sides of his nose. Or was it hot tears? He wasn't sure. He tried to orient himself but couldn't figure out where he was. One by one the elephants started to disappear. One even slid down his nasal cavity and out through his left nostril. Several of them tried to stampede down his throat, but Alec outsmarted them by coughing them up and spitting them into the cup that was on his nightstand.

A soft tapping at the door jolted him back into the real world. "Yeah." His voice was craggy as if he'd spent hours at a Van Halen concert. The door opened, and his father walked in. The elephants were gone, but the sight of Manny reminded him that his head hurt like hell.

"Don't you think you should get up? Join the rest of us out there?" Manny waved his arm toward the open door as if Alec had no idea where 'out there' was. "Kathy's little friend brought a bucket of fried chicken."

So that's who had been sitting in his living room earlier. His sister-in-law's 'little friend.' What the hell does that mean? Little friend. It was so like Manny to describe someone like this. Someone he obviously didn't think much of or would want to try to get to know. This 'little friend' of Kathy's didn't look so little. She probably stood several inches over everyone in the house.

"What time is it?" He said this more to himself than to his father. He turned toward the clock on the nightstand and regarded the numbers. His vision was a bit blurry, but he could make out that it was almost eight-thirty at night. He got up and shuffled to the bathroom. He could sense Manny following closely behind him. He was tempted to jab him with his elbow but decided to ignore him instead. It seemed to take forever to walk the short distance from his bed to the bathroom. When he finally arrived, he felt victorious. He opened the medicine cabinet and grabbed the bottle of Brenda's migraine pills. He knew he shouldn't, but he popped two in his mouth and swallowed them without water.

***

The lights in the living room threatened to resurrect the elephants. Alec rubbed his forehead and turned them off. The TV, which seemed permanently set to CNN, was muted and provided more than enough light. Plus, it was better for Henry, who was asleep on the couch. Alec started to walk away but went back to the TV and changed the channel. He'd rather have Henry wake up to *Nick at Nite* than yet more yellow journalism regarding the attacks. He stood over his son and was struck with how little - how much like a baby - he looked when he slept.

"I'm trying to help." Manny sat down on the arm of the couch. He looked at the floor when he spoke. Alec turned and walked into the kitchen without responding. This time, his father didn't follow.

Alec sat down at the kitchen table and massaged his aching head. The pills hadn't entirely kicked in yet. Maybe if he added some alcohol to the mix. Yes? He went to the fridge to grab a beer and saw the plate, wrapped neatly in plastic, with his name written on a hot-pink Post-it Note. He wasn't aware of himself enough to know if he was even hungry. He figured he must be since he hadn't had a bite of anything in what felt like forever. He removed the Post-it, then carefully removed the plastic wrap. Two chicken thighs and a breast. A mound of mashed potatoes with a well in the middle filled with gravy. Green beans. Two biscuits. He doubted he could eat it all. Still, he covered the food with a paper towel and stuck the whole thing in the microwave. Thank God the microwave had a 'reheat dinner plate' option because he would have had no idea how long to cook this massive amount of food. He pushed the button and watched his dinner rotate. Around and around. It was hypnotic. He couldn't take his eyes off the plate. He could see gravy seeping through the paper towel. Around and around. It had a calming effect. Around and around. The soul-piercing beep made him jump. It seemed to echo through the apartment. He thought about Henry sleeping on the couch, just on the other side of the doorway. He didn't want to wake him. Because the boy needed the sleep. But mostly because he needed the alone time.

He eschewed sending the plate through a second cycle and carried it to the table. The beer he'd taken from the fridge a few minutes ago was still unopened and sweating. He decided to trade it for a cold one. He opened the refrigerator and as if for the first time, noticed the 'wish you were here' postcard that his father and stepmother had sent from their Mediterranean cruise about this time last year. The card showed a map with a line indicating the route: Barcelona, Toulon, Livorno, Rome, Naples, Mykonos, Izmir, Istanbul, Athens, Venice. He pulled the postcard off the fridge and took it to the table with him.

"Good, you found the food."

The voice was unfamiliar. Alec looked up and saw that it was Kathy and her friend.

"Alec, this is Robin," Kathy said. "The food was her idea."

He wiped his right hand on the leg of his jeans and extended it to Robin. "Thanks. And nice to meet you."

Robin glanced down at the postcard. "Izmir. Istanbul. I've been there." She looked at Kathy. "You should go sometime." Kathy looked at the floor and didn't respond. "Well, anyway, nice to meet you, Alec. I'll try to come back tomorrow. Kathy and I have some ideas regarding your wife. We think she's alive. We won't stop looking until we find her."

"Thanks." Alec stood. "Be careful going home."

Robin nodded and quietly let herself out of the house.

Alec arranged a single green bean and some mashed potato on his fork and slowly nibbled until the fork was clean. He put the fork down on the table without attempting another bite. He pushed his plate away. He looked at Kathy, who seemed to be studying her cell phone. What a waste that she wasn't straight. She was cute. Maybe even prettier than Brenda.

"What's up with you and the Doc?" Kathy said.

"What are you talking about?"

"You know what I'm talking about. Your Dad. It's obvious that you have some deep baggage with him."

"Yeah, I do, and it's none of your damned business."

"Look, he's here to help. That's all. Maybe you should embrace that. Let him help us find Brenda." She put her head in her hands and started to sob.

He didn't offer any words of comfort. Nor did he put his arm around her like an ordinary brother-in-law might. He just sat there staring at the postcard. Barcelona, Toulon, Livorno, Rome, Naples, Mykonos, Izmir, Istanbul, Athens, Venice. He said the cities names, in succession, in his mind. Over and over. He liked the rhythm of them. He even liked the way they looked, lined and connected by the black line that showed the cruise's route. Barcelona, Toulon, Livorno, Rome, Naples, Mykonos, Izmir, Istanbul, Athens, Venice.

Maybe he needed to make a list of places to see with Brenda. Maybe next year, when she was home, and all this was behind them. Maybe by then, the cancer would be in remission. Maybe, unless she's already dead. No! She's not dead! He would choose to believe what Robin said. That Brenda was alive. He picked up a pen that had been left on the table and started writing a list. Denver. San Francisco. Seattle. Reno. Pittsburgh. Jackson Hole. God, it felt good to make a list. London. Toronto. Paris. Frankfurt. Rome. He kept going. The Great Wall. Mount Fuji. And with that last one, he thought of Jenn. It was the first time he'd thought of her in days. Damn. He crossed Mount Fuji off the list and focused on his wife. Yes. He would put this list on the fridge and add to it. They would spend the rest of their lives seeing these places together. He looked up and saw that Kathy was staring at him with red, swollen eyes.

Alec got up and hung his napkin on the fridge with one of their many magnets - selecting a heart-shaped masterpiece that Henry made in pre-school. He suddenly didn't care that the door was a cluttered mess of magnetic tchotchkes. He suddenly loved all the magnets, the cheesier, the better. He would make a point to buy a fridge magnet in every one of the places on his new list. He returned to the table and hugged his sister-in-law. He was feeling hopeful for the first time since Tuesday.

"Let him help you, Alec." Kathy hugged him back. "This is about Brenda. And Henry, really. We need to find her. Your Dad can help. Please let him."

"I don't know." Alec picked up the postcard and twirled it in his hand. "It's complicated."

"Yeah. I'm familiar with complicated. Hey, do you mind if I crash here again? I could sleep on the floor in the living room."

"You can sleep in my room. I'm wide awake now. I'm not going back to bed tonight."

"Nah. That would be too weird for words. I'll be okay in the living room. I think your father claimed Henry's bottom bunk."

"Okay, whatever."

* * *

Alec continued studying the postcard. If Brenda wasn't dead, as Kathy and Robin suggested, then where the hell was she? What was she doing? Why wouldn't she answer her phone or at least call to say she was alive. He understood her wanting to run away from him. He takes full responsibility for that. Can't blame her one bit. But Henry. How could she do this to their son? He turned the postcard over and read what was written on the back. *Dear Little Arnstein's* (he hated that his stepmother referred to his family that way), *We're having a great time. Venice is amazing. Wish you were here.* Right. Like hell, you wished we were there.

"You gonna eat this?" Manny pulled out the chair next to Alec and sat down. Before he could answer, Manny was out of his chair, plate in hand.

"You might want to stick it in the microwave." Alec's mouth formed the tiniest of smiles.

"I'm so glad you told me. I never would have thought to do that." Manny smiled back.

It had been a running joke between them. Alec was away at college when Manny and Susan got their first microwave. From then on, during every meal, Susan would announce that if anyone's food wasn't hot enough, they could *stick it in the microwave.* He suddenly felt a tenderness for his father that defied logic. He hated his father. Had for a very long time. How could he feel tenderness toward someone he hated? He would get to that later.

Right now, he had more urgent things on his mind. Find Brenda. If he was going to allow himself to believe that she was alive, then he had to focus on that. Solely. He'd deal with his familial baggage later.

"Someone called me." Manny popped the microwave door open and sat back down at the table. The chicken and green beans looked shriveled, but Manny shoveled things into his mouth like he hadn't eaten anything in days. Alec got up and got him a beer. "Nah." He waved the beer away. "You got any red wine?"

Alec disappeared into the dining room and returned with a dusty bottle of merlot. He set it on the table in front of Manny and went to get the corkscrew and two glasses. Might as well join the old man.

Manny eyed the bottle disapprovingly, then nodded. "It'll do." He opened it and poured two glasses without the performance and affectation that he usually displays when opening wine - acting like the wine maven of the world when really, he hadn't a clue. They clinked glasses and gulped it like it was water.

"It's not the best I've ever had." Alec set his glass down on the table.

"It basically sucks." Manny lifted his glass back to his lips and took a slower, more deliberate sip. "Someone called me, Alec. Someone called about Brenda."

"What do you mean?" Alec stared at his father.

"When you and Henry were hanging the posters, I hung a few of my own, with my number on them."

"Why the hell did you do that?"

"Alec, just hold on. Don't do this. I don't know what the problem is between you and me. Been trying to understand it for years. Now isn't the time. We'll get to that later. Because I really want to know. I really want you to enlighten me."

Alec took a deep breath and tried to think of the five things he's most proud of in his life. His mind was blank. His trick wasn't working. He took another gulp of wine and nodded his head for his father to continue.

"Someone thinks they saw her in New Jersey. They're not completely sure it was her. But they wanted to call anyway."

"Where in New Jersey?"

"Across the river in Jersey City."

"That makes no sense. Oh, wait a minute. Maybe she's looking for Kathy."

"We thought of that. Kathy and Robin are going there first thing tomorrow."

"Why wait?"

"Daylight."

"Did the person leave a name or any other contact info?"

"No. No, she didn't."

"Dammit, Dad. Why didn't you get a name and number?"

"What difference would it have made?"

"I don't know. None of this makes any sense. Why wouldn't Brenda just call me? Why won't she just fucking call me?" Alec felt like an idiot. He knew why she won't call him. But Henry. That was the part that didn't make sense.

"I don't know. Look, if Brenda was down there when it happened, anywhere near there, well, she was traumatized," his father offered.

"I'm not so sure. I'm not so sure of anything. Does Henry know?"

"No. I don't think it would be a good idea to give him hope. I mean, hope is a good thing, but I want to see what we can uncover tomorrow." He refilled both glasses. "So, it's okay then? That I'm here?"

Alec nodded, took his wine glass, and left his father alone at the table.

Hope - Kathy

FRIDAY - A DAY KATHY ASSOCIATED with anger and hatred. Her father had died on a Friday. And Friday was pizza night
during her childhood. Pops always picked up the pizza from Red
Moon on his way home from work. Brenda was barely out of di-
apers and too young to remember pizza night as anything other
than thrilling. It was Kathy who bared the brunt of her father's
sins. It was Kathy who tried, in her own pre-teen way, to console
their mother. Yes, Mother put on a face for the girls and pretended that she couldn't smell the cigarette smoke or booze. Yes,
Mother pretended that Pops had indeed been at work all day and
didn't skip out early to squander a portion of his paycheck and
murder the productive hours of the afternoon at the corner bar.
And when he was so plastered that he couldn't make it home
without dropping the pizza box, Mother would scrape the cheese
off the inside of the box's lid, redistribute it over the pizza and
heat it up under the broiler for a few minutes. Yum. Delicious.
Thank you, dear, her mother would say, picking at her slice,

making herself a gin and tonic with no gin, and retreating with her daughters to the living room. Then Mother usually read to Brenda, or colored with her. Kathy sometimes colored with Brenda too. It drove Kathy crazy though, to watch Brenda use colors that didn't seem right for whatever inane picture she was coloring. A purple duck, for example. Or a green man. Makes sense now, of course, given the breadth of Brenda's artistic expressions.

Friday. A day that, over the many years of her life thus far, gradually became less of something to dread and more of something to look forward to. She supposed that working full time would certainly do that to a person. *Everybody's working for the weekend.* Kathy was no different. Except that she loved her work and never particularly looked forward to Friday, because there would be no work the next day. Over the years she began looking forward to Friday because everyone else looked forward to Friday and, at least as a young woman, her friends were always in a better mood Friday than any other day of the work week. Now in her mid-forties, Kathy couldn't remember why she ever hated Friday.

Friday. Today, this very Friday had the potential for altering the day off its current axis. There were so many moving pieces to today. So many ways the day could go. So much potential for joy or sorrow. Robin said she would stop by this morning to help her look for Brenda. Today. Friday. They would either find her or they wouldn't.

Today would be telling too. The first step into a potential relationship with Robin. The thought exhilarated her. And her exhilaration would propel her into the depths and corners of Jersey City that she had always been too buried in her work to care about exploring. The tip about Brenda was promising. Sort of. Manny's poster sported a much better, much more recent head-shot than the poster Henry made. There wasn't much chance of anyone recognizing Brenda in the beach picture that Henry had picked out.

Kathy looked at her watch. Robin would be arriving any minute. She fluffed the throw pillows on her living room couch and took a step back to examine her efforts. She wondered suddenly if she had too many pillows. Yeah, she did. She started to gather several up when the doorbell rang. Damn. She quickly put them back in place and went to meet her fate.

* * *

The first few minutes were awkward. They went through the usual round of greetings and the obligatory hug. Kathy would have been happy for the hug to linger a bit longer but given the circumstance of this visit and the mission at hand, well, all that other stuff could wait. Never mind that they had planned to go out tonight. They had planned it before. You know, before the world changed. Everything was different now, and she was afraid to mention their pre-planned date.

Robin set a box of Dunkin' Donuts down on the table. Kathy was grateful for the diversion and put on a pot of coffee.

"I'm actually a tea drinker." Robin looked around the kitchen as if searching for a teapot, teabags, or even a microwave.

"Strike one against me, I guess. Never touch the stuff." Kathy shrugged. "I used to keep a few teabags handy for Brenda, but she goes both ways, you know, coffee or tea. Me, I'm strictly coffee."

Robin chuckled. "It's okay. I can go both ways too."

"Really?" Kathy figured Robin didn't mean coffee versus tea and wondered if it was apparent that she liked things one way, and not the other.

"Yeah. But, at least for now, I've kind of sworn off men. Bad deal the last time. Like what happened with your sister, only my guy left me. I'm guessing if the attacks hadn't happened, your brother-in-law might have done the same thing."

Kathy made the coffee without responding. She was disappointed. At her age and the ages of the women she dated, well, she was under no illusions that people didn't come with baggage. She just wished that Robin was one way or the other and that she hadn't just come out of a relationship. Her earlier buoyancy sunk under the weight of this news as well as the weight of the reality that faced them today. For the first time, she felt raw fear at what she might find out.

"I have both sets of posters here." Kathy pushed them out of the way to make room at her small kitchen table to sit, have coffee and donuts, and map out their game plan.

"You have any sugar?" Robin found the mugs and brought them over. "It's the only way I'll tolerate coffee. Massive amounts of sugar."

"Now that I can do." Kathy smiled. She made up a tray with a small bowl of sugar, a carton of table cream, and two spoons.

"This is great coffee." Robin held her mug with two hands as if to warm them after being outside in the snow. Only it wasn't cold out, not even close. It was a breathtakingly clear, warmish mid-September day, one more in a string of days that were incongruent with the sadness that seemed to envelope the world.

"You don't have to say that." Kathy teased. "Really, it's okay if you don't like coffee."

"I never said I didn't like it. I simply said I'm a tea drinker."

Okay, so this was how it was going to be. Kathy kept that in the back of her mind as the front of her mind began formulating a plan.

"Here's what I think we should do. I say we go around to every bar, restaurant, hospital, convenience store, coffee shop within a five-mile radius of here. We give the posters to people. I'm not a big fan of hanging them, although hanging them has its merits. I just think that if my sister is here, well, I want people to be forced to look at the pictures with us standing there. And I think we should hand each person a set of the two posters."

"Yep, I was thinking the same thing." Robin still had her hands wrapped around her mug. "After a while, people will become blind to the ones plastered all over the city." She took a slow sip then set it down. "Yeah. Handing them to folks is a great idea. Brilliant, actually."

They sat quietly, each taking in the posters and their own thoughts. They filled their mouths with donuts and coffee to avoid having to fill the space with words.

"He's adorable, by the way." Robin poked a hole in the silence. "Your nephew."

"Yeah. I love that kid."

"If this person really did see your sister, and if your sister is here in Jersey, well, why? I mean, why not just come home?" Robin emphasized the *why* and searched Kathy's face.

"I already told you. It's complicated."

"I get that her husband's an ass. And yeah, that was my first impression of him yesterday - that he's an ass. An arrogant ass." She looked at the ceiling as if contemplating what she would say next. "But the kid. Her son. Her flesh. Her blood. If she's hiding, why would she hide? Why would she hide from her son? Who does that kind of thing?"

Kathy clenched her teeth and silently counted to ten. Anger and frustration today would be counterproductive. She'd get to that later. After hearing Robin ask these things, Kathy wasn't sure she was interested in seeing her again after today. She knew she was being unfair - Robin's questions were reasonable questions that anyone might ask. But Kathy felt like she had to be Brenda's protector, advocate, and defender of her choices. And because of this she was tempted to end things with Robin right then and there. Being with Robin suddenly felt like a betrayal to Lydia, as crazy as that sounded. She missed Lydia terribly, even after all this time. Yeah, she wanted Robin out of her apartment, out of her life, but really wanted - really needed - someone to help her look for Brenda.

"She was just diagnosed with cancer too, on top of everything else. Oh, and she had a miscarriage two weeks ago. She's pretty messed up in the head at the moment, or did I forget to mention that the other day?"

"I know, I know. You mentioned it." Robin shook her head. "But the kid! Seriously."

"His name is Henry." Kathy was two seconds away from asking her to leave. Robin's reaction to Brenda was so typical of someone who doesn't have kids or hasn't spent a lot of time around them. Judging a mother for letting her own problems overshadow and dull her instincts to nurture her child. Kathy figured it happened more often than anyone was willing to admit. "Look, I know that from the outside looking in, my sister seems like a selfish bitch."

Kathy held her breath. She didn't want to cry in front of Robin, especially now. Without the possibility of a relationship with her, and Kathy was certain she did not want to pursue Robin beyond today, there was little point opening up and being vulnerable. No point.

"She's not selfish," Kathy continued. "And she's not a bitch. She's a good person, a good mother. If she is deliberately staying away, she has her reasons. I'm not about to judge her for it." She glared at Robin then got up to put her empty coffee mug in the sink.

"I'm sorry." Robin followed Kathy to the sink. "I get preachy sometimes. I guess that's not something I wanted to show you so soon." She gave Kathy a quick hug and went back to the table for the tray.

"Thanks." Kathy sighed and went about loading the dishwasher.

***

They laid out a street map of Jersey City and made a circle around Kathy's apartment that stretched a mile all the way across. They initially thought to do a five-mile radius but in the end, decided to start small. They would each cover opposite sides of the pie and meet for lunch at noon, after which they would set out again if they weren't fruitful. But when noon came, Kathy didn't feel like she'd covered enough ground or talked to enough people. She called Robin's cell and asked if they could meet at two instead. They'd agreed earlier to meet at a place Robin knew: an Irish pub called Shorty O'Rourke's.

Kathy walked into the pub and was struck by how dark it was in contrast to the blindingly bright day. She wished they'd picked a light and airy cafe, something with a salty, beachy, feel. The dart boards, booths, pub tables, and bar - all a dark stained knotty pine - did not create the right tableau for generating the hope and positive vibes Kathy needed to get through this day. She immediately crossed it off her list as a place she'd take her next date, which would not be with Robin. The place was at least clean.

"Go ahead and sit anywhere you want." A tall man with limp walked toward her while taking in the entire place with his arm. "As you can see, we're not busy. Things haven't been the same the last few days if you know what I mean." He looked serious. "You never know though. We were mobbed Tuesday night. It's tapered off quite a bit since then."

She looked around the empty pub. She saw a booth in the corner near the back and pointed to it. "Can we sit there? I'm expecting someone." The man grabbed two menus and followed her to the booth. "Are you the owner?"

"Now that's relative." He laughed. "I'm here so often that it seems like I own the place. But no, my good friend is the owner. I help him whenever I can, which is pretty much all the time. Can I get you a drink, or do you want to wait for your friend?"

"If you have Fat Tire, I'll take one."

"Sure thing." He started to walk away.

"Wait." She was surprised by the apprehension she felt. All morning she'd been handing her sister's face to everyone and anyone. She'd stopped at the library and made a hundred more copies of both versions. "Never mind."

"What is it?" The man tilted his head toward the opposite bench. "May I?" He didn't wait for a response before sliding in. "I'm John, by the way."

"Kathy." She heard the door open and saw Robin. She pointed. "And that's Robin." She worried now that Robin would launch into a diatribe about their mission and hoped that she wouldn't. This guy seemed different. He seemed real in a way that the others all morning weren't. The people they'd handed posters to were nameless, faceless people. Bodies. The masses to spread the word. Nothing more, nothing less. The more people who saw Brenda's face, the better the chances of finding her. Much to Kathy's relief, John got up.

"Can I get you something to drink?" He handed Robin a menu.

"I'll have what's she's having." And after he left: "Did you ask him if he's seen your sister?"

"Not yet. Please. I want to take my time with this one. I'm not even sure why. Just following my gut."

"Whatever."

John brought the beer to the table and left to take care of group of soccer players who had just come in. Kathy was relieved that he didn't sit back down.

"Thanks for doing this." Kathy was sincere, despite her decision to not take the relationship further. Robin waved her hand as if brushing off Kathy's gratitude. "No, I mean it. Thank you. You barely know me. You took a day off work. You schlepped all over Jersey City on a warm day." Robin shrugged, and Kathy laughed. "Seriously. Look at you. You're a sweaty mess." Robin laughed now too. Kathy suddenly felt those damned tears welling up again. Damn tears. She was moved to tears by Robin's gesture. Go figure. "Anyway, thanks."

"Hey, glad I could help."

"I'm guessing you weren't fruitful today?"

"Depends on your definition of fruitful." Kathy pointed to her envelope, which was thinner than it had been that morning. "I handed out a bunch, so in that sense, I was fruitful. But not a single person said they'd seen her."

"It sounds like you're looking for someone. Someone missing from, you know, Tuesday?" John was standing at the table with Robin's beer. "I'm so sorry. Maybe I could help." He sat down at the table next to Kathy and studied the two posters. He picked up the one with Brenda's head shot - the professional looking one that Manny's wife had made. He considered it for what seemed like a long time. He put that one down and picked up the other one and studied it even more intently. He finally put it down and ran his finger over Henry's words. He looked ashen, and it unsettled her a little.

"Have you seen her?" Kathy's voice was bordering hysterical. "I'm sorry. Have you seen my sister?"

He drew a deep breath and exhaled slowly. "Your sister. She looks very much like someone I know."

"Could it be her?" Robin was a bit gentler with her tone than Kathy had been.

"Tell me about her." John's voice seemed far away. "She seems like someone everyone loves."

"Yes, yes. Everyone loves Brenda. But I don't care about that right now. I just want to find her. Is this the person you know? Is her name Brenda Arnstein?" Kathy was desperate.

"My friend's name is Annie."

Kathy took a deep breath. "My sister, Brenda, she, well, she's beautiful. She's an artist. Married to a jerk. Has a wonderful ten-year-old son named Henry."

"Henry made these." Robin held up Henry's poster. John nodded. "About the jerk Brenda's married to. You see, that's part of the problem. We think she was in the process of clearing her head when the attacks occurred. She'd been at the World Trade Center." She turned to Kathy. "What was she doing? I forget."

"Some sort of artwork. Brenda is an artist." She looked directly at John. "Her husband was cheating on her. Or was about to. Or was thinking about it. The attacks shook him up. The fact that Brenda was at the Trade Center and hasn't come home yet is really shaking him up. It's shaking us all up, actually."

"But don't you think if she were alive she'd want her son to know she's okay?" John picked up the Henry poster again, then put it back down. "Wouldn't she have wanted to go home to her son? Deal with the jerk husband later?"

"Oh God, not you too." Kathy chugged the last of her beer and set the glass down hard. "I am getting so sick and tired of everyone assuming she'd want to run home to her son. She loves her son, okay. Loves him more than life." She looked at Robin, then back at John. "I think that's it. She loves him more than life. I think she'd rather have him believe she died a 'hero' in a terrorist attack than have him watch her die a slow, painful death-by-cancer. Yeah. She has cancer. Bad cancer. Aggressive cancer. She was recently diagnosed."

"I'm so sorry." John closed his eyes and when he opened them he put a finger on Henry's poster and slid it toward his side of the table. Then he put his hand over Kathy's hand. She didn't pull away. She just sat quietly crying. "Can I have a few of these?" Kathy nodded. "I'll hang them up in here, and I'll ask around. I'll call you personally if I hear anything. Are these your numbers?"

"No, here." Kathy scribbled her home and cell numbers on a napkin and handed it to John.

"Thanks. I'm really sorry." He said. "I hope you're right about her being alive and just hiding until she sorts things out." He got up and walked toward the bar, then, as if he'd forgotten something, turned around and went back to Kathy and Robin's table.

"Why are you looking for her here? Why Jersey City? Why would she come here?"

"I live here. She lives in Brooklyn. Someone saw one of these things in midtown and called her father-in-law. That's his number there. The person thought she saw Brenda here. I mean, not here, at this bar, but somewhere in the area. I guess I'm a little bit surprised that Brenda didn't come to my apartment. I live not too far from here. She knows she could have come, and I would have respected her wishes if she wanted to hide. Why didn't she just come to me?"

"I'll do what I can. And I will call you." John squeezed Kathy's shoulder, and told her that the drinks were on him.

Robin slipped out of the booth and slipped back in on Kathy's side, putting her arm around her and pulling her close.

Loafers - Alec

THE SHOE DREAM AGAIN. Alec found himself sitting up in bed, sweating and shaking. A pair of brown shoes in front of a closed, white door. The exact same shoes his grandfather Joe always wore. Alec will never forget those shoes. Joe called them penny loafers, although they didn't have the iconic slot to store pennies. The shoes in Alec's dream sat neatly in front of a door that was one of hundreds of similar entries in a long, endless hall. The hall was also white. Bright, nauseating white. The person belonging to the shoes was absent from the scene. Alec was confident - during the dream and now, reliving it - that the shoes were his grandfather's shoes and that his grandfather was behind the door. The shoes were clean and shiny as if they had never been worn. He tried to yell for Joe, but his mouth produced no sound. He banged on the door, but no one answered. Yet he knew Joe was behind the door. Could feel it in his very core.

The shaking began to subside. Alec wiped the sweat off his forehead with the bedsheet. He felt strangely connected to his grandfather, who had been dead for a long time. Joe had been the only one who tried - albeit weakly - to reassure Alec that his brother's accident was not his fault. He wondered now if two souls could ever be connected and in communication, separate and apart from the conscious, physical bodies that house them. In Alec's dream, Joe seemed to be trying to tell him something through his shoes, yet was afraid and hid behind the closed door. At least this is the explanation he might have given if one of his patients had come to him puzzling over this dream.

Alec needed a distraction. Henry. He would fix breakfast for Henry. Maybe waffles. Yes. Waffle sandwiches. Henry loved those. Squirt syrup in every hole. Place a fried egg on top of the waffle and bacon slices on top of the egg. Pour lots of syrup on the bacon. And finally, top the whole thing with another waffle. Alec looked at the clock and was shocked that it was nearly ten. He threw on his robe and bolted for the kitchen, certain that by now Henry would have fixed himself a bowl of cereal. Or maybe Manny made something for him. He smelled the coffee, so he knew Manny had to be around.

"Oh. Hi Dad." Alec was glad to see his father sitting at the table with the newspaper and a cup of coffee. It was odd to feel happy to see the great Dr. Manny Arnstein.

"I hope you don't mind, but I sent Henry to school." He spoke without looking up from the newspaper.

"I wanted to keep him home. I even told him yesterday that we'd hang more posters today."

"I know. But he insisted. Who am I to argue with a kid who wants to go to school? It will be good for him to get out of the house, away from that damned television. I was ready to unplug it last night. Anyway, he took some posters with him. He said he wanted to give them to his teacher and some of his friends to give to their parents."

Alec sighed. He poured himself a cup of coffee and sat down at the table across from his father. "I dreamed about Joe last night." He thought about this for a second then clarified. "It was more like I felt his presence. I didn't see him in the dream. I saw his shoes."

"The loafers?"

"Yep, the loafers." He looked down at his own bare feet. "Why did we call him Joe?" He looked up at his father. "Why not Zayde? We called your mother, Bubbe. So why not call him Zayde? Or even Grandpa."

Manny sat quietly, looking at Alec as if looking at someone he had just met. Alec suspected this was going to be one of those awkward conversations. And the level of discomfort was going to be caused by Manny. Alec calculated the possible scenarios: Manny would change the subject; Manny would pile on a load of crap; Manny would entertain him with an elaborate tap dance. He readied himself for the unknown.

"He wanted to be called Joe. He wasn't Jewish."

This is not what Alec expected to hear. "But what about our name. It's as Jewish as they come."

"He comes from a line of Jews. But his grandfather - my great-grandfather - married a Catholic girl. The family disowned him. Joe was raised Catholic."

"But he converted right? Joe, I mean. He personified Jewishness."

"He acted Jewish for Bubbe. He never converted."

"Well, this is news."

"I'm sorry I never told you. I just didn't think it was important. And you never asked."

"You see, this is what stuns me. Why would I have to ask? How did this never, ever come up in conversation?"

Manny lifted his hands and slammed his palms down on the table. "When was the last time that we had a conversation? A real conversation?" He stood up, red-faced and cartoon-like. He started to step back from the table then sat down again. "Tell me?"

"When you blamed me for what happened to Seth." He shook his head. "And then you broke my heart by lying to me about visiting Mom for Hanukkah. Do you even remember that?" He felt his throat tighten and willed his eyes to remain dry. "Dammit, Dad."

"You have no idea what it's like to lose a child. No idea. It changed all of us. It destroyed your mother. It destroyed Bubbe and especially Joe. Because he felt like he should have been watching you and Seth. He hid it well, but Joe never recovered. Never."

"But he was the only one in the family who never made me feel like it was my fault. He never acted like he didn't love me anymore." Alec didn't try to stop the sobs. He let them come. Wave after wave after wave of them. If Manny was saying anything, Alec couldn't hear it. He finally caught his breath. "I never recovered from Seth either. I'm a mess. My life is a mess. I've been a lousy husband. I've been a lousy father. I almost cheated on Brenda last week, and she knew it. Now she's either dead, or she's soon to be dead. She has cancer. She just found out last week, apparently. I yelled at her. I didn't believe her." The sobs again. Fucking sobs.

"Alec." Manny stopped. He scooted his chair closer to Alec's and put his arm around him. Instead of recoiling, Alec sat and continued sobbing, feeling comforted for the first time in a very long time.

"About the dream," Manny continued. "Joe's loafers. I think Joe was trying to tell you that he's gone, Seth's gone, your mother is essentially gone, but the shoes remain. The memories remain. Those could have been Seth's shoes. Nobody blames you, Alec. Not then, not now. I think you've been blaming yourself, and stuffing that blame away so that you could function in the world. You were five years old. You were just a baby yourself."

"I don't know where to start." Alec pulled away and looked at his father, seeing him, possibly for the first time as a person and as a very skilled doctor.

"Start with me. I'll call Susan and tell her I'm staying a while. If that's okay with you."

"I could sure use the help around here."

"I'll buy you a pair of loafers. We have a lot more posters to hang. We'll find her. I want to promise you that we'll find her, but I know you'll see right through me."

"You're right about that." Alec chuckled. "I don't think loafers are quite my style. Do they even sell them anymore?"

"Damn straight they do."

Guilt - John

WHEN SHORTY SHOWED UP at four-thirty to prep the pub for dinner, John didn't explain why he needed to leave, and why it needed to be right then. Shorty just shrugged, not sure what kind of crowd (or lack thereof) to expect. It was likely to be empty. But this being the first Friday after, well, who knows. Maybe people would feel ready to let loose. Not John. Nope. He needed to be alone, to reflect, and to understand what happened a few hours ago. He needed to get to the bottom of why his heart felt like it was ripped out of his chest, thrown on the ground, and stomped on. This wasn't fair, and he knew it. He barely knew her. In fact, he knew her even less than barely. His reaction stunned him. His emotions jumped out of the bushes like a lion pouncing on its prey.

Shorty knew him well. Too well. Well enough to know not to ask. Well enough to say yeah, go ahead, do what you must do, or something like that. Earlier this afternoon, John waited until the two women left before taking all the fliers and folding them in quarters then sticking the entire wad in his pocket. He felt only a little bit guilty about this. His guilt was based solely on the fact that he gave his word that he'd hang some and distribute the others. John liked to think of himself as a man of his word. Yeah right. He hadn't kept his word to love, honor, and cherish his wife. He'd let the aftermath of her rape and his resultant anger color his view of everything. It all threatened to suffocate him at times, particularly at night.

It wasn't that long ago, at least it seemed like it wasn't that long ago, when John used to treasure the end of the day. These days, the end of the day is when the guilt-elf on his shoulder reminds him of everything he's ever done wrong in his life. It's been three years since his divorce, and he was mostly okay. He had his moments, and right here, right now is was of them. The guilt-elf was taunting him in a particularly lousy way tonight. Guilt over his past, guilt about not being straight with Kathy - Annie's sister. Or was it Brenda's sister? He didn't care. She was Annie to him, and he wanted to hold her in his heart as his alone for just a little while longer. So, he could hardly call himself a man of his word.

This knowledge of his own dark side made it easy for him to flick the guilt-elf off his shoulder and abscond with the fliers. He'd poured over Annie's painting after her sister left. When he was talking to her, or rather, when she was talking to him, all he could focus on was the woman whose face adorned the fliers. He considered showing her Annie's painting. Her sister would surely recognize the style, wouldn't she? That genuine possibility - that Annie's sister would realize 'Brenda' in the brush strokes -

sealed it for John. He bound and gagged the guilt-elf and decided, quite hastily, not to show, distribute, or hang posters. As soon as Annie's sister and her friend left he ran behind the bar and moved the painting out of sight. He'd stood and looked at it for a long time and imaged what Annie might have been thinking when she painted it. The desperate look on her sister's face, well, this made him feel guilty too. Quite guilty. Maybe he'd go to confession tomorrow. Maybe. Or not. Probably not. Maybe what he really should do is shoot the damned guilt-elf.

Unglued - John

JOHN WANTED TO SEE ANNIE. He felt somewhat of an obligation to talk to her and let her know that her loved ones were searching madly for her. He walked toward the boat but found himself still walking an hour later. He somehow ended up on the rooftop deck at The Salty Dog but didn't quite recall how he got there.

The bell tower on the church down the street chimed seven times. It was still light out, but barely. He ordered a scotch, something he seldom does, and looked at the water below. The commercial fishing boats were long tucked in for the evening, and yet the drawbridge went up and down with regularity. A sailboat here, a power boat there. People out enjoying what's left of their lives after what happened on Tuesday. He swigged his scotch, dropped a ten-dollar bill on the table, and jogged all the way back to Liberty Landing, down the C Dock, and practically leaped aboard *Three-Ring Circus*.

"Annie!" All he wanted to do was hug her. No words. He just wanted to hold her in his arms. He wanted to bury his head in the crook of her neck and inhale her. He wanted to remember her. With all his senses. "Annie." He expected to see her sitting in the cockpit, but it was eerie and quiet. "Annie?" He knocked on the companionway hatch and waited. "Annie, are you down there?" Nothing.

It seemed strange that the companionway hatch was closed. Annie never closed it before, plus, it was warm and breezy tonight - the airflow would have been pleasant. And that's when John noticed the envelope on the bench, weighted down with three oyster shells. He didn't have to open it to know what was inside. He could feel the outline of the companionway hatch key. He sat down and stared at it. So, she's gone. Just like that. Without saying goodbye. The ache in his chest wasn't justified. She had a life, a family, a child. And she needed medical care. He willed his heart to stop breaking. He missed her terribly already, and he didn't even really know her. He was fearful that her hologram would fade in and out of focus, causing him to question his ability to recognize her at a distance or in a crowd. What did he expect? That she would stay on his boat forever? That she would fall in love with him? The guilt-elf's cousin, the illogical-elf took up residence on his other shoulder. Yeah, he's illogical, and he knows it. He flicked the illogical-elf into the water. So, he misses her. So, the wind shifted unexpectedly. So, she's tacking back to her life. *Ready About? Helms alee.* He pulled the folded-up fliers out of his pocket and looked at the one that showed just her face.

"Annie," he held the picture close to his mouth and whispered to it. "Annie, in your eyes I see everything my heart wants to say."

He ripped open the envelope and pulled out the key. It was wrapped in a piece of paper - a flier. The missing person flier that her son had made. She'd scribbled something on the back. He opened the companionway hatch, climbed down the short ladder, and turned on the cabin lights. He looked around, not really expecting to find her down there, but wanting to convince himself that was really gone. He sat down at the navigation table and read:

John,
I should have told you. I'm sorry. I'm a bit unglued right now and need to go home. Thank you for everything. I won't forget you.
Annie (Brenda)
P.S. Keep the moth painting - it's yours.

He sat for a long time. He needed another scotch. He had a bottle tucked away in a cabinet above the instrument panel. He fumbled around for it. When he found it, he took a long, slow swig.

"You're not the only one unglued right now." He said to the empty cabin. He ran his fingers over her scribble and turned the paper over to look at her.

Morticia - Brenda

FOUR HOUSES TO THE LEFT, then turn the corner (also a left). You'd come upon two identical houses - the only difference being that one had a purple door and the other had a standard white door like most of the homes in the neighborhood where Brenda grew up. The house on the left, the one with the purple door had a chain-link fence around the entire quarter-acre property line, like a moat. A large, gangly dog with a forbidding countenance lived within the confines of that fence. Anyone who dared come near that fence got growled and barked at. Except for the nine kids who lived in that house. Two of the boys were in Kathy's class, and the youngest girl was in Brenda's. These kids always had the unkempt look of not being well cared for.

Brenda remembered her mother having had an ache in her heart for those kids. The father was a bald, angry looking man with a huge belly. Never said much. Just grunted and yelled a lot. The mother had long black hair and looked a lot like the *Addam's Family* matriarch, Morticia.

One day without warning, the talk on their street was that Morticia had run away. The house was boarded up, and the dog, the kids, and the big-bellied father were gone. Brenda's mother made some calls and tried to take some of the kids in but was told the younger ones were sent to relatives. The older ones would stay with friends. And the dad, well, no one ever knew what happened with the dad. The concept of a mother "running away" puzzled Brenda back then. How did a mother run away? Kids ran away from home. Mothers didn't. Or did they?

Brenda hadn't thought about that family in years. Not until now, sitting on the front stoop of Kathy's apartment building. She didn't know where Kathy was, exactly, but she suspected that she was out looking for her. The fliers were proof of that. Some woman saw her wandering around the marina this morning and approached her. Brenda gasped when she saw the fliers. She'd taken a walk to clear her head and think about her time with John. The conversations they had. How gentle he was with her. The look in his eyes.

She felt like someone dumped a bucket of ice on her head. She couldn't face John. Not now. He was certain to have seen one of the fliers by now. She felt like a fugitive. What would she tell him? How would she even begin to explain why she'd been hiding from her family.

Your decisions had a funny way of writing the story of your past. Those children in her old neighborhood were known as *the poor children whose mother ran away*. What might the story have been had Morticia stuck around? Brenda couldn't do that to

Henry. No matter how she justified it, the outcome would be the same: she would forever be known as the mother who ran away.

The real unknown was her relationship with Alec. She didn't know what awaited her or how angry he would be. She felt her body tense just thinking about his reaction. The fact that she'd put him - all of them - through this would overshadow all of Alec's transgressions - the big and the small. She would be the bad guy, the one juggling flaming bowling pins, the one tiptoeing on broken glass, the one solely responsible for repairing their marriage. But even with all of that, she couldn't, wouldn't be like the mother of those children from her childhood. She wouldn't be the one who ran away.

She felt cold and pulled the balled-up wool sweater out of her bag. John's sweater. She hoped he wouldn't miss it because she wanted to keep it. She had known him for such a short time. A breath, really. Yet in that tiny fragment of time she knew that he was a man she could trust. Easily. He was comfortable and familiar, and it seemed like they'd known each other longer than a few days. She figured these things happen in chaotic times: disparate people being thrown together who would have otherwise never met. Could this be part of a larger plan? She didn't know. All she knew is that she deeply regretted that she hadn't told him her whole story - the truth. That she'd pretended to be someone else. She regretted it so very, very deeply. She felt like she made a mockery of his kindness. She could think of nothing else to do but leave him her hastily written note and her painting. She had nothing else to give, except maybe her heart. If only.

She opened her phone to call Alec and was reminded of the call she'd received - the one from her oncologist. Her diagnosis was hard for her to believe. She didn't feel sick. In fact, in the weeks leading up to all this, she'd never felt better. Even with all the emotional upheaval with Alec. Even throughout her very short pregnancy and losing her baby, her Annie, she felt healthy and robust. Even now.

Even now, when she saw Kathy walking up the sidewalk. Even now she felt strong. Kathy's form came into the foreground and suddenly all the "even nows" crumbled. She felt weak and small. So small. Tiny. She could tell Kathy had spotted her because her walk became urgent. The urgent walk turned into a run. And within a second the sick, tiny, exhausted, spent, "even now" girl was wrapped in her sister's arms, and nothing - not even a silly little thing like terminal cancer - could harm her.

Promises - Brenda

IT WAS DECIDED THAT HENRY would not be told right away that his mother had been found. It was decided. These were the words Alec used toward the end of their emotional phone call yesterday. Henry had been at school and Alec, with the help of his father, made this decision with zero input from her. The decision infuriated her, although she understood why they made it - sort of.

All she wanted to do now was wrap her son in her arms and tell him how much she loved him and how sorry she was that she'd worried him. She wanted to explain things to him that were beyond his years to understand. She knew this. And apparently, so did Alec, because Alec invented an entire cockamamie story to tell him. When he told her what he'd planned to say to Henry, the whole thing sounded so ridiculous that even a ten-year-old would have a hard time believing it. She looked at her watch. By now the great Dr. Manny would have sat Henry down at the kitchen table. She pictured the scene: Henry at the head of the table with his back to the window and Alec's father flanking him on the left. The story would go something like this: *Yes, your mother was in the north tower. But good news! She left before anything happened. She had a doctor appointment in Jersey. Do you know what Breast Cancer is, son?* Brenda absolutely hated when Alec's dad called Henry "son."

She felt hostility wrapping around her body like a boa. Alec's right hand was resting on her knee as he drove them toward Brooklyn. If not for Henry, her home was not a home she wanted to go back to. This startled her. There's no place like home, right? She repeated this mantra to herself and even visualized her feet adorned with sparkly ruby slippers. *There's no place like home.* And just for fun, she let a tiny dog leap into her arms. *There's no place like home.* Click, click, click. *There's no place like home.* Maybe if she repeated this to herself and pretended to really mean it, well maybe, just maybe it would work. *There's no place like home. There's no place like home. There's no place like home.*

"How is it that I went to a doctor appointment and didn't call or anything? Why couldn't I get home?" She stretched her legs for the sole purpose of getting Alec's hand off her knee. "You know he'll ask."

"I don't know Brenda. You tell me. You didn't come home. You're the one with all the answers." She expected tone and vitriol from him but instead got something that was far away and wistful. A quick glance at his profile as he kept his focus straight ahead revealed a spot of moistness under his right eye. Like a thin puddle on the sidewalk that was quickly drying in the hot sun after a late afternoon thunderstorm. She suddenly felt guilty and filled with shame.

They rode in silence for what seemed like an eternity. She felt physically ill in the deepest part of her heart like she was being torn away from something she never even knew she needed. She found herself missing John so much that she wanted to take the steering wheel from Alec, push his foot out of the way and slam on the breaks, open the door so he would roll out, then turn the car around and drive as fast as humanly possible, back, all the way back to a place where she could just forget the world for a little while longer.

There's no place like home. Click, click, click. *There's no place like home.* Maybe if she repeated this to herself and pretended to really mean it, well maybe, just maybe it would work. *There's no place like home. There's no place like home. There's no place like home.* The only problem was that aside from being with her son, she didn't want to go home.

***

Brenda had been away from home for four days. When she walked through the door, it was the typical yellow-ribbon, teary, happy reunion that you sometimes see on the news. Soldiers coming home from war. Patients waking up from comas just seconds before the doctor pulls the plug. Survivors being lifted from the wreckage of Name Your Disaster after three days without food or water or the medications needed to keep them alive. People who went missing on the day of the attacks appearing out of the mist the next day. Or the day after that. Or four days later.

Rejoicing. Answered prayers. Hugs. Kisses. Promises to do better. Promises to be better. Oh yes, such promises to do better.

Alec, on his knees, promising to be a better husband. Without admitting to any wrongdoing with Jenn, he promised he would take steps to cut off any and all communication with her. He promised to put in his notice, leave the practice, and go out on his own. He explained he was already on the path to starting his own private practice and showed her all the lists and research he did when he wasn't frantically searching for her. He promised to respect her in whatever choices she made, about anything and everything. He promised to love her and to be at her side through her cancer treatments. And, if all went well with that, he vowed to try and give her another baby. Not at all what she'd expected from Alec. No blaming, no beating her up for putting him through hell. No need to juggle flaming bowling pins or tiptoe on broken glass. At least not yet.

And then there was Kathy. Her precious sister. Kathy didn't promise anything. Kathy just held her. Long and tight. Kathy would love her, unconditionally, forever.

Henry didn't promise anything either. He seemed nonplused - as if she'd been on a four-day getaway - one painstakingly long weekend - rather than presumed dead. Manny had pulled her aside and reassured her that this was normal - that the past few days had been profoundly frightening for Henry. At his age he wouldn't process her return in the same way that an older person might. Now that she was home Henry's mind would start to relax - his body and soul could return to the normalcy of being a kid. At least until she started her cancer treatments, which would set

Henry back a few steps. He will need therapy. *Sooner rather than later*, Manny said, stressing the sooner.

Part 3 - After

Turkey Day - Brenda

A WEEK OR SO AFTER BRENDA returned home, Alec suggested they drive to his dad's house in Connecticut for Thanksgiving. Apparently, Alec and Manny had made peace and were in the process of rebuilding their fragile relationship.

On Thanksgiving morning, they were in the car, making their way up the Hutchinson River Parkway. Alec's head bobbed in time with the song on the radio. Brenda had just finished eating a cinnamon raisin bagel and felt like a piece of the raisin was jammed between her central and lateral incisors. She lifted her chin to look into the rearview mirror. Her eyes met Henry's. It was a flash really. The time it takes for a firefly to turn on and off its light. She knew more about fireflies than she needed to because as a kid she had researched them for a science fair project. Like the fact that fireflies are neither flies nor bugs, but are coleopteran, which means they have hardened forewings that cover their body. They are, essentially, beetles.

And so, like the stupid, useless facts about fireflies, the look in Henry's eyes as she met them in the rearview mirror etched itself in her brain. A snapshot in time. A glimpse into Henry's heart that she stumbled upon by accident. A glimpse that was raw, innocent, and troubling. She couldn't quite define what she saw. But it pierced her soul, and she wondered if they - mother and son - would ever recover. In the rearview mirror, in the time it takes a firefly to cycle its light on and off one time, she saw something in Henry's eyes. His eyes were studying her as if seeing her for the first time. Like he suddenly realized a stranger was in the car, sitting next to his father, someone alien who maybe looked a little like his mother but wasn't entirely his mother. In that tiny flash of time she saw emptiness in her son's eyes. Perhaps Manny had been right and Henry needed to talk to a therapist. She and Alec had decided on a watch and wait approach. She made a mental note to talk to Alec about it after the holidays.

She leaned her head against the headrest and closed her eyes. Since returning home, she'd made a real effort to tuck her four days on John's boat away. But now, with the radio on and zero conversation in the car, she couldn't keep the memories from taunting her. She tried to remember John's eyes, which had a gentle, fanciful, introspective intensity about them. At first glance, there wasn't anything spectacular about John's eyes. They were quite an ordinary color brown and the whites around them were a little bit weathered, as if he'd spent too much time in the sun without proper eyewear or too much time in the dust and grime of having been a cop. His lids were the kind of lids that, even when open, covered almost the entire surface of his eyes. Because of this and possibly in spite of it, he often looked like he was far away. She thought she saw a glimpse of her future in those intense eyes. A future that, in light of her illness, was fleeting - the horizon of it much, much too close.

She looked in the rearview mirror again. Henry's forehead was pressed against his window. She twisted herself to get a better look at him and reached her arm through the crack between the two front seats. She patted his ankle - the part of him within closest reach - and then wrapped her hand around it. He looked at her briefly then resumed staring out the window.

"What are you studying out there?" She employed the lightest, the most sing-song voice she could muster.

"Just counting cars. Red cars. I'm up to seventeen."

"Now that's a lot of red cars." She smiled, and Henry nodded. "Oh look, there's another one. I guess you're up to eighteen now." She used to count cars with him when he was a toddler. They'd go out for walks, and to keep him entertained they counted cars. Sometimes the color didn't matter. Other times he was very specific in what he wanted to count. Blue ones. Or "lellow" ones. She chuckled at the memory of Henry trying to say yellow. So, he was reverting to something comforting. Counting cars. She knew then that she would need to tread very lightly and give him a lot of hugs in the coming weeks.

She closed her eyes again and considered her health. The way her body felt despite having cancer was no different than it had been during her four days as a runaway. Her oncology team had her on a cocktail of drugs that would purportedly slow the progression of her cancer without the harsh effects of more aggressive treatment. She would die from this cancer. That much was universally certain. But for now, it was being held at bay, if that is even a thing with cancer. She didn't know. All she knew was she needed to be physically and mentally present for at least the time being. She needed the time the cocktail of drugs was providing so she could repair the hairline fractures that her days as a runaway had created in their family dynamics. Fill the fractures with glue and sand them smooth before they became full-blown breaks.

But the thing that kept her up most nights was that she didn't die the day of the attacks. Why? Was there a reason? She would die from her cancer. Why didn't God just take her on that day? Her death would then at least be memorialized in a way that it wouldn't when the cancer took her. She could easily have still been in the north tower when it was hit or when it came crashing down. She'd been on the ninety-second floor! She might have been instantly pulverized. Or trapped and burned to death. Or succumbed to smoke inhalation. If she'd been trapped above the fire would she have chosen to jump to her death, the way many brave souls did? She often found herself thinking about the jumpers. They were heroes in her mind. It was as if they were telling the world that they were going to die their way. In jumping, they were essentially giving the terrorists the finger. They were not going to burn or suffocate for those assholes. They were going to have ten seconds of freedom. They were going to free fall to their deaths in one last act of dignity. In choosing quality-of-life over an aggressive chemo regimen, at least for now, Brenda was choosing to jump rather than burn or suffocate.

"Hey, we're here." Brenda woke to Alec gently nudging her shoulder. She sat straight up startled and confused. Her seatbelt contracted. She'd fallen into a solid sleep, something she often did on long road trips. Only this trip to Connecticut was not that long. Or was it?

"What time is it?"

"Mom, there was a ton of traffic. You slept through most of it though." Henry was out the door then and running up the driveway. Alec's father and stepmother were waiting on the front porch, arm in arm.

* * *

Dinner prep was already underway when the three younger Arnstein's walked through the door. In a pleasant way the smell of turkey overwhelmed Brenda and seemed to permeate the universe.

After coats were taken and bags placed in guest rooms, they all gathered around the big kitchen island and fell into a comfortable banter as Susan gave each of them a small task. Brenda and Henry worked together cutting the ends off fresh green beans. Alec and Manny ignored the potatoes that needed quartering and stood leaning against the island with their scotch.

"Tell me about this new project you're working on, Brenda." Susan pushed Manny and Alec out of the way and started quartering potatoes herself. "Manny said the poster I made for you inspired it."

"Sort of."

"Mom, can I go watch TV?" Henry carried his pile of green bean detritus to the garbage disposal.

"Yes, of course!" Susan answered for Brenda. "There's an *I Love Lucy* marathon on!" Henry seemed unimpressed but plopped himself in front of the TV anyway.

"You can change the channel if you want," Susan called after him. She turned back to Brenda. "Now. About your project. I'm all ears."

Brenda didn't respond. She just kept hacking at the green beans, her pile of tips growing quite large. She looked at Alec's stepmother and momentarily didn't recognize her. It struck her, how little she knew Alec's family. She didn't really know them at all. Not on a deep level, anyway. How could she even begin to convey what she was hoping to accomplish with her project?

"Well, it's complicated." She put down the knife. "I want to do a few paintings of some areas in the city where people put up pictures of their missing loved ones." She picked up a handful of green beans and tossed them into the large pot that was on the counter next to her cutting board. "So, in a sense, your poster inspired me."

"What I want to know is this." Manny broke away from Alec and broke into the women's conversation. "I'd like to know what in God's name you were thinking, hiding out like some fugitive. Your family was worried sick." He looked at Alec, then back at Brenda. "There should have been no need for a damned poster."

"Dad." Alec slid next to Brenda and put his arm around her. She instinctively recoiled, but it was so imperceptible that she wondered if she'd imagined recoiling, and didn't, in fact, recoil. "Dad, we've been through this a million times. Let it go. Please."

"Manny, enough of this. Stop. Just stop." Susan walked over and kissed him on the top of his head.

"Dad, we've been storming and norming here. Me, Brenda, and Henry."

Brenda glanced in the direction of the family room. Thank God, Henry seemed oblivious to anything but Lucy and Ethel trying to contain a thirty-foot loaf of bread that was bursting out of the oven.

"They have a lot going on, Manny," Susan said. "Let them sort through everything."

Brenda decided to not engage or jump to defend herself or excuse her actions. Manny was right. She should have gone straight home that day. But she didn't. And she would likely never be the same for it. This 'storming and norming' stuff that Alec was always talking about made some sense. He explained it was a team-building type of thing - storming, forming, norming, and performing. The stages that all groups go through for the duration of their group-hood. She did her own research and found another stage, not nearly talked about as much. Mourning. Yep. When she dies, she will leave the "group," and the group will be left to mourn. Then Alec and Henry will go through another cycle of storming, forming, norming, and performing. She, however, was in mourning now. In mourning for her family - the way it had been a year ago. Before cancer, before Alec and Jenn, before 9/11. And before John. Life was normal then. While not perfect - far from it in fact - it was stable and predictable. It was a pure joy compared to now.

"Like I said, I'm doing a series of paintings on missing persons from 9/11," Brenda said a bit louder than she had intended. They all stopped to look at her. She didn't realize it, but she had been crying. Susan handed her a tissue. "Yeah. I'm painting pictures of missing-person posters."

"Who'd want to look at something like that? Everyone wants to forget."

"Manny! For God's sake!" Susan shot Brenda a sympathetic glance, and in a soft tone asked: "Why?"

"Because I could relate to them," she said directly to Susan, avoiding eye contact with Manny. Then: "And I don't want to forget. It's important that nobody forgets." She stared at her green beans. There was so much more she could have said. She could have explained in vivid detail how and why she came to be a missing person. Oh, they all had their own ideas, their own theories, but they couldn't really know. She didn't really know what had possessed her to worry her family like that. She cringed when she thought of it. At times she felt lower than scum at the bottom of a pond. On that day, faced with the thought of facing the raging fire at home, she did the only thing her panicked brain allowed her to do - she disappeared. "I was one of them. I was a missing person." She said this, mostly to herself. Everyone had stopped what they were doing to listen. They were expecting more. Like the old EF Hutton commercials. Without looking at her audience, she put the rest of the green beans into the pot, wiped her hands on her jeans, and went into the family room to watch *I Love Lucy* with Henry.

***

Everyone was "happy" again. Polite against the backdrop of the comforting sounds of plates being passed, glasses being filled. Turkey. Stuffing. The green beans. Not walking on eggshells exactly, but careful avoidance of sensitive topics. There were genuine attempts to keep things light and fun. The topic of storming and norming came up. Alec and his father had a healthy, albeit short debate - saved by the candied yams. Thankfully, the issue of Brenda's heath did not come up.

"Why did the turkey cross the road?" Manny asked this of the table, but the riddle was really directed at Henry, who had been quiet throughout dinner.

"Um, to get to the stuffing?" Susan laughed at her own attempt at the answer.

"To get to the other side," Alec said.

"Nope, I think you're both wrong." Brenda chimed in. "The turkey crossed the road because that's where the couch was, and he needed a nap." She exaggerated a yawn.

"You're all wrong!" Manny seemed pleased with himself. "The reason the turkey crossed the road was that..." He made a drumroll on the side of his plate with his knife and fork. "Any last takers?" He looked at everyone around the table, all mute. "Okay. Because the chicken was on vacation!" He put the emphasis on *chicken*. Lots of moans and eye-rolls ensued.

***

Susan set out a massive spread of desserts. It seemed like the entire neighborhood could partake and there would still be leftovers. Champagne was served, and Brenda was struck with its unusual color. She held her glass up to the light and tried to identify the color. It wasn't gold, exactly. Nor was it pink. Salmon? No, not salmon. She worked hard to imprint it in her memory. Over the weekend she would try to recreate it. She couldn't help but think that this color, very sparingly applied, could become a sort of ethereal glow around the faces in her missing persons paintings. She envisioned her paintings lining the perimeter of a gallery. A place that was yet undetermined. It would need to be solemn enough for people to come in and reflect. Very minimal. Dim light as to be smoky the way it was that day. Smoky enough that the champagne color glow would stand out.

"Where are you?" Alec waved his hand up and down in front of Brenda's face.

"Huh?"

"You're in your own world again."

"I'm always in my own world." Her reverie pierced, she took a long, slow, sip of her champagne.

"More so lately." He whispered.

"You're driving me crazy Alec. Please just let me be. I was just admiring the color of the champagne. Trying to figure out how I can recreate it with paint." In her own head she'd sounded snappy and then felt terrible about it. He was hovering. But lovingly. She had learned over the past couple of months that giving him something, anything was better than just shutting him out. But still, he drove her crazy with all the hovering.

"I'm sorry. I'll try to do better." Alec kissed her lightly on the lips. "Look who's asleep over there." He pointed to the couch in the family room, where Manny was asleep - head tilted back and mouth wide open. Henry was sleeping in the crook of his arm.

"I'm glad you and your dad are making amends. Today was nice." She set her glass down and stood up. "Let's go help Susan in the kitchen. Then I'm heading up to bed."

* * *

The gentle sounds, muffled voices rising and falling, laughter, a cabinet closing, the clink-clank of a rogue dish being put in the sink. Brenda tried to sleep but couldn't. It wasn't just the fact of Manny and Susan's old house or the sounds being carried through it. It was what all those sounds represent. Life. A life that, for her, will be cut painfully short. Her future Thanksgiving dinners in her house with Henry and his wife flying in from whatever exotic place they happened to be living. Maybe even the sounds of little voices. A granddaughter, perhaps. A granddaughter named Annie.

She worked hard, very hard, to not succumb to these kinds of thoughts. She felt so good, even with the pain in her back, that it was hard to think of herself as a woman dying of cancer. She appeared vibrant and healthy. It was a cruel slap of reality when she remembered she had cancer and would die from it.

"Hey." Alec floated through the door that Brenda had left partially open. "I hope I didn't wake you."

"No, you didn't. Where's Henry?"

"My dad carried him up to bed a little while ago." Alec climbed into bed and sat up against the headboard. He handed her a small black box.

"What is this?"

"Open it." She did, and inside found a pearl necklace. "It was my grandmother's apparently."

"It's beautiful."

"My dad gave it to me tonight. He said Bubbe would have wanted me to have it and that she never blamed me for Seth."

"Of course, she never blamed you."

"But it felt like everyone blamed me." There was pain in his voice. "Anyway, I was going to give you these for Christmas, but then I thought 'what the hell,' it's almost Hanukkah. So, it's an early Hanukkah present. Even though I haven't done Hanukkah in forever. I'd like to start. So, happy early Hanukkah."

"Happy early Hanukkah to you too." She laughed. "I didn't get you anything."

He wrapped his arms around her and kissed her. But when she felt his interest going from Hanukkah to her body, she stiffened.

"So, you don't want to?"

"Actually, I don't. Not really."

"Because this bed squeaks?" He bounced on the mattress, and it let out a long, slow squeal.

"Alec, stop!" She was laughing now. "Stop!"

"Not until you say yes." He was bouncing harder now.

"Okay, okay, okay!"

They made love then, gentler and more tenderly than she could have imagined. And they were very, very quiet.

Split - Brenda

BRENDA WORE HER PEARLS every day. She wore them to her doctor appointments. She wore them out jogging. She wore them when she was painting. She wore them to her art therapy sessions. She wore them when Ted and Donald threw a "gotcha" party for their newly adopted son. She wore them when Kathy introduced her to the new love of her life, an older woman named Dee. She wore them when she took Henry out for pizza. She had her pearls on when her oncologist read her latest scan - the drugs were indeed slowing the cancer, and it had not yet spread beyond the one place in her back. *We can switch to a chemo protocol at any time,* he said. Brenda knew it would likely come to that, but for now, for beautiful now, her life was back in balance. Her life was good. Except for one thing. Alec left her. She'd been wearing her pearls then, too. And, for a few weeks before that, in a futile attempt on their part to try and fix things, she wore them to marriage counseling.

Their first session, shortly after Christmas, was laughable. Alec's practice had recommended a woman who had a track record of repairing broken promises, broken hearts, broken marriages. This woman even, allegedly, stopped a couple from divorcing after an affair. An affair! Alec emphasized this as if there was never, ever any recourse or reconciliation for a mistake of that nature. He even reminded her, often, that he didn't actually have an affair. As if to convince her that this doctor, this Edna, as she insisted on being called, would wave a magic wand and take away the fact that Alec had not only one toe, but an entire leg over the line of being unfaithful. Brenda was skeptical but agreed to go for Henry's sake. She wanted him to grow up in a stable, loving household. For whatever amount of time she had left on earth, she wanted Henry to feel safe and secure.

"You don't mind if I eat, do you?" Edna walked into the waiting room to collect Brenda and Alec. She was holding a freshly nuked frozen entree. Alec mumbled *no we don't mind please eat.* They followed her and the pungent steam into her office.

No introductions, no pleasantries exchanged. Just Edna and her dinner, sitting in a chair almost knee to knee with the miserable couple. She looked to be in her early sixties and had short auburn hair in a Buster Brown cut. Only she didn't quite look like the little boy of the old comic strip. No, Brenda thought that this woman, this doctor who came highly recommended and had a magic wand, looked more like Mr. Magoo.

"So. Tell me why you're here." Edna barely looked up from her plastic tray.

"Well, where to start." Alec produced a notebook from his briefcase and started to read a list of things he either did or is currently doing. "First, I'm trying to go out on my own, you know, leave the practice where I'm currently..."

"Back up." Edna interrupted him. "Back up. You need to go way back."

"How about we introduce ourselves." Brenda found her voice. She was incredulous at this woman's demeanor. "Don't you want a bit of our background?"

"That's exactly what I asked for when I said to tell me why you're here." She turned her fork upside down and scooped up the last bits of sauce with the handle.

"That's it, I can't do this." Brenda stood up but sat right back down when Alec looked at her like he might cry.

"Brenda, please. Dr. Boggs at work highly recommends Dr. Edna." He pleaded.

"Edna. Just Edna. I'm a doctor, yes. But please. Just. Call. Me. Edna."

An hour and a half later Brenda and Alec ate their own dinner a few blocks away. Chianti and pizza - the food and drink they'd bonded over so many years ago. It was evident that they had a lot of challenging work ahead of them. It appeared that the name of the game was rehashing everything that was ever wrong between them. Everything they'd stacked on a high shelf to be dealt with another day. It was exhausting, and Brenda couldn't imagine another hour and a half with this woman, let alone the ten sessions that Alec's health insurance covered.

They attended two more sessions, each followed by Chianti and pizza. It was in the car on the way to their fourth session that Alec blurted out: *It's no use. I can't do this.* The fissures were too broad. The magic wand didn't have enough magic. *It's no use.*

They bypassed Edna's office and went straight to the pizza place. They ordered their usual and Alec poured out his guts in a way he hadn't seemed able to do in their sessions with Edna. He begged her to believe him that there was no more Jenn. *Jenn was just a smoke screen*, he'd said. *A diversion from his own misery*, he'd said. *It's not you*, he'd assured Brenda, explaining that he was tired and could no longer keep up the charade of going through the day to day motions of ordinary life. She resisted the urge to scream that he had no idea what it really meant to be tired.

He begged her forgiveness for the broken promises. Ironically enough, he made yet another promise: that he'd be there for her when her health started to deteriorate. No matter what. No matter where he was or who he was with. He'd take care of her. She appreciated the sentiment but said she didn't need him. She had her sister. And new friends: three women she met at her oncologist's office, also with breast cancer. She was under no illusions that someday - either sooner or later - her health would take a nosedive and she would die from this disease. She suddenly realized that she'd rather live alone with her son then live with a man who didn't want to be there, even if having that man there would make things easier.

Two weeks later Alec moved out. When the door closed behind him, she wasn't even that upset. How telling was that? She didn't ask him if he wanted the pearls back.

***

The smell of garlic permeated the apartment. Brenda and Henry were in the kitchen making fresh garlic bread. She sautéed six garlic bulbs, three for the bread and three for the spaghetti sauce that was bubbling nicely on the stove. It was the third weekend since Alec moved out, and the first one where Henry was with her.

"I think the garlic for the bread is ready. Let's melt some butter in the microwave, then brush the bread with it, and spread the garlic." She wrinkled her nose. "It smells amazing.

"It smells garlicky," Henry said. "But I guess since it's garlic bread, it's supposed to be garlicky." He put a stick of butter in a bowl. "How long should I nuke this?"

Hmm. Let me see." She looked at the bowl. "A whole stick?" She raised an eyebrow at him.

"I like it buttery." He bent his neck over the stove and sniffed. "And garlicky."

"Okay then. A whole stick of butter it is." And then, in a playful tone: "I'm sorry arteries. I promise never to do this to you again." She turned to Henry. "One minute in the microwave should be more than enough."

Henry brushed the liquefied butter onto the two halves of their freshly baked loaf. Then she dotted each one with the sautéed garlic. She turned on the oven and took off her apron.

"Can we invite Mr. Ted and Mr. Donald over?" Henry reached into the cabinet for extra plates.

"I don't know. I thought it would be nice if just the two of us ate together tonight. Aunt Kathy and Dee are out. So, it's just us."

"Is Aunt Kathy gay?"

Brenda hesitated. The topic of Kathy's sexuality had never explicitly come up. Kathy was just Aunt Kathy. And Aunt Kathy had a lot of friends who were also women, friends whom she dated. But until Dee, there hadn't been anyone serious in her sister's life. Not since Lydia.

"Yes. Aunt Kathy is gay. Just like Mr. Ted and Mr. Donald. They both love each other. Aunt Kathy loves Dee like Mr. Ted loves Mr. Donald."

"I kind of knew. A boy, Simon, in my science class has two moms. They're gay. Will Aunt Kathy and Dee adopt a baby? Simon's two moms adopted him when he was a baby."

Brenda picked up a wooden spoon and aimlessly stirred the spaghetti sauce. Round and round, the contents bubbled and swirled. The desperation in Kathy's heart when she and Lydia were trying to have a baby. All before Henry was born. Never talked about. The highs, the lows, the walking on eggshells. And in the end, when Lydia left, the darkness that engulfed her sister was almost too much to bear. She had never seen Kathy such a raw, jumbled mess.

The nine months of her pregnancy with Henry was perhaps the happiest, most content period of her life. She reached for the salt shaker and pretended to shake some salt into the pot. She lifted the spoon to her lips and pretended to taste the sauce. She stared at the simmering concoction as if contemplating whether all the flavors had sufficiently mingled. She was stalling. Biding time to let the lump in her throat work its way down. Anything to keep from allowing Henry to see her cry. What she really wanted to do was curl up in a ball and sob over the loss of her baby girl, the demise of her marriage, and the fact that the sands were rapidly slipping through the hourglass of her life. She took a deep breath. She needed to be strong. Henry needed her to be strong.

"Well, I don't know if Aunt Kathy and Dee will adopt a baby. I don't think we should ask them because it's very personal and they might not want to talk about it." She cleared her throat, feeling better, feeling able to resume the tenor of the evening. "But, you know, they can also have a baby naturally. They could get the dad's seed from a special doctor and have the seed implanted into the mom. Sometimes a baby will grow. Sometimes not."

"It's called sperm. The dad's seed is called sperm." Henry said.

"Okay, okay. I guess Dad talked to you about these things?" She continued when he didn't answer. "Anyway, some moms and dads use a sperm donor when they have trouble making a baby. And this is what some moms do when it's two moms. Like Aunt Kathy and Dee." Brenda was ready for this conversation to end. She didn't feel like she had the emotional strength for an in-depth talk tonight.

"How come you and dad stopped loving each other?" Henry changed the subject, choking back tears.

Brenda was afraid of this. She knew it would happen but didn't think it would be this soon. She and Alec thought they'd done all the right things: Sitting Henry down. Telling him that this wasn't his fault, that they both loved him very much and would do everything they needed to do to take care of him. That Mom and Dad just needed some time apart. Brenda regrets that they'd left things open-ended with Henry. They both knew that the separation would be permanent. That there was no going back, no turning back time. No retracing footsteps. No getting back on a course that they had begun to veer slightly off years ago. And now here they were, in the middle of a vast ocean with no navigation equipment. They'd gotten so far off course over the years that turning back, trying to get back to the exact place in the ocean where they began to veer, was impossible. She hadn't believed it at first. But she believed it now.

She put her arm around her son, and he asked through sobs: "Did dad leave because you're sick?"

"No." She reassured him with a tight hug and a kiss on the top of his head. "Dad did not leave because I'm sick. Sometimes couples do better when they don't live in the same house. Your dad and I will always be connected by you. We both love you very much and always will. But he and I will be better to each other, and to you, if we don't live in the same house." The sobbing subsided just enough for her to say: "It will be okay, I promise."

She didn't tell him that Alec offered to come home to care for her when the time came that she needed help. She didn't want Henry's hope to hang in the balance of whether she was sick or well. On the one hand, he'd want his father to come home. On the other hand, he'd want his mother to be well. The last thing she wanted was for guilt to engulf Henry over her failing health and ultimate death.

"I am so happy I met and married your dad because we made you. Our marriage will forever be priceless because of that."

Henry's sobbing slowly abated. She could see that he's had enough of the in-depth talk, for now. With her face in his hair, she suggested that they eat their dinner in front of the TV and watch the movie of his choice.

Exhibit - Brenda

"I FOUND THE PERFECT VENUE." Ted sat down at Brenda's kitchen table. He helped himself to two beers from the fridge and handed one to her.

She had finished her series of paintings depicting the missing persons posters a week before Alec moved out. Ted had opened a new studio just a few blocks away and gave Brenda carte blanche to use it to paint. She'd carved out her own corner, which was littered with the detritus of her frantic burst of inspiration.

"I think we need to change the name of the exhibit." Ted looked cautiously at her. "Missing Persons as a title is just too bleak, too hopeless. If you get my drift. We need a name that will give people hope."

"Hope about what? Hope that their loved ones are still alive? After all this time, figure the chances. Zilch." She caught herself. She might still be a missing person had she not decided to return home. Brenda didn't want to minimize the importance of having a meaningful title for her exhibit, but honestly, she was so focused on finishing the series that she hadn't given the title too much thought.

"You were a missing person. Your family got you back." He echoed her thoughts and took a long, slow sip of his beer. "Who's to say there aren't other people who, for whatever their reason, decided to disappear. Maybe this would inspire them to come home. Okay, scratch that. I'm guessing that anyone who lost a loved one and sees your paintings may feel like the lost person is being memorialized, even though your missing persons are fictitious."

Brenda's chest tightened. She didn't like feeling this way, feeling like she committed an egregious sin by putting her family through a few days of pure hell. She was fearful that Henry would be forever scarred because of it. She tugged at the pearls around her neck.

Ted continued: "Your paintings are surreal. They tell a story of hope. Not hope in the sense that any of these people survived or were found but hope in general. Real hope."

"I get what you're saying." She couldn't keep her fingers away from the pearls. It was physically painful for her to not touch them. "I feel a sort of kinship with the people in the posers." The pearls that Alec gave her were so much more than a family heirloom. So much more than a peace offering from her husband, or rather, soon to be ex-husband. The pearls represented the beauty that comes from suffering. A little grit of sand. A piece of foreign debris. The tumor of an oyster. A beautiful tumor. She had cancer - had her own tumors. But she was determined to live beautifully. To make pearls.

"I know you do." He touched her arm. "Let me tell you about this venue. Better yet, are you free tomorrow? I'd like to just show it to you."

"I can't tomorrow. I have doctor appointments." She raised her eyebrows and sighed.

"I'm so sorry. I know you're sort of riding a good wave at the moment. Sometimes I forget that you're sick."

She got up and put her empty beer bottle in the sink. When she returned to the table, Ted was pulling papers out of an envelope.

"I was wondering when you were going to tell me what was in there." She started reading what would be the narrative of her art exhibit. More of a memorial. Ted's partner, Donald, copy editor by trade, had written it. It was moving. Very. "I don't know how to thank you. Both of you." She grew quiet. "I'm having second thoughts about this. What if it offends people?"

"There's always going to be someone offended. Doesn't matter what you do. You have to live your life. You can't please everyone."

"I agree with you about all that. But, I want to be careful. I don't want to be perceived as glorifying a horrific moment in history." She tugged at her pearls again. She added a string of pearls around a woman's neck in one of her paintings. "We need to make sure people know that my paintings are a metaphor - each one the shadow a real person who was missing. I want to make sure we stress that the people in the paintings are fictitious." She tugged at the pearls again, this time more forcefully. "I don't want someone coming in and thinking the person in the painting is their son or wife or friend."

"Don't worry. I'll ask Donald to rewrite the narrative to emphasize all that. Now, about the venue. It's in a loft on Mercer Street."

Brenda looked carefully at the pictures of the venue that she'd pulled out of the envelope. She liked it. It was very industrial, very minimal. She wanted to keep the sights, sounds and smells somber. There would be no cocktails or hors-d'oeuvres offered. Any donations collected would go directly to affected families. Maybe a scholarship fund for surviving children.

"Oh, and Donald wants to interview you. It will be a part of the 'coming soon' campaign. We want to run it in the Times a month out from the anniversary."

She dreaded the interview. But knew it was necessary.

Tired - Brenda

ONE OF THE UNFORTUNATE side effects of Brenda's palliative cancer treatment was fatigue. She was tired. Bone tired. It was a small price to pay for the quality of life that this approach was affording her. She'd researched the options extensively. The sad truth was that having a mastectomy and chemo would extend her life for only so long, and with horrific side effects. She'd rather be exhausted but otherwise able to live her life the way she wanted to live it. And living it her way meant that she wouldn't give in to the fatigue.

Mornings were the worst - usually because her sleep was fitful. She wasn't about to let her disease define her so she willingly got out of bed most mornings before the whole house woke up, which usually meant five o'clock sharp. And now the whole house included not only Henry but her sister too. Kathy had been nonchalant about the fact that she felt Brenda needed help, and spun a tale of practicality and sensibility: Kathy and her now very serious girlfriend Dee wanted to buy a place of their own and both of their apartments sold quickly. They planned to take their time looking. They weren't even sure if they wanted a little house in suburbia or an apartment in Manhattan. *Blah blah blah.*

Brenda didn't believe a word of it. They moved in to help her with Henry. Plain and simple. And for that, she was secretly grateful. Mostly, she was grateful for the laughter and chaos that filled the once empty spaces. Before Kathy and Dee moved in, the weekends that Henry spent with Alec were unbearably quiet.

Funny how you covet what you don't have. Now that the house was filled with life, Brenda sometimes longed for quiet, which was another motivator in getting out of bed before dawn. Cup of strong coffee. Sometimes a sketchpad, sometimes not. Lately a leather-bound journal where she captured all the things she wanted to tell Henry before she died. A memoir of sorts so he could carry her with him when she was gone. Words that he was too young to understand now. Her notes shed a little bit of light here and there about her four-day disappearance last year. Alec frequently reminded her that they need to stick to the story they'd told Henry - that she'd had a doctor appointment and couldn't get home. For now, she would honor Alec's wishes. But not forever. Plus, she sensed that Henry didn't believe the story. Someday he would realize that the pieces didn't add up. And he would question it. And the answers would be contained within the pages of the journal. Hopefully many journals.

This particular morning the coffee didn't help. She felt like an eighteen-wheeler had run over her sometime during the night. She slipped the journal and pens in her special corner cabinet and padded over to the couch. When she eventually opened her eyes, it was no longer dark outside. She was ravenously hungry, and the house was eerily quiet. And then she saw it: her moth painting on the fireplace mantle, leaning against the wall at a slight angle. She sat up to get a better look and saw that Dee was sitting on the other end of the couch studying her.

"It's beautiful." Dee waited until Brenda registered some recognition of her presence. "Your sister told me about it, but her description didn't do it justice."

"I'm confused. Why is this here? I gave it to John. For his pub."

"We went over there yesterday. Kathy wanted to tell John about your exhibit next month. Please don't be angry with her. She thought he might like to see it." She moved closer to Brenda and reached for her hand, but Brenda recoiled.

"Why? She knows I'm trying to put that whole episode behind me. I wasn't in my right mind. I don't want to see him. I don't want to relive all that."

"Well, you don't have to worry because the other guy, what's his name?"

"Shorty."

"Shorty said John's gone 'on walkabout.' He took the boat. Doesn't know when he'll be back." Brenda felt her stomach sink in a way that startled her. She had done an outstanding job of pushing John so far into the background that sometimes she felt she had dreamed the whole thing. That those four days with him never happened. That he had been a ghost. Or an angel.

"Did Shorty say anything else?"

"No, not really, just that your leaving hit John pretty hard." Dee paused. "Shorty gave the painting to Kathy. He said he thought you might want to have it back now, with the upcoming anniversary and all. Kathy thinks this might work well as part of your exhibit."

It hit Brenda then that John hadn't been a ghost after all. "He was good to me. He didn't need to be. There was something so familiar about him." Brenda looked hard into Dee's eyes. "His hands were the first thing I noticed. They reminded me of my father's hands. Where did you say he went?"

"I don't know. He just left. Shorty doesn't know."

"Did Shorty say when he might be back?"

"He doesn't know."

Brenda didn't realize, until that very moment, that she'd been pinching an invisible thread between her thumb and forefinger. She'd been doing it since coming home. A strand of hope. Hope that she'd reconnect with John at some point. Hope that he might even try to find her. The realization of this thread she'd been pinching rolled over her like waves in the ocean. Why hadn't he wanted to see her? In fact, her first split second semiconscious thought when she saw her painting on the mantle was that John himself had delivered it. Her heart sank a little when she saw Dee. She'd half expected to see John sitting on the couch or maybe even sitting on the hearth, or, on the floor with his head in her lap and her arms around his neck. Tears sprung anew at the thought of him leaving - going on walkabout like a seafaring Crocodile Dundee - without a word, without a goodbye. This punched-in-the-gut reaction was unjustified. Completely unjustified. The thread she had been subconsciously holding had severed. He owed her nothing.

"Why did you sign it Annie Wells?"

"What?" Brenda wiped her eyes with the back of her hand. If Dee had been talking to her, she was completely unaware.

"Nothing," Dee said. "It's okay. I'm sorry for all of this. I'm sorry he left without saying goodbye."

"How can you be so damned perceptive?" She let the remaining tears flow and then smiled. "I can see why Kathy loves you."

Brenda willed her heart to stop hurting. She needed it to stop hurting long enough for her brain, however foggy and jumbled it was, to stabilize and come back to reality. Even if - and this was an 'if' the size of the Empire State Building - even if John felt the same odd connection to her as she did to him, he had no reason, no right even, to pursue further contact with her. Yes, her brain did a great job of laying out these not so fun facts before her. But the pain in her heart trumped the logic in her mind. She ached at the real possibility that she may never see him again.

"Where is everyone, anyway?" Brenda was desperate to fill her mind with anything other than this unexpected change in the wind.

"We wanted to let you sleep. Kathy took Henry to the movies to see *Spy Kids* 2." Dee rolled her eyes.

"What, you didn't want to see it with them?"

Dee rolled her eyes again, then: "Are you hungry? I can make grilled cheese."

Brenda nodded, and they went to the kitchen, a happy diversion, yet, the rock in her chest was still there. She figured it would be there for a long time.

Yellow Boat - Brenda

ALEC OFFERED TO BE WITH her today. *You shouldn't be alone,* he'd said. But alone was exactly what Brenda wanted to be. She told Alec not to come. He then offered to pick Henry up from school and keep him for the night. That offer, she accepted.

The exhibit opening was set for tomorrow and was called, simply, *Hope* - a name that Ted had eventually talked her into. Kathy and Dee were at the loft on Mercer Street helping Ted with last minute preparations. They understood, more than they should have, really, that Brenda needed to spend the day alone.

She got up early and retraced her steps. She didn't go to ground zero, didn't want to be among those who were grieving their loved ones who, unlike her, were never found. Instead, she went to Battery Park and sat on the bench. The same bench she'd fallen asleep on the year before. Unlike the year before, she was fully alert, wholly in control of her heart and head. At least that's what she told herself. She sat still and allowed whatever thoughts wanted to come, to come. And of course, they came. And all involved John.

She felt silly for letting the ghost of someone she'd know for a few days have such power over her. They'd spoken so little during those days. Like negative space in art, referring to the shapes that form between objects - a patch of sky between two trees on a hillside, for example. Life was like that too. So many things unspoken, unrevealed. Sometimes this led to regret, and Brenda knew, unequivocally, that regret was never good. She was convinced though, that there were times when the unspoken was beautiful. Like the patch of sky. Unadorned and beautiful.

The morning was sunny and bright, almost a carbon copy of how it had been on this day last year. The hole in the skyline where the twin towers once stood was negative space filled with sadness, regret, and hope. Planes flew freely overhead and boats dotted the river before her. And then she saw it. A sailboat. Yellow against the blue sky. It was too far away for her to make out the name. She didn't need to see the name. She knew.

Anniversary - John

MY EX-WIFE HAD THIS DREAM about restoring her dead father's boat. I hated boats back then. I still hate boats, really. But I've come to respect them. We have an understanding, boats and me. We will never go into the ocean together. That's a given. And if we can't use each other for some sort of good, well then, it's just a waste of time - my time and the boat's time. She was crazy, my ex-wife, Marina. Of all the women in the entire world, I would have to marry a woman with a reference to boating built right into her name. Did I mention that I hate boats? But I don't hate Marina, not anymore. I hated her all over again last year when I finally got through on the phone, you know, on the day of the attacks, and I heard the kid crying in the background. She named him Luke. Of course, she did. She named him after a song from her favorite band, a band that sings about boats. *Lukey's boat is painted green, ah ha me boys a-biddle-aye-day.* What the hell does that mean, anyway? She loved that band, Great Big Sea.

"Why do we have to listen to this?" Shorty snuck a few Great Big Sea tracks into this afternoon's mix. Mari-Mac is the current gag-inducing thing I'm being forced to listen to. Again, with the crazy lyrics.

"This is an Irish pub, John. People like this kind of shit. You know sea-faring songs. Drunken sailor songs. Songs that make them happy instead of sad. Today that's important. Real important, if you know what I mean." Shorty was behind the bar wiping a mug. He filled it with Sleepless Pale Ale, my newest experiment, and handed it to me.

"This stuff tastes like cat piss." I reached over the bar and poured it in the sink.

"What are you doing?" Shorty grabbed the glass out of my hand, filled it with Sam Adams and handed it back to me. He held a tasting glass over the Sleepless tap, filled it, chugged it, and wiped his mouth with the back of his hand. "Okay, so it tastes like cat piss," he said. Then: "Maybe I'll use it to marinate that cheap stew meat I bought from Shop Rite. It's tougher than rubber but a day or two in this cat piss beer, and it will melt in your mouth."

* * *

Shorty and I sailed back into Liberty Landing this morning at around ten-thirty which was around the time the north tower fell last year. It was surreal being out there on the water today. Clear and calm with no hint of last year's tragedy except a gaping hole in the skyline and all the news coverage over the past few weeks leading up to today. Last weekend there was even a big cycling event to commemorate this first anniversary. I was in Atlantic Highlands picking up several cases of a new beer Shorty was considering when I saw the bikers. There were hundreds of them, most of them wearing patriotic spandex. Some even had pictures of people they'd lost in the attacks pinned to their backs. Three guys stood in the grass changing a tire, and I asked them where they were headed. *To the Pentagon*, they said.

I spent the morning trying to remember every last detail. The sounds, the smells, the feelings. The people we picked up and dropped off. Mostly though, I spent the morning desperately trying to remember Annie. It's not that I could ever forget her. I can't. I won't. But the details of her are fading fast. Like the way her hand felt when I lifted her onto the boat. And the timbre of her voice. For months after, the sound of her voice was the loudest thing in my head. Now her voice is barely a whisper. I have to be completely quiet and full of focus and concentration to recall the subtle nuances of her voice. But if I ever heard it again I would instantly recognize it.

Shorty had a steady stream of customers today. He alternated between local coverage and CNN on the TV until people couldn't stand it anymore. And people became unable to stand it faster than I would have thought. By two o'clock someone tapped me on the shoulder and begged for some music. Shorty always selects the music. Our tastes are vastly different. When I first started working at the pub, he told me I could liven up the music a bit, if I wanted. So, I brought in a few of my favorite hand-selected obscure oldies mixes. After about an hour he handed them all back to me and said *never again*. So today Shorty chose the most lively, upbeat, raucous, drinking songs, many of them Irish, many of them Celtic rock - too many of them Great Big Sea.

"I'll be out back." I swallowed the last of my beer and left the glass on the bar for Shorty to deal with. It wasn't quite time for the dinner crowd, and there were only a handful of people at the bar. Most of the tables were empty. He didn't need me.

"You okay?" Shorty looked concerned. Or annoyed. I couldn't tell the difference. And I didn't care.

"Yeah. No. Not really." Shorty wasn't about to budge on to-day's music choice, so I'm stuck with Great Big Sea. Problem is, it's filling my mind with Marina and pushing Annie out into left field somewhere. Annie doesn't deserve that.

"I'll change the music," he said, reading my mind.

"It's too late, the damage is done."

***

A few years ago, Shorty paid his nephew a nice little sum to paint a mural on the side of the pub - the wall in the alley between his place and Moonstruck Pizza. Yeah, it's a terribly corny reference to the movie, but people seem to like the place, and I must admit that the pizza is great. It's rumored that Cher and Nicholas Cage have eaten there, but not together. Who knows? I suppose it could be true. Right now, it smells so good out here that I might just be forced to go in and order a large pepperoni-sausage-mushroom. With extra cheese. I could sit on the ground against the mural and eat the whole thing. Not many people are eating at Shorty's right now, else the smell of his fish and chips would likely compete - fried fish the most likely winner. Sometimes though, when the wind is just right, the aromas from both places greet each other kindly, their invisible molecules mingling like the lonely regulars at Shorty's happy hour.

The mural looks just a little too kitschy today - the ocean, way too aqua, the sun way too yellow. Why did Shorty's nephew choose those colors? This is New Jersey, not Key West. The sails on the sailboats are too graceful looking, too perfect. And what's with the seagulls? Smiling seagulls? You're kidding me, right? Some of the paint is chipping too. A more muted painting - perhaps one featuring a gray misty day with an old lighthouse casting a beam across the water - would have been more realistic and might even look good over time with a bit of a patina and chipping paint. This damned painting is happy. It makes people happy. It makes kids happy. It's just the wrong thing for today. Just so wrong. Like those damned drinking songs. Not today. Any day, just not today. Shorty must have turned up the music because I can hear it. I can feel the beat. He must have it out for me today - he's such a dick.

* * *

"Marina." I'm not sure why I dialed her number. Damn. I came out here to clear my head and now here I am, listening to the sounds of life - TV, clattering flatware, kids laughing, and Nester's deep voice interspersed with several other unrecognizable voices. She must be having a party.

"This isn't a good time John. Are you okay?"

"Yeah, I'm okay. How's Ness?"

"He's dealing. Lukey's a good distraction. It's his birthday today, you know."

"Yeah, how could I forget. Hey, tell Ness I'm sorry. Tell him he's on my mind."

"Look, why don't you just come over. You can say whatever you need to say to him in person."

"I don't think so, Marina."

"We already did the memorial thing for his cousin. A lot of engine companies came for support. So, Nester is okay. He's okay. We're grilling later. Think about it, at least."

* * *

I told myself I needed a dose of reality. At least that's the only justification I came up with for why I left Shorty to run the pub alone and why I'm now parked in front of my old house. Maybe it's closure I need. Or something. I thought I'd moved on. But now I feel stuck in some sort of strange limbo. Damn, the lawn looks freshly cut. It looks good. Nice and green. Much greener than it ever did when I lived here. It looks like the pavers leading to the front steps have been redone. I wonder if Nester did that or if he contracted it out. Probably contracted it out. Ness was never into all that happy homeowner horse shit. I'm guessing he has a lawn service come too. That must be why the grass is so green.

What I really wish I had was the super power to become invisible. I'd sit in the corner of the kitchen and watch. That's the dose of reality that I need today. I need to see Marina happy. I need to look at her in her new life, the life without me. I need to look at the kid and see that yes, he really does look like Phil Riley, only he looks nothing like Riley and everything like Marina. I kind of wish he looked like Riley, because then I could justify my anger. I'd be able to say that I can't look at the kid because he looks like the man who raped my wife and destroyed my marriage. Maybe I could have gotten past the fact that the only reason the kid even exists is that Marina was raped. Logically I know that the kid was not conceived in love. Marina was raped. I know that. I know that! The bastard entered our house with a key I had given him years before. Always provide a trusted friend a key, isn't that what the police tell you to do? Yep. I was the police, and I followed my own advice. I trusted Phil. I liked Phil. I drank beer with Phil. We broke bread together. Frequently. I've scratched my head and beat myself up over this since it happened. How could I have missed it? What didn't I see? He's dead now. After the rape Marina's survival instinct kicked in and she fought back. It was her perfectly executed elbow strike to his trachea that killed him. The autopsy confirmed this.

"What are you doing out here, I'm about to light the grill." Nester reached into my truck through the open passenger side window, unlocked the door, and climbed in. He just sat and looked at me. "It's damned good to see you." He hugged me hard. I could tell that his eyes were wet.

"I'm so sorry about Joey. I'm sorry I wasn't there for you last year."

"Meh. Look, I don't think I would have been receptive of you then. I was still wrapped up in the hurt you caused Marina."

"She caused me a lot of hurt too, you know."

"That's between the two of you. Hey, I don't want to be strangers anymore over this. I've made my peace. Marina has too. You and I have known each other too long to let this hang. And I'm sorry I wasn't more of a friend to you during that time."

"I'm over it."

"No, you're not."

We laughed. A little.

***

Everyone in the house seemed to be expecting me. Most of the neighbors. Some of the folks from the station. No one paid much attention to me, though. Except for Mel. The guy across the street who survived a run-in with a train and severed his spine in the process. He's in a wheelchair but has regained almost full use of his arms. Wow, he's improved in the last three years. I'm floored by the sight of him and find myself on the verge of tears. He wheeled up to me and squeezed my arm and gave me a knowing look. Like he gets it. The others pretty much ignored me. I could almost hear the whispered discussions that took place after I called Marina earlier today. The aspersions cast. The ass I must be for walking out on a wife and baby.

Did any of them have any clue how hard it was to be me back then? To not only have to deal with the fact that my wife was raped by a trusted friend, but also to go through all the shit that comes with the fact that my wife killed the trusted friend? Or that she killed him after being raped, not before when it would have mattered. I know, I know. My wife was raped. It wasn't her fault. I know it wasn't. Yet at the time, I couldn't help but think that she should have reacted differently. She should have gotten directly into her fighting stance - the one I taught her, and we practiced in the kitchen occasionally. She should have yelled - in a deep and reverberating voice - to stay back. She should have yelled. She said she screamed for me. I tell you, I didn't hear any of it. I'm a light sleeper, but I was three floors down - in the basement, below the surface of the earth. I might as well have been in hell. Still, I should have heard her. I can say with absolute certainty that I would have heard her if she'd yelled adequately. Screaming is too high pitched. She knew better. All of this could have been prevented. She should have yelled. Then I would have heard her. And I would have been up those three flights of stairs in an instant, and I would have killed the bastard before the rape. I would have killed him quickly and quietly. He wouldn't have known what hit him.

The ugly truth is that even if she'd yelled differently, I wouldn't have heard her. Of course, I wouldn't have, no matter what. I was passed out on the couch. In the basement. Sound-proof. The whole damned thing was my fault. I should have rescued her. And I couldn't because I'd had too much to drink and passed out on the couch. Fuck.

The kid materialized at my feet and was looking up at me. Of course, he doesn't remember me. I've only seen him a few times over the past few years, and just in passing. He looks nothing like Riley. And everything like Marina. He looks like a kid we could have created together.

We stood sizing each other up for a few seconds, then he ran through the kitchen to the sunroom, and for some reason I don't quite understand, I followed him. He pointed to a Lego tower that climbed almost to the ceiling. Clearly, Nester was involved in its construction. The kid handed me a red Lego, the kind that looks like a window. I started to place in on top of the tower, but instead, I handed it back to him, lifted him up, and let him put it on. I helped his little fingers press it into place. He tried to wiggle his way out of my arms, so I lowered him to the floor. The grin he flashed me as he leaped away for more exciting surroundings made me question my sanity: for hating him, for leaving him, and for coming to this damned house today.

"He's a handful." Marina apparently was watching me from the archway between the kitchen and sunroom.

The sunroom looked like it belonged to a young couple, not the mid-life couple that Marina and I had been, or Marina and Nester now are. A long, gray couch was pressed up against the main wall, and across from it, instead of a TV, an entertainment stand filled with toys. There was a drafter's table in one corner, my guess is it's where Marina draws and paints when the kid is building Lego towers. In the other corner is a multi-drawer plastic bin, probably for art supplies. A toddler-sized art table sat neatly under the window. Next to the art table stood a small easel chalkboard contraption.

"It looks like he's taken over your world. Look at this place. This used to be our sanctuary."

"Priorities change when you have a kid. You wouldn't know that John."

"Wait a minute. I wanted to know that. I wanted to know that all the years we were together. I just wanted it to be my kid, not some rapist's."

"That's not fair."

"How the hell is it not fair? It is fair. It's very fair."

"John, lower your voice."

I moved over to where she was standing and pulled her across the threshold into the sunroom.

"What are you doing?"

"We need to talk, Marina. I certainly didn't come here today with the intention of talking, you know, about the big stuff in life. I came here, well, I'm not entirely sure why I came here."

"It's too late to talk about any of that - the big stuff or the little stuff. It's too late John."

"Well, I'm here, and we really should talk."

"But my guests."

Nester appeared. He had the kid in his arms. "Everything okay in here?" He glared at me. Like he'd mess up my good leg if he thought I was being unkind to Marina.

"We're just talking, Ness," Marina said. "It's okay. We'll just be a minute, I promise." Nester held me in his death stare as he slowly backed out of the sunroom.

I sat down on the couch and forced myself to take a deep breath. I had to bite my tongue, hard. I'd wanted kids. Badly. She never did. Sure, we were careless more than a few times, but nothing ever happened. She badgered me about getting snipped. So, I did. I never should have. I deeply regret that decision.

"How can you look at Lukey and imagine my having aborted him?" Marina reluctantly sat down next to me.

"We wouldn't have known him."

"You saw the sonogram picture, John."

And there you have it. That damned sonogram was her reality. My reality today is either going to be that I made a huge mistake in leaving her or I did the right thing in leaving her. But what about the kid's reality? He has Nester as a daddy. The kid will have a good life. It's not like I left him destitute.

"I'm sorry I came here today." I tried to get up, but my body wouldn't cooperate. "Do you have any idea how it made me feel that you wouldn't have a baby with me, but you had one with the bastard who raped you?" Again, I had to force myself to breathe. Again, I had to bite my tongue. This time, I think I tasted blood.

"The bastard that I killed. I killed him, John, remember? You know how I felt about killing him. You know the only way I was ever going to make peace was to have the baby."

"I agree that you didn't have to have an abortion. But you didn't have to keep it either."

"I know, but I had already lost you in the process."

"Not really. Not necessarily." If only she had yelled properly. If only. Then I would have heard her, and I would have rescued her, and I would have killed the bastard. Then the guilt would be on me, not her. Dammit, there I go again. If only I hadn't been in the basement, half-crocked, passed out on the couch.

"You hadn't lost me yet. Not then. Not yet."

* * *

The night my wife was raped I was in the basement fixing a vacuum. The next thing I remembered was a football game on TV. I didn't really need the third beer I'd opened. She came down looking for me quite a bit later, but by then I was watching some dumb movie that I can't even remember. I told her to go to bed without me, that I would come upstairs later.

"I'm sorry, Marina. I'm sorry I failed you that night." I was shaking and babbling and choking and sobbing. She put her arms around me and squeezed me. She told me it was okay and that she's made her peace. I have no idea how long we sat like that. When I finally drew the last of my shaky breaths and choked out the last of my sobs, I got up to leave.

She followed me out of the sunroom and through the kitchen, through the dining room, through the small foyer, and onto the stoop. When she tried to follow me to my truck, I held up my hand and shook my head. I left without saying goodbye to Ness.

* * *

It was still light outside. Both Shorty's and Moonstruck were busy. I could smell the evidence of the two kitchens competing for the best aroma award - the aroma most likely to lure in the passerby who had not previously planned to eat out. Moonstruck's alley tables all were occupied, despite an early fall crispness. Shorty should put some tables on his side of the alley. There's plenty of room. They would back up against the mural, but so what. I think I'll mention it to him tonight. I know there are permits and required approvals to have an outdoor eating area, but I think it would be worth it.

"You okay dude?" Shorty handed me an O'Rourke's ball cap and motioned for me to follow him. Inside the pub, there was no music, no Great Big Sea, just CNN on closed caption. The place was nicely busy but not crowded.

"If you don't need me, I think I'll just go sit on the boat for a while."

"You deserted me today man. I need you here, now, behind the bar with me."

Leave it to Shorty to find a diversion. Anything to keep me off that boat. Anything to keep me from wallowing in whatever it is I had been wallowing in since the attacks last year.

Straggler - John

I HATE THIS TIME OF THE NIGHT. It is morning, I suppose. Two in the morning. The dead hour. The drunk hour. The sad hour. The depressed hour. The post-break-up-call hour. The suicide attempt hour. The let-me-take-you-home hour. The hour when the darkness seems so thick, you nearly choke. The hour that your personal demons like to taunt and poke you with their ugly accusations. The hour the stragglers get kicked out of bars. Not at Shorty's. Shorty will stick around with any and every straggler. He'll stop serving them the potions they desperately hope will make them forget whatever it is that they are drinking to forget. He'll make them a pot of coffee and drink it with them. He'll help them stagger over to one of the booths and lay them down on the vinyl covered bench as if tucking in a toddler for the night. And, like a toddler, sometimes thumb sucking or drooling is involved. Shorty has even been known on occasion to experiment with new recipes during these hours, often using the stragglers as taste testers. Not that any of them could ever give a coherent assessment given how drunk they sometimes were.

Two in the morning and I'm the only straggler. Just me. I begged Shorty to go home. Told him I'd clean up. I'd get everything ready for tomorrow. I'd wash and dry all the glasses. I'd mop the floor. Anything to avoid going home and facing my demons. So here I am, sitting at the bar, listening to Frank Sinatra (yes, Shorty loves Frank), nursing a beer (Shorty's rule of no alcohol for stragglers apparently doesn't apply to me), watching Shorty wash and dry all the glasses, and jousting with my demons.

"I need to move on."

Shorty ignored me. He hung four wine glasses upside down in the rack at the far end of the bar, right where a guy with a hair weave had been sitting a few hours ago. It looked like a recent hair weave. I'd been helping Shorty behind the bar and served the guy a burger and fries. He bent over his plate and carefully cut the burger into four, uniform quarters. Meticulous, the way he cut that burger. Kind of like the meticulous tufts of hair sprouting from meticulous rows on his shiny scalp. The clumps of hair were spaced so evenly that I don't care how thick it grows in, well, his head will always look like a garden plot. My mother's gardening philosophy was to always plant things in groups of three, or other odd-numbered combinations. *You never want your garden to look orchestrated*, is what she says. It should look like every plant came by naturally, with zero human intervention. My mother seemed to spend every summer morning, before the heat became too much for her, tending her precious flora. Yet it never looked orchestrated. It always looked like it had been placed there by God himself. The guy with the hair weave should have met my mother. Then he'd have a beautiful garden of hair instead of the ridiculousness that I saw today. Maybe I should talk to him. Perhaps if he ever comes back, and I'm here, I will. Yes. I will.

"Move on from what, exactly?"

I guess Shorty was paying attention after all. I shouldn't be surprised. He's a bartender. Restaurateur, if you will. Pub master. Master Chef of the greasy kind. De Facto therapist. Quietly social. Socially quiet. He kind of sneaks up on you when you least expect it. He doesn't miss a beat. Unlike me. I've been missing beats a lot lately.

"Nothing. Everything."

"Annie?"

"Yeah. Annie. And Marina. And the craziness of this world. I don't know. I can't sit here anymore. I always thought I'd be a good father. Seeing my ex-wife with that kid. Shit. Maybe I should've stuck it out. Maybe I would have forgotten eventually that the kid isn't mine."

"Do you still love her?"

"No. I don't. Maybe. I don't know. Sometimes I think I still love her. I want to hate her, I guess, but I can't seem to find a reason to hate her anymore if that makes sense."

"It makes sense. Sort of."

You see, I won't say this to Shorty, but I'm afraid if I stop hating her, I'll realize I never stopped loving her. And if I allow myself to love her, then what?

"You still love her, don't you?"

Dammit. Like I said. Shorty never missed a beat. "I don't want to love her. I don't want to hate her either, but I don't want to love her. I want to love Annie."

"John. Annie isn't here. Marina is. Marina's not married. Annie is. Annie isn't even Annie. What the hell are you doing?"

"Marina might as well be married. Her life is completely intertwined with Ness. You should have seen the house. I never thought Ness would become such a happy, pappy, hubby homeowner."

And therein lies the problem. Seeing him in my house with my former wife was like coming back from the dead and seeing my life from the outside, or on a movie screen, only the lead actor wasn't me. It was my best friend.

I wasn't kidding when I said I don't hate her anymore. But allowing myself to love her just isn't an option. I'm even telling myself that maybe, just maybe, Ness and Marina had something going before all this. Before Riley broke into my house. Before the rape. Before the pregnancy. Before, before, before. If I tell myself that she and Ness, you know, well, it makes the whole thing easier. Nah. Marina was as faithful as they come. Ness and I were of one mind. I would have known if something was up. I mean, we've only known each other for what, almost three decades? He couldn't have hidden something like that. At least I don't think he could have. In the matinee of my former life, he played the role of me, flawlessly. He is a good actor. If he could be that good of an actor now, how do I know our entire friendship wasn't an act? But, if he was acting today, maybe Marina was acting today too. I'm sure she's hardened herself toward me. It's been three years since I left her. I'm crazy for even having these thoughts.

"Shorty, it's over. I know where you're going with this. I'll always love her. But that's buried now. It came out a little bit when I saw her today. Mainly driven by jealousy, I think."

"So, what are you gonna do then?"

"I think I need to get out of town."

"On a boat?"

"Going to the Southern Islands.

"Sailing a reach, upon the following sea."

"Alright already! Enough!" Shorty and I do this thing where a conversation will literally turn into an exchange of song lyrics. "Southern Cross" is one of our favorites and frequently happens when one or the other of us starts to get too serious. I say "it happens" rather than "we do it" because it really does somehow just happen without conscious thought beforehand. And it almost always breaks the impasse or changes the direction of the wind. We usually end up laughing, but for some reason tonight, while it was successful at lightening the mood, it didn't result in the deep gut laughter that it often does.

"Hey, I'm out."

"Wait." I knew exactly what he wanted me to wait for. He's crazy, and I love him. I got up and started toward the door, and then I heard what's been circling in my head for the past few minutes. Yep. Crosby, Stills & Nash. "Southern Cross" pulsing from the speakers. I stopped and listened. The tune made me smile. Yet, much to my dismay, it reminded me of Annie. Not that the song ever came up between us. I'm sure that in the few days I knew her we never even discussed music. She seems so real to me, even now, that it's hard to imagine that she graced my life for less than a week.

I glanced over at Shorty. He was back at the sink, head down, concentrating on his task as if his life depended on it. He must have sensed that I was halfway out the door because he stopped what he was doing and gave me one of his looks. With my eyes, I acknowledged his concern, then totally ignored it as I stepped outside.

Mercer Street - John

SHORTY SAID IT WAS AGAINST his better judgment to tell me. He said he couldn't believe that I didn't notice that the painting was gone. Truth be told, I'd grown blind to it. Shorty had found an excellent place for it - on a wall at the left side of the bar. In the beginning, I obsessed over it. I'd wanted to take it home, after all, she gave it to me, not Shorty. But the bastard fought me tooth and nail. Said I'd wallow. Said I'd obsess. He was right. So, I let him hang it up in the bar. In the end I was okay with him keeping the painting. I knew I could see it every day. More truth be told - what I obsessed over more than anything was the note she'd left me. One morning I spilled a cup of coffee on it and decided enough was enough. Spilling the coffee was a sign. At least that's what I'd told myself. I couldn't bring myself to throw it away. I took it back to the boat and ceremoniously placed it between the pages of the ships log.

That's when I decided that I needed a walkabout. I took the boat down to Florida and kept my mother company for a few months. I kept myself happily distracted fixing things around her house, repaying her for all the time she'd spent with me when I was recovering from my leg surgery and my ruined marriage. I never told her about Annie. How could I when I went running to my ex-wife's sister before the ink on my divorce papers was dry. My mother knew about, and encouraged apparently, my obsession with my ex-wife's sister. The thing with Dale, I've come to realize, was years and years of feeling like I'd made the wrong choice - listening to my head instead of my heart, choosing practical over passionate. The tragic irony is that I had indeed married the right woman. Marina was perfect for me in every way. There are times when I miss her so much it hurts. So, the last thing my mother needed to know was that I was obsessed yet again. Maybe obsessed is the wrong way to put it. It was different than that. I wouldn't call it love or even infatuation. And I know this will come across as sounding terribly cliché, but it's like I'd known Annie before. In a past life? Nah. I'm much too sensible to believe that.

I figured she had died by now, and did a pretty good job of putting her out of my mind. It was hard. I'd wanted to search for her a million times between then and now. I'm not even entirely sure what stopped me. It wasn't that I was afraid of what I'd find - Annie bald and emaciated. I wasn't afraid of that at all. I would have given anything to see her, to know how she was doing. Anything.

I thought her sister might come back to the pub at some point. For lunch or a beer, if nothing else. I kept her number all this time and even called once or twice to check in and ask over

Annie, but of course, hung up after the first or second ring. Last month I called, and the number had been disconnected. So that was the end of that. Chances that I'd ever run into her sister were less than zero.

The thing is, Annie wasn't Annie at all. Annie was someone else. Someone who was married and had a kid. Someone who had more than enough to get through without me coming along and complicating her life.

I showed up for work this afternoon, just in time for the happy-hour crowd. Shorty sat me down and told me. About Kathy coming to get the painting. About Annie's health. And about her divorce. Then he handed me an article about her exhibit from the *Times*. And now here I am in SoHo, standing in front of an obscure building on Mercer Street, afraid to go in.

But I did go in. Up the stairs and to the entrance of the loft. I stood in the open doorway, and this is what I saw: Annie standing in front of her painting, the one she gave to me, wiping away tears, talking to the three people who were standing around her. She wore a black dress, a string of pearls, and a simple sweater draped around her shoulders. My raggedy old sailing sweater. I didn't even realize the sweater had been gone all this time. That sweater hanging off Annie's shoulders made me happier than I care to admit. Not because I had any particular attachment to it. It was the fact that she took it with her when she left last year like she wanted to take a piece of me with her. I wiped away tears as I walked in and slowly made my way around the room, one painting at a time.

ACKNOWLEDGEMENTS

Story ideas come to me in unexpected ways, and often end up very different from what I'd initially set out to write. For this novel, I started out wanting to write a story with 9/11 as the backdrop. I didn't personally know anyone who perished that day, yet the day still knocked my world a bit off its axis. And the company I worked for at the time - Booz Allen Hamilton - lost three colleagues at the Pentagon.

In the years since the attacks, I often thought about the boats that ferried people away from Lower Manhattan that day. That's where I decided to begin writing the story - with my character John on his sailboat in the midst of the 9/11 chaos.

I also wondered about the people on the ground in New York City during the attacks. Someone who perhaps should have been in the towers but for some reason wasn't. What if that person had problems they wanted to run from? Would they let their loved ones think they died that day? That thought intrigued me, and thus, the idea of Brenda was conceived. I needed to figure out what her problems were and why she felt compelled to run from them. And why she would put her loved ones through the hellish days of not knowing.

While mindlessly surfing the internet, I came across a story about a woman diagnosed with cancer who eschewed aggressive treatment in favor of a palliative approach. She wanted quality of life over length of life. Last I checked, that woman was still alive - seven years after her diagnosis. I had my answer: Brenda would receive such a diagnosis a few days before 9/11. That, mixed in with a few other things, pushes her over the edge and she disappears.

I want Brenda to stick around for a bit (and maybe be in my next novel) and not be ravished with the side effects of harsh, aggressive treatment. To appease me, she chooses a palliative approach to deal with her cancer. I took some artistic liberty with this because the advanced cancer drugs available today didn't exist at the time of 9/11.

Many thanks to my husband, Mike (aka Sweet Petunia), for reading and commenting on the many drafts of this novel. It was tedious for you, I know. I love you!

In memory of Gerald Fisher, Terence Lynch, and Ernest Willcher

ABOUT THE AUTHOR

Lynn Stewart lives in Cambridge, Maryland.
This is her second novel.